HARD POWER

J. B. TURNER

HARD POWER

A **JON REZNICK** THRILLER

THOMAS & MERCER

Published by Thomas & Mercer, Seattle

www.apub.com

Amazon, the Amazon logo, and Thomas & Mercer are trademarks of Amazon. com, Inc., or its affiliates.

ISBN-13: 9781542039819
eISBN: 9781542039826

Cover design by @blacksheep-uk.com
Cover image: © Joanna Czogala / ArcAngel; © Zsolt Hlinka / Getty Images

Printed in the United States of America

To my brother, Andrew

Times Square Subway Station, New York

They were watching her. She sensed it.

Amy Chang stood on the packed subway platform, "Paranoid Android" blaring in her ears. She was trying to block out her surroundings. She tapped her phone to turn up the headphone volume, noise cancellation on. The music was like a wall of sound washing over her. A barrier to the outside world. She stared across the tracks at the dirty white-tiled wall as the music overpowered her senses. The vibrations from passing trains and the throng were making her more anxious than usual.

Amy's heart beat faster. She wondered if they were close by. Watching and waiting. Her fear never seemed to subside. She wondered if today was her final day on earth. More and more, she saw threats everywhere, sometimes real, sometimes imagined. A fear gripped her deep down in her soul. Gnawing away at her.

Her boyfriend and her brother had both told her to get therapy. She resisted. It would not save her from her fate. It was like a sixth sense she couldn't turn off.

She couldn't see them today. But she felt their presence.

She saw them in the dark shadows, lurking on subway stairs. In a passing reflection in the mosaics around the station. She knew they wanted to take her back, but she wasn't going. Not now. Not ever.

Amy closed her eyes and tried a meditation exercise she had been working on, learning to disassociate herself from the mass of people all around her. She hated the subway. She hated its chaos. Its grime. She especially hated Times Square, underneath the heart of Midtown Manhattan, with its heaving, twisting, winding paths through the byzantine corridors.

The heat. The pungent smell of weed. The stench of pee. The reek of shit in subway carriages. Cardboard boxes of broken men and women, needles stuck in their rotten, blackened veins. The homeless shouting. Whispering threats. Talking to themselves.

It was like no one was in charge. A postindustrial society, hollowed out, having to fend for itself. A dystopian dog-eat-dog world. A dangerous place.

Amy hadn't imagined freedom being anything like this. Her mind had constructed a utopian reality of New York City from the synthetic version that appeared on social media.

Maybe she was naïve. She wondered if she needed to live outside of the city, head out to Westchester. Or maybe she simply missed her boyfriend, the cool gamer she had met online.

Amy wanted to see him badly. He worked out of the state most of the time, in cybersecurity. He moved around. A lot. A digital nomad. They met up three or four times a year at most. God, she missed him. Her way of coping without having to resort to Xanax was meditation and loud music. She switched on her playlist the moment she left her Midtown office. It quieted her mind, just a little.

The smell of fries and more weed smoke wafted in her direction. She choked back nausea.

Truth was, she wasn't sleeping too well. She had finally agreed to see a psychologist for her anxiety. She felt like she couldn't relax. Not totally. Once or twice a week, she saw faces in crowds she thought she'd seen before. A friend asked if she was having flashbacks to childhood trauma. She said no. She believed she was being watched. And followed.

Her brother told her to just relax. He said he understood her fears. He felt the same. But she felt it more acutely.

The more she thought about it, the more she feared they were closing in and that they wished her harm. She glanced around. Anxious faces, most staring ahead. Etched with tiredness. Talking into phones. Gray pallor. A muffled loudspeaker announcement penetrated the noise cancellation headphones.

Her mind flashed back. She had first started noticing them a month earlier. The same faces. Different locations. Sometimes on the R train home. Sometimes at a street corner near her tiny Upper West Side studio. She thought at first it was just a coincidence. But no. A pattern was emerging.

The ominous rumble of the train began to sound like a jet engine, even with her music blaring. Were they playing mind games with her? Were they just trying to make her scared? Maybe that was what it was. Just a way to try and intimidate her.

Amy tried to push those thoughts to one side. She felt people pressing against her as the train approached. But it wasn't stopping.

She felt her breathing grow rapid. Closer and closer. Bony fingers pressed against her lower back. She stumbled forward onto the tracks, headfirst. Screaming, she looked up as the train hurtled toward her.

One

Jon Reznick stood outside JFK's Terminal 4, dying a little inside. He hated goodbyes. He always had. And this was going to be a long one. He wouldn't see his beautiful daughter in person for a couple of years.

He took Lauren in, all grown up and self-assured. He beamed. "I'll miss you."

Lauren had one hand on a cart piled high with her luggage. Tears welled in her eyes. "I'll be fine."

Reznick hugged her tight. "You look after yourself, honey."

"I can look after myself. Don't worry."

"I know you can. But I'm your father. I worry. You're going to be ten thousand miles away from home. From me. And it's not America. They have different rules."

Lauren hugged him tightly once again, as if she didn't want to let go. "I'm going to miss you so much, Dad. I'm going to miss Mom too."

Reznick wiped away the tears on her face. "I know."

"I can't believe we thought she was gone, and now she's back in our lives. And now I'm the one who's going away. Just when we finally found her again."

Reznick held his daughter close. He and Lauren were still coming to terms with the shocking discovery that Elisabeth Reznick—the mother and wife they believed had died on 9/11—was actually alive and well. She wasn't a high-flying New York tax lawyer, mom, and wife who had tragically died more than two decades earlier. Instead, she had been living and working in Switzerland as a CIA agent.

It was true that Elisabeth had worked for years as a tax lawyer in the Twin Towers. But unbeknownst to her husband, Jon, a young Delta operator at the time, she had been recruited by the CIA to begin work in a secret office in New York, also based at the World Trade Center. The Agency had used the massive attack and loss of life on 9/11 as a cover for Elisabeth Reznick to disappear and begin her new life as a CIA agent with a new name in Switzerland, as part of a covert spying operation.

"I know it's been tough on you," he said.

Lauren closed her eyes. "I really wanted to start to get to know her."

Reznick had only found out Elisabeth was alive after a high-level security breach. The deception was almost too shocking to comprehend. Now, all these years later, Elisabeth was back, living under another new name and identity in rural Connecticut. But although they had found her, Elisabeth could not really be in their lives, even though she was alive. She had promised both of them that she would be able to make a secret visit to Rockland, Maine, twice a year to see both Lauren and Reznick.

"I was looking forward to starting again with Mom," Lauren said. "I can't even FaceTime her, obviously. I can't text her. I just want to sit with her. I want to hold her hand. Sounds crazy."

"It's not crazy. You'll see her again. I promise."

"Just the three of us, right?"

"Just the three of us. When you get back, and you *will* get back, we'll have her over. Me, you, and her. No one else."

"I'd like that. But in the meantime, I've got my first overseas assignment to focus on."

"Remember this. You have any problems, you contact me, no matter the time of day. Text, email, phone, FaceTime, OK? You hear me?"

"I'm ready, Dad."

"I'm serious."

"You're always serious, Dad."

Reznick felt a deep sense of trepidation. His daughter had left the FBI six months earlier and joined the CIA. It was the last thing he wanted. Her first overseas posting, in goddamn Jakarta. He had posted there once in his life. A hellish operation hunting a jihadist cell living in the mountains. Bad memories flooded back. "The Agency is not the FBI. It's a whole new set of rules. A whole new way of doing things."

"The Agency has trained me well. I'm prepared."

"Remember what I said. Trust no one. Not even the ones you work with."

"Things have changed since your day, Dad."

Reznick had checked her flight times and schedules. She would fly United to Qatar. A three-hour layover. Then on to Indonesia. He looked at her three large suitcases. "Wow, you packed a lot."

"I'm going to be away for two years. I need stuff. Besides, I'll buy more over there."

Reznick hugged her one last time. "I will miss you, Lauren Reznick."

"I'm coming back, Dad."

"Damn right you are."

"One thing, Dad."

"What?"

"Try and stay out of trouble. Is that too much to ask?"

"I'm fine. Look after yourself."

"I will. Love you, Dad."

Reznick pecked her on the cheek. "Give them hell."

And with that, Lauren spun around and pushed her luggage toward the terminal elevator. Without a final glance.

Reznick's mood was low as he got in his car and drove from New York back to Maine. He had a grueling six-hour journey due north. It was like his penance. Mile after mile, skies darkening all the way. He would miss her like crazy. He tended to catastrophize, imagining the worst things she would face. The fact that she worked for the CIA concerned him. A foreign posting was always a challenge. He remembered in 2009 there were al-Qaeda–inspired bombings, killing eight, injuring dozens more, of two hotels in Jakarta frequented by Americans. He knew full well, as she would have been briefed, that Indonesia had the largest Muslim population in the world and had seen a rise in Islamist terrorism in the last twenty years. His fears were partially assuaged knowing she had been trained by not only the Feds at Quantico but also the CIA down at the Farm. She would have had to pass numerous psychological, physical, and shooting tests before being deployed. She was capable. More than capable.

He stopped off at a gas station and refueled his car, then had a snack and a couple of cups of strong coffee before he got on the road again.

Reznick was around twenty-five miles from Rockland, Maine, when he saw a sign for a regular haunt of his—an outdoor gun range.

He pulled up at the isolated club. He went to his locker, took out his ear protectors, and headed through to the deserted range. He took a few moments to compose himself. Then he aimed his 9mm handgun at a life-size wooden cutout target fifty yards downrange.

He squeezed the trigger again and again and again, quickly emptying the magazine. He had obliterated the chest of the wooden target and punched a fist-sized hole through where the face was. He spent another thirty minutes shooting out on the range. He did a little close-range shooting. Ten yards. Twenty yards. Then he went indoors and did the same again.

He checked that the chamber was empty, then flicked on the safety and holstered his handgun.

Ex-Marine Dave Courtney, who ran the range, walked over, shaking his head. "Nice work, bro."

Reznick nodded. "Hey, Dave, how's the leg?"

Courtney was suffering pain from a twenty-year-old shrapnel wound in his left knee he got while serving in Iraq. "We march on, Jon. Nothing else to do. Haven't seen you for the last week or so."

"Been busy."

"Yeah, you working?"

"A few days away. Just got back from New York."

Courtney shook his head and grinned. "What a nuthouse."

"It has its moments."

"How's Lauren settling into life in the big city?"

Reznick sighed. "She's just been posted overseas for a two-year stint. So, I was seeing her off at JFK."

"That's tough, man. Anywhere interesting?"

"Indonesia."

"Shit. Jakarta? Been there. Not going back."

Reznick said, "Anyway, I'm home. And I need to kill some time."

"The next time I'm in Rockland, we'll grab a beer. What do you say?"

"Anytime, Dave."

Reznick shook Courtney's hand and climbed back in his truck and drove off. He arrived back in Rockland half an hour later. It felt good to be home. He made himself a strong black coffee and a ham sandwich and sat out on the deck.

He stared across Penobscot Bay and wondered how he was going to cope with his beloved daughter being away for so long. They had grown closer and closer over the years, especially since she had joined the FBI after college. Now he was going to have to adjust to not having her in his life for a long period.

The more he thought about it, the more he wondered about the direction of his life. He didn't see many people these days. He kept mostly to himself. Maybe it was just the way it was. Maybe it was by design. Maybe the fact was he liked it that way. He hadn't even seen Martha Meyerstein in a while. The FBI Assistant Director had been a fixture in his life for years. He had worked with her and her team on national security assignments, top secret investigations, and all manner of intelligence operations. And over the years, their relationship had become more than platonic. But in the last year, the relationship seemed to have petered out. Either he was out of the country or she was assigned to another high-level case in DC. He never seemed to find the time. Maybe rediscovering Elisabeth had played a part. He sensed that she could no longer tolerate his, at times, illegal and violent actions. He was an ends-justify-the-means kind of guy. She was also under pressure from the FBI Director, who wanted her to stop using Reznick, an ex-CIA assassin and Delta operator, as part of any investigation. He felt in his bones that it had run its course. But maybe they had just drifted apart, both more comfortable in their own individual lives.

He was very fond of Martha, but he always returned to what he loved and craved: his solitary life. He enjoyed his space. Time alone. Time to think. But also to forget. It helped him decompress if he headed up to the North Maine Woods. The isolation was a balm for his soul.

When it all came down to it, for Reznick, only Lauren really mattered. That was the truth of it. Now she was gone.

Reznick ate his sandwich and drank his coffee as he watched the last remnants of the sun drop behind the horizon, a tangerine sheen rippling over the dark waters. The view would never change. The same view his late father had seen when he returned from his twelve-hour shift at the sardine packing plant on the far side of town.

He remembered his father would wash and scrub his red-raw hands with warm water. Then afterward, he would grab a cold beer and sit out on the deck, the same deck his son now sat on all these years later.

The beautiful wooden deck, along with the entire New England colonial house behind it, had been built by his father with his own bare hands. Night after night, he worked. Long into the night. Reznick would watch him. He marveled at his father's toughness. His pride in hard work. His resilience. His father had picked the wood. He had designed the house using his rudimentary carpentry skills. A man with no education. He got a few friends to help on weekends, but by and large, his father had built it himself. A home. His home.

Reznick felt his mood lighten. The house still sat proudly atop the rocky shoreline of Rockland. Surrounded by a stillness, beauty, and serenity that was hard to match. Waves crashed onto the sand and rocks below.

His phone rang. Reznick checked the caller ID. He didn't recognize the number. "Yeah?"

"Jon?" said the tentative voice of Trevelle Williams, the brilliant ex-NSA hacker.

"Trevelle? You OK?"

All he could hear were sobs.

"What's wrong, man?"

"Jon, something's happened. Something terrible. Turn on your TV. NBC."

"Give me a minute; I'm outside." Reznick went back into the house and switched on his TV. He got to the channel. "Subway accident in New York? A girl died."

"That girl . . . that girl was my girlfriend. I loved her."

"Oh my God, Trevelle, I'm so, so sorry. That's awful."

Trevelle began to sob like a little boy, lost in grief. "I don't know who else to call. I feel shattered. I feel sick."

Reznick stared at the screen as cops and paramedics swarmed the platform. He was devastated for his friend.

"I was planning to surprise her by turning up unannounced in New York in the next day or two. I just can't . . . I can't comprehend this, Jon. I can't deal with this."

"What can I do? Do you need anything?"

Trevelle began to cry again. "I thought I had a future. I was going to propose. I swear to God, I wanted her to be my wife. Now she's gone. She told me they would get her. She told me that repeatedly."

"What?"

"She told me they would find her."

"What are you talking about, Trevelle? Who's 'they'? I don't understand what you're saying."

"Her brother said she told him the same thing. I'm close with him too."

"Her brother?"

"Yeah, he lives in New York as well. He's a computer genius. I don't know what I'm going to do. I'm scared."

"Where are you?"

"I'm headed to New York. But I don't know if I should."

"Why not?"

"I'm worried."

Reznick was concerned that Trevelle thought his girlfriend had been targeted. "How did you hear about it?"

"Her brother messaged me. But he's gone silent. He's freaking out of his mind."

"When you say he's gone silent, what exactly do you mean?"

"I mean he's scared for his life. Really scared."

Reznick listened as Trevelle cried and cried. It was painful to listen to. His friend was analytical. A cold, detached geek. But he was showing a side of his personality now that Reznick had never truly seen. A young man, crushed by grief.

"It wasn't an accident. You need to believe me."

"I'm listening."

"He thinks she was pushed."

"Your friend needs to go to the police. Right now."

"Jon, this wasn't a random event. It wasn't a drugged-up panhandler shoving someone onto the tracks. This was targeted."

Reznick didn't know what to say. "Trevelle, I'm going to level with you. Shit happens. Maybe it was terrible luck that she was in the wrong place at the wrong time. Nutcases are all over the subway. We all know that. It's bad."

"Jon, you're not listening! Amy was pushed by people who wanted her dead! They killed her. My friend is freaking out. He thinks he's going to be next. That's why he's in hiding."

"So, your friend believes his sister was murdered? I don't know . . ."

"Amy was assassinated. I swear to God, she was murdered. Not by a freak accident. But a very calculated assassination to look like a random subway push. It wasn't."

Reznick wanted to be there for Trevelle. His friend had helped him out countless times in the past.

"I need a favor, Jon. A big favor."

"Name it."

"I'm going to New York to see her brother. He's my friend. I need to be with him. He was my last connection with Amy."

"That's a nice thing, man."

"But I'd like you to be with me when I meet up with him."

"Me?"

"Just to reassure him. He's spooked. And I'm hoping your presence along with mine will reassure him that he's not alone. We can get through this. And that he's not going crazy."

Reznick closed his eyes. "And he's in New York now?"

"Lower Manhattan."

Reznick had just returned from there. "I see."

"Is that a problem?"

"It's not a problem. Just that I just got back from New York."

"I'm sorry, I didn't realize."

"It doesn't matter. I'll be there. Count on it. A bit of moral support, right?"

Trevelle began to sob hard again. "I hope so."

"I'll be there."

"I don't know how I'm going to get through this."

"I'll be there before you know it."

"This wasn't random."

"I know."

"They got to her."

Reznick watched the TV footage of a cop being interviewed.

"She told me over and over again that they would find her and kill her. And now they have."

"She told you that? Didn't she go to the cops?"

"She was afraid."

"What else did your girlfriend say?"

"She called me a couple of nights ago."

14

"And what did she say?"

"She thought she was being followed. I tried to tell her that she was just paranoid. But she insisted she wasn't. She thought people were going to kill her. We had decided that it would be best in the future if I could be based in New York to be close to her. I guess . . . it's not going to happen now."

"That's horrible, man. I'm so sorry."

"Jon, I'm going to level with you. I don't want you just to reassure my friend. I don't just want you to be with me for moral support."

"So, why do you want me to come down?"

"I want you to help me find the people who killed my Amy."

Two

It was late morning when his plane touched down in New York.

Reznick took a cab from JFK to a boutique hotel in Soho. The cobblestone streets familiar under his shoes. He checked in, quickly showered, and changed. Then it was a ten-minute walk to the diner.

He headed east along Spring Street and hung a right onto Mott. Past Vietnamese restaurants, Thai diners, Korean travel agents, until it was all Chinese restaurants, cafés, delis, and supermarkets. The pungent aromas of Asian cooking filled the Lower Manhattan street. His father had developed a taste for Vietnamese food during the war. And after coming home from Hanoi, he had cooked Reznick similar meals. They were strange for Reznick's young tastebuds. But over the years, he enjoyed the *bún chà*, Vietnamese meatballs, which grew to be his favorite.

Reznick spotted the neon sign for the tiny café. He was in the heart of Chinatown. Inside sat Trevelle, hunched over a cup of coffee, checking his phone. Reznick laid a hand on his shoulder as he passed behind him.

Trevelle turned around anxiously and looked up, eyes bloodshot. "Hey, man, thank you so much."

Reznick slid into the seat opposite. "How are you holding up?"

"Not too good."

"It must have been a terrible shock for you."

Trevelle closed his eyes as if trying to block out the thought.

"I'm here for you. I just wanted you to know that."

"Thank you."

"How long had you known Amy?"

"Eighteen months, give or take. I was introduced to her by her brother, Kevin. He's devastated. They were really close."

"That's tough."

Trevelle shook his head. "I feel numb. Absolutely numb."

Reznick hadn't seen the normally impassive, composed, and highly rational hacker in such an emotionally disturbed state. He felt so bad for this guy he would consider a friend. Not a going-out-for-a-beer friend. Not even a college friend type of friend. But more just a guy he could rely on. A guy who hadn't ever let him down. Now his life had fallen apart. He knew the suffering and anguish Trevelle was going through all too well.

"I'll get through this. But it's Amy's brother I'm worried about. He's freaking out like you wouldn't believe."

"It's tough. Losing someone. I know."

"Kevin is talking about hurting himself. I don't know what to do. And that's why I wanted you to come with me. I'm just hoping you can try and help him in some way, maybe reassure him as well. I know you're friends with Martha."

Reznick nodded. "I'll do whatever I can."

"I appreciate that, Jon."

Reznick stopped a passing waitress and ordered a couple of cups of coffee for him and Trevelle, along with steamed shrimp and pork dumplings for each of them. "The flight was delayed. I would've been here earlier."

"I haven't slept since I heard about Amy. My brain is scrambled. What I told you probably sounded insane. I'm on the spectrum, and this thing has really thrown me."

"It's understandable."

The waitress returned with the coffee and the food.

Reznick waited until she was out of earshot. He took a sip of his coffee. "I'd like to know a bit more background on everything."

"What do you want to know?"

"I suppose my main question is, first of all, why doesn't your friend just go to the police? If he thinks this wasn't an accident but foul play, he needs to go to the cops, right?"

Trevelle sat in silent contemplation.

"I was thinking about this last night. He should go to the cops. You both should."

Trevelle eyed his food and picked at the dumplings. He took a gulp of his coffee. "Here's the thing, Jon. It's a delicate situation. Kevin has Asperger's. He has an incredible IQ, but emotionally he's a closed book. Reclusive. Finds it difficult to relate to other people. So, he views this situation through his own prism."

"I understand."

"Going to the cops is not an option. At the moment, it's just a theory he has. How his sister was killed."

Reznick said nothing.

"A theory I believe."

"Listen, if you and your friend think there was more to this than a random push, he has to go to the cops, whether he has Asperger's or not."

"Not right now."

"Why not?"

"The main reason is that he's scared shitless. He doesn't know many people. He moved to this country with his sister a year and a half ago. He doesn't want to get into trouble."

"I'm starting to follow your drift."

"My mind is going crazy. So is his. I'm not thinking straight. That's one of the reasons why I called you. I know you've worked in all sorts of places and situations. I know you have connections to the FBI. I can't figure it out. Neither can he."

Reznick took a large bite out of the steamed shrimp and wolfed down a dumpling. He washed it down with a large gulp of the strong, black coffee. "Here's the thing . . ." He dabbed his mouth with a napkin. "I need to know if Amy had enemies. Does her brother? I get the impression that you didn't tell me the whole story on the phone."

Trevelle averted his eyes.

"Which is fine, I guess. But I need you to lay it on the line for me now. What are we really dealing with? It's all a bit . . . a bit sketchy, if you don't mind me saying."

Trevelle leaned closer across the table. "It's sketchy alright. It's a mindfuck. I'm going to lay it all out. I'm scared."

"Let's take a step back. What did you work with him on?"

"I've been using my cybersecurity skills, working with foreign political activists and those with high skills, like Kevin and his sister, helping them get out of their countries. Working with NGOs to get them safely into our society. Companies in the tech sector need qualified people from overseas. Amy and Kevin fit that bill."

"So, you're working pro bono?"

"Absolutely. They want to live in a free society."

"Who doesn't?"

"You'd be surprised, Jon."

"So, you think me turning up with you would reassure him?"

"That's the plan."

"I know he's not from this country, like you say, but again, why not simply go to the police and say he fears for his life? What about the FBI? Let them deal with it. They can help."

"He doesn't want to attract undue attention about what's happened. He believes they have spies watching him. He is fearful he will be extradited to his country. What's happened to Amy has shocked him so much. He was literally screaming on the phone. He thinks they will come for him. Just a matter of time."

"Who's trying to kill him? A foreign government on American soil?"

"I don't know if he's exaggerating, not exactly sure, but he talked about malignant forces at work. Maybe from his government. Maybe working for that government. Maybe here in New York. I don't know."

"Let me get this straight," Reznick said, taking a sip of coffee. "He's a stand-up, regular guy who just wants to live in America?"

"Correct. He's already worked as a contractor for the State Department."

"That's interesting."

"Amy was the last surviving member of his family. You couldn't meet a nicer person than Kevin."

"I could put in a call. NYPD or the Feds. We'd get the ball rolling. He really does need help—personal, psychological help, as well as support from law enforcement."

Trevelle shook his head. "That won't work. That definitely would not fly with him."

"Your friend, does he work in the city?"

"New York?"

"Yes."

"Yeah. He works from home. He has a green card. He's a permanent resident. But he's not an American citizen. At least not yet. Maybe in a year or two. There have been some delays. And he doesn't want to jeopardize his status. He feels very fortunate."

Reznick finished his food, wiped crumbs from his mouth, and shrugged. "Listen, Trevelle. I want to help. That's why I'm here. I can contact Martha Meyerstein directly and explain the situation."

"He's already ruled that out. He's super-paranoid."

"Where is he now? Is he at his apartment?"

Trevelle shook his head. "He's not far."

"Where?"

"Staying at a friend's house, down here in Chinatown. He had a place in Midtown, but he moved because he was convinced they would quickly track him down there. He packed a bag and was gone."

Reznick leaned back in his seat. "Tell me more about this guy."

Trevelle showed him a copy of that day's *New York Post* and pointed to a picture on the front page. "That's her. The one that died."

"She's very pretty." Reznick studied the story. "It says here it was a random push from the subway platform."

"Jon, you're not listening. My friend says—he insists—that is absolutely not the case. Besides, Amy was also convinced people were watching her."

"Was she maybe a bit paranoid too?"

"Maybe she was."

"I don't mean any disrespect."

"It's fine."

"What else do I need to know? You said they're from China, right?"

"Amy and her brother are from Hong Kong." Trevelle took out his phone and scrolled through photos. He showed Reznick a photo of a young Chinese man and woman. "That's them. Taken in Hong Kong shortly before they fled."

Reznick studied the features of the handsome young man and his stunning sister at a demonstration.

"They should have been safe here. They fled Chinese oppression. They were both students who were active in the movement against China taking control of their lives. They wanted to live free. They were getting harassed in Hong Kong for protesting the government. That's why they traveled to the other side of the earth to get to a place of safety. At least it should have been a place of safety. They just wanted to be free."

"And you want me to head on over to where your pal is staying? And then what?"

"I don't know exactly. I suppose I guess it would be useful to get him out of New York. Maybe to my place in Iowa, my compound. I thought you could help me with that."

"I want to help you. Really, I do. But I think the best bet is for your friend—"

"Kevin. Kevin Chang."

"Right, for you and Kevin Chang to go to the FBI. I'll go with you. The cops. Anyone. For what it's worth. And we can go from there. We can also talk about getting police or FBI protection if he's in danger."

"If you're with me, he might listen to you. You worked with the Feds, right?"

Reznick nodded. "You know I have. My concern is that he won't listen. You think he'll go for it coming from someone else?"

"There's only one way to find out."

Three

The run-down fourth-floor walk-up on Forsyth Street sat above a Chinese grocery store.

Reznick noticed the intercom had been ripped out of the wall, hanging loose. He pushed open the door and he and Trevelle headed up the dingy stairwell, past graffiti sprayed on the peeling walls, past the pungent smell of cooking, past cigarette smoke and weed in the air.

Frightened shouts were coming from a fourth-floor apartment.

Trevelle had fear in his eyes. "Shit."

Reznick's senses heightened.

Trevelle pointed to the graffiti-daubed door straight ahead and whispered, "Sounds like Cantonese."

Reznick wondered if the frightened kid was arguing with someone on the phone. He signaled for Trevelle to move away. He put his finger to his mouth, indicating for Trevelle to be silent.

Trevelle nodded.

Reznick approached the door and paused, listening. Then there was the sound of a piercing scream from the room. Panicked pleading, as if begging for mercy. He signaled again for Trevelle to step away. He took a step back and kicked the door wide open.

Reznick burst in, crouched down, handgun drawn. He rolled into a room where a besuited Chinese man pointed a weapon at a kneeling Kevin Chang.

The man spun around and faced Reznick, gun pointed straight at him.

Reznick fired off two deafening shots to the guy's head and one to the chest. Blood splattered the wall. The guy collapsed.

Chang cowered on the floor, trembling.

Reznick stepped forward and reached out his hand. "I'm a friend of Trevelle. Come with me."

Chang cowered and shook.

"Now!"

Chang stared up at him. "Please don't kill me!"

Reznick grabbed his arm and hauled him to his feet as Trevelle entered the room and hugged his friend. "We need to go! Now!" He checked the guy's pockets. He pulled an ID out of the wallet. A Chinese diplomat, based in New York. Shit.

Trevelle whispered softly to Kevin.

"What are you saying to him?" Reznick asked, staring at the body on the ground.

"I'm saying we need to get out of here, to someplace safe. That you're here to help."

Reznick thought he heard whispered voices down in the stairwell. He moved softly through the open front door. The voices were faint. Chinese. Maybe a couple of floors below. It wasn't surprising after screaming and three loud gunshots.

He spread-eagled, ear to the floor, sensing the vibrations of movement farther down. But he couldn't be sure if it was on the stairs or vibrations from traffic outside.

He crawled to the landing of the fourth floor and peered down through iron stair railings. The sound of angry whispered voices rose back up. He craned his neck and looked down. A Chinese man and woman on the stairs. The man had his gun drawn.

Reznick waited until they headed up a few more steps. "Freeze!" he shouted.

The man spun around, gun trained on him.

Reznick gunned him down with a single shot. The noise reverberated and echoed around the old stone stairwell.

The Asian woman with him fell to her knees on the stairs, hands on her head. She began to plead, speaking in Chinese.

"Don't fucking move!"

The woman flinched, right hand moving to her side. Suddenly, she reached into her jacket and pulled out a gun.

Reznick fired off two quick shots at her head. She collapsed on the stairs, blood and brain matter splattering the walls. The gunshots echoed like firecrackers in the enclosed space. He got to his feet and leaped down the stairs to the two bodies. He rifled in the man's pockets and pulled out a wallet. The guy was a private detective from Queens. James Lan. Then he rifled inside the women's jacket and pulled out ID from her pocket. He scanned the details. The woman was a Chinese diplomat. She worked in the Overseas Chinese Affairs office at the Chinese consulate in New York. This was fucked-up. Not good. Not good at all. He quickly ran back up the stairs and into the room. "We need to go! Now!"

Trevelle looked at him, arm around his friend. "What happened?"

"I'll explain later." Reznick led them down the stairs, past the bodies.

"What the hell, Jon?"

Reznick said, "Ignore the mess."

Chang was a quivering wreck as he clutched Trevelle's arm. He glanced at the bodies.

Trevelle said, "Why did you kill them?"

"They were carrying guns, and pointed them in my direction."

"Oh my God! What have you done?"

Reznick tucked his gun into his waistband and hustled Trevelle and his terrified pal out to the street. He quickly hailed a passing taxi and bundled Trevelle and his friend in the back, before sliding into the passenger seat up front.

The driver flicked on the meter. "Where to?"

"We're going to Queens."

"Queens is a big place, pal. Where in Queens?"

"I don't know. Just drive."

"I need a destination."

"Just drive, will you?"

Four

It was dark when Meyerstein's plane touched down at LaGuardia. She received constant updates to her phone on the flight up from Washington, DC. Her brief was simple: she had to close this down, find Reznick, and make sure the fallout from the killings couldn't be traced back to an occasional FBI operative.

FBI Director Bill O'Donoghue was red in the face as he read her the riot act in his office. She was ordered to fly up immediately when it was clear that Reznick was at the center of the storm.

She needed to get a grip on the situation before it escalated further, becoming a diplomatic and political scandal.

Meyerstein was picked up by a team of special agents and shown into a waiting SUV. She was whisked across town toward the FBI's field office in Lower Manhattan. The SUV headed onto the expressway, through the Queens Midtown Tunnel. Before she had even reached Manhattan, her phone rang.

She checked the caller ID. Her heart sank. It was Bill O'Donoghue. She had a good relationship with the long-serving Director. But in the last few years, there had been a noticeable deterioration. And she felt herself under increasing pressure and on the defensive when it concerned Jon Reznick. What had transpired earlier in Chinatown had chilled an already lukewarm relationship to downright frosty.

She stared out the window at the passing traffic, phone pressed to her ear. "Meyerstein speaking."

"ETA?"

"Hi, Bill. I'd say we're twenty minutes out, depending on traffic."

"Martha, I just want to reiterate how toxic this relationship of yours has become."

"Excuse me?"

"How many fucking times does the name Reznick come between us? I mean, seriously? He's going to be the death of me."

Meyerstein sighed. "As I said earlier, I'm on it. I just got here. I'm going to get up to speed. I don't know the chain of events. But I'll find out."

"It might be too late."

"What does that mean?"

"I just got off a very, very heated conversation with the Attorney General. He is losing his mind over this. Reznick is finished. You and Reznick as well, that's finished."

"Let's not be hasty."

"It's over. The Department of Justice has flipped over what happened. They know the links with Reznick and the Bureau. Now Reznick is a wanted man. Meanwhile, two Chinese diplomats are dead. One other is also dead. Do you understand the problem this creates for the Bureau? The State Department?"

"I saw the message from the State Department."

"The Chinese government is going to want blood for this."

Meyerstein closed her eyes as she sat in shock in the back seat. "Sir, I know it's bad. It's as bad as it gets, but I want to establish the facts."

"Too late. And that's not all."

"What?"

O'Donoghue sighed. "The Attorney General wants you out."

"Me?"

"He has given me a week to fire you, or he will fire the whole senior executive team of the FBI himself. That includes me."

"That's ridiculous."

"Is it? I don't blame him."

"Have you agreed to this already?"

"It's a done deal."

Meyerstein felt as if she was drowning in quicksand. Her career was over. It had been her life for the better part of twenty-five years. A life of service. A life of devotion to duty. A duty to her country.

"Look, I'm sorry. This is brutal, I know. But no one apart from me, you, and the Attorney General knows about this."

Meyerstein snapped out of her shock. "I want to find out where Reznick is. I have another week, right?"

"That's right."

"Well, I want to try and use whatever leverage and influence I have with Jon to bring him in."

"New York is taking the lead on this. But you can have your say, of course. Understood?"

The car emerged from the tunnel.

"I understand, don't sweat it."

"I'm sorry it had to be like this."

"Whatever. But for what it's worth, Bill, I don't think the Attorney General should be getting embroiled in day-to-day FBI operational matters."

"Bullshit. He can do whatever he goddamn wants! Reznick has already been formally identified by a witness going into and leaving the walk-up in Chinatown. And I'm hearing that we have him on surveillance video taken outside the Chinese grocery store below the walk-up."

"Shit."

"Yeah, shit. It's all gone to shit. It's a mess."

"I will fix this."

"Find him. Bring him in. This is on you, Martha."

The SUV pulled up in the underground parking garage beneath the FBI's New York field office in Lower Manhattan. Meyerstein rode the elevator with a couple of agents to the twenty-third floor and was escorted to her temporary office.

A young agent handed her a cup of coffee as she was shown into the meeting room for the latest briefing.

Meyerstein sat down and introduced herself, notes spread out in front of her. She looked around the assembled faces. "I appreciate the opportunity to sit in and hear what we're facing. First of all, can I have the latest update on this shitshow?"

Special agent in charge of the FBI's Criminal Investigative Division in New York, Don Laslow, got up and stood in front of a huge TV screen on the wall, the remote control in his hand. "This is what we've got, Martha." He pressed a button and the footage began. "So, we've got this frame by frame. We've pieced together the movements of when Reznick arrived with Trevelle Williams at Forsyth Street in Chinatown."

Meyerstein began to take notes.

"When they were first spotted. We have them here." He pointed to Reznick and Trevelle headed down Forsyth Street. "Jon Reznick and Trevelle Williams, genius, ex-NSA." He paused the video, showing two men entering the run-down walk-up apartment. "The shooting of a Chinese diplomat occurred in the apartment less than two minutes after Reznick's arrival. We don't have footage of the shooting inside the apartment. We are also dealing with the execution of another Chinese diplomat and a private investigator from Queens in the stairwell. Forensics is all over this. Three confirmed dead. Three Chinese. Gunshot wounds from a 9mm."

Meyerstein watched the footage as Reznick led Trevelle and Kevin Chang out of the apartment building and to a passing cab. "Where did the cab go from there?"

"We could trace it using traffic cameras, heading across to Queens. The cab driver we still have to talk to. Can't seem to find him or the cab. Just seemed to disappear."

Meyerstein studied the others at the table: special agents taking notes, analyzing real-time data.

"Reznick has dropped off the grid," Laslow continued. "He's as tough as they come. Along for the ride are Trevelle Williams and Kevin Chang, a green card holder originally from Hong Kong. We've got to assume they're together, on the run."

"I'm assuming that the Marshals Service is up to speed?"

"Total cooperation. They're linked with us on this. It's gone high priority for them."

"Any leads from anyone?"

Don shook his head. "It's early . . . but we'll find them."

Meyerstein looked around the sea of determined faces. "I can't stress this enough. They must be caught and detained. I don't want any media leaks on this. If there is a leak, you'll be dealing with me."

"We all know that," Laslow said.

"I'm just restressing the point. This is to be kept under strict wraps here in New York. This is already a diplomatic incident. How did this happen? What brought Jon Reznick to New York?"

"We have no idea, Martha. Reznick is friends with Trevelle Williams. They both use and access military-grade encrypted phones. Reznick is a trained killer, we know that. Trevelle has worked with us in the past on off-the-books jobs. So, you can see how these links to not only the FBI but also the NSA could be explosive if this got out to the media. I don't want to see this story blowing up on Fox or anywhere. You got me?"

The team nodded dutifully.

Meyerstein looked up at Laslow. "I know Jon well, better than anyone. I know what he's capable of. But I don't understand how this situation has evolved."

Laslow ran his hands through his hair. "He's crazy. Must be."

Meyerstein stared at Laslow. She detected an irritation in his tone of voice. Was it sarcasm? "That's not the man I know. Yes, he's a trained killer. But he's not crazy. He wouldn't go and gun down Chinese diplomats just for the hell of it. So, I want to find Reznick."

Laslow went quiet for a few moments. "I've got to be up front, Martha. I'm concerned that this wacko has any sway with you or the FBI."

"He's no wacko, Don. And let me be very clear, he has no sway with me."

"What I mean is that we can all see what sort of guy he is. He's a damaged ex-Delta nutcase."

"I don't care for your language."

"Oh come on, Martha. We all know he's certifiable."

"That's where you're wrong. He has high intelligence and is considered one of the most brilliant CIA operators over the last twenty years. He has brought down drug cartels, jihadists, and terrorists. He has helped out the FBI on highly classified operations. So, do not underestimate him or call him crazy. He's far from crazy. But, yes, I agree he is dangerous."

"Point taken," Laslow said, changing the direction of the discussion.

Meyerstein sat in stony silence. She knew it had to stop. Enough was enough. She had had her fill of Jon Reznick. It seemed like every year there was another crisis. She faced losing the job she loved. She believed in the FBI. What it stood for. The problem was that Reznick, a man she very much admired, maybe even loved, seemed to push the boundaries of her tolerance to the breaking point. Reznick as a man couldn't give a damn about the FBI. He didn't respect it. She thought at one time he did. But it was clear from his actions that he held the organization in contempt. He was a maverick. A rogue operative. She'd known that all along.

Meyerstein looked across the table at Thomas Kelly, the FBI's head of counterintelligence in New York. He wore a well-tailored single-breasted navy suit, a white shirt, and a pale-blue tie that matched the color of his eyes. "What's your take, Thomas? Where are we?"

Kelly looked up from his note taking and fiddled with the gold cuff links on his starched white shirt. He sat as if in quiet contemplation. "Reznick is as tough as they come, as you say," he said. "We all know that."

Meyerstein nodded.

"The problem is," Kelly said, "Reznick is getting enmeshed with stuff he doesn't understand. This is not his usual theater of operations. His modus operandi. In this instance, we are dealing with the People's Republic of China, after all."

"You're referring to the diplomats?"

"Correct. I don't believe they're diplomats in the true sense of the word. And these people, they operate on a whole other level than what Reznick is used to. A world of spies."

Meyerstein glanced at Laslow.

"To put you in the picture, Martha," Kelly said, "my last report concerning China's nefarious activities in and around New York was pretty conclusive. They're probing. The tempo has changed. They're upping the ante. They're testing us. They want to see how far we go. What happened down in Chinatown might be the latest example of that. And that's why we need to find Jon Reznick, for his own good."

Meyerstein nodded at Kelly, impressed with his summary. "So, what happened might be linked, indirectly or directly, to Chinese spying in New York?"

"High degree of probability."

"If that's the case, do you believe the three people Reznick killed had their actions officially sanctioned by Beijing?"

"Maybe tacitly approved. Hard to tell. But the mood is different. China's taking its first steps in the last year or so. Crossing boundaries. And the mask has slipped."

The meeting broke up then, and Meyerstein headed back to her office and shut the door. The threat to Reznick from the Chinese operatives was clear. She wondered what on earth had possessed Reznick and Trevelle to become fugitives.

A few moments later, her phone rang.

"Meyerstein."

"Well, well, well, Assistant Director." It was a voice she didn't recognize.

"Who's this?"

"My name is Robert Chow, consul general at the Chinese consulate here in New York."

Meyerstein's blood ran cold.

"Assistant Director, I just got off a call with your boss. He said you are the most senior person in New York, although the Kevin Chang investigation is being led by the Special Agent in Charge of New York. Am I correct?"

Meyerstein shifted in her seat. "Mr. Chow, that is correct. How can I help?"

"I want answers."

"I think it best to direct your questions to Special Agent in Charge Laslow. He is in charge of the New York FBI."

"I talk to the most senior people only. I will talk to you. And that's why the Director passed on your details. I trust that is not a problem."

Meyerstein sensed a migraine coming on. "Not a problem at all."

"Two of my diplomats, one a friend from university, are both dead. I've just spoken to their families back in Shanghai. They are devastated. They want answers. The Chinese people require answers."

"First of all, I would like to express my condolences for this terrible event. We are at an early stage trying to establish the facts."

"Enough! How dare you try and placate us. Do you think we Chinese will simply turn the other cheek? This is an outrage!"

Meyerstein wondered if this guy knew more than he was letting on.

"Do you know the person at the center of this? His name is Kevin Chang. He is from Hong Kong. He is a criminal and fugitive."

"I'm not at liberty to discuss details of this case. But is there anything else you would like to share with us?"

"Yes, I would. I have been in touch with ICE and Homeland Security."

Now Meyerstein definitely realized this guy knew more than he was letting on.

"They agree with us that Kevin Chang should be removed from this country and deported to China. I'll be holding you personally responsible if this Chang is not brought to justice where he belongs, behind bars, in China."

Five

It was nearly midnight as the stolen Mazda traveled north through Queens.

Reznick glanced in the rearview mirror as Trevelle and Chang hunkered down in the back seat. The three of them had taken a cab to an abandoned warehouse in Far Rockaway. They had laid low for hours. Then Reznick decided it was time to break cover. He had stolen a parked car two streets away.

The mood was tense as Reznick sped on.

"Where exactly are we going, Jon?" Trevelle asked.

"I'm still trying to figure it out. We can't hide forever."

Chang began to sob. "I'm scared. I didn't want this. I didn't want any of this."

Reznick glanced again in the mirror. "Just hang in there, Kevin. Here's the deal: I'll take you straight to the nearest police precinct if you want. Right here, right now. It's your call."

"No. Please don't."

"Are you absolutely sure, Kevin?"

Chang nodded vigorously. "I know what will happen. The cops will arrest me, and further down the line, I will be deported to China."

"This is not China."

"I will be arrested. And they will throw me out of the country. They will torture me. Maybe they will send me to a reeducation camp."

Reznick nodded. "Let's take it easy. I see where you're coming from. But this is on a whole different level now. I killed those people. At least two were diplomats. But you did not kill them."

Chang said, "I will be the one to blame."

Trevelle shook his head. "I wish I hadn't gotten you involved, Jon."

"Well, I am involved, OK? So, we need to move on. And both of you need to compose yourselves. We need to figure this shit out. And quick."

Trevelle sighed, "What a mess."

"I don't want to hear any more bullshit negativity. We need solutions. This is not the time for morose thoughts. Think!"

"So, what do you propose?" Trevelle said.

"Here's my plan. I believe we should reach out to the FBI."

Chang said quietly, "I don't know."

"Kevin, can I at least try and speak to the FBI? Maybe cut a deal."

Chang was quiet for a moment. "What sort of deal?"

"A guarantee that you would not be deported under any circumstances. That's our red line."

"That would be a smarter move, I think, than going to the police. That's for sure."

Reznick drove on, through a desolate area not far from Rockaway Beach. "I'm going to get a new pair of wheels, OK?"

Trevelle said, "Sure thing."

Reznick pulled up on a near-deserted side street behind a Ford Transit Van. He got out and pried open the passenger door of the van. He reached over and took a couple of minutes to hot-wire the van. He climbed in and revved up the vehicle as Trevelle and Chang climbed into the back seat. "Bit more spacious, guys? Buckle up!"

Chang said, "Let's go."

Reznick sped away and drove for ten miles through northern Queens until he pulled up beside a rare pay phone. "This is as good a place as any. I'm going to make the call to the FBI. Sit tight."

Chang sat quietly, head bowed.

"You OK for me to do this, Kevin?"

"It's the best plan."

Reznick reached over and ruffled his hair. "We'll figure this out, don't worry. I'm not going to bail on you." He got out of the van, looking around the deserted street before he tapped in Meyerstein's phone number. He waited a few moments as it rang.

Eventually, it was picked up.

"Who's this?" Martha Meyerstein sounded stressed.

"It's Reznick."

"Jon . . . my God, what the hell is going on?"

"Long story."

"You need to turn yourself in, along with Trevelle and Kevin, Jon."

"That's why I'm calling. We need to talk."

"Where are you?"

"You need to listen to me, Martha."

"I'm assuming you know the whereabouts of Kevin Chang?"

Reznick stood, filthy pay phone pressed to his ear. "I don't want to get into that."

"Jon, you are in serious trouble."

"Tell me something I don't know."

"What the hell happened? Maybe I can help you."

"Forget about me. I want to talk about Kevin Chang."

"Tell us where you are. Is Kevin with you?"

"I have a proposition."

Martha exhaled loudly. "What sort of proposition?"

"I will hand myself in. But I need a cast-iron guarantee that Kevin Chang will be safe from deportation to China if I hand him over. He wasn't involved in this."

"I don't do guarantees."

"Bullshit, Martha. You guys cut deals all the time."

"Immigration officials and Homeland Security, not to mention the State Department, as well as the NYPD and the FBI are interested in Kevin Chang. He is not an American citizen."

"I'm trying to come to an agreement. I'm reaching out to you. I'm helping you if you can help me."

"That's not how it works, and you know it."

"I want you to trust me."

"Jon, trust is earned. The fact is, I *don't* trust you anymore. I don't trust you not to go crazy and get involved in all this madness. I can't take it. I can't do this."

"Let me explain what went down. I arrived and heard shouting inside the apartment. I kicked down the door. What I saw was a man with a gun to Kevin's head."

"So, you killed that guy?"

"Yes, I did. I was responsible. I want to go on the record. I'll take my chances. But Kevin isn't responsible. I was trying to save him. I was defending him."

"Tell me where you are, and then we can talk. You killed two Chinese diplomats. Do you even understand the ramifications of your actions?"

"I know full well."

"This is the final straw. And you need to know one thing—we will find you."

"You're not making this easy for me. I'm giving you a heads-up. The diplomats were threatening Kevin. They tried to kill me. I was acting in self-defense. I had to take the fuckers down."

"We can talk about that. We can work something out there. But right now, it's a diplomatic nightmare. The Chinese government will not take this lying down."

"They were going to kill Kevin. All I'm asking is for the FBI to give me a guarantee that Kevin will be safe and not deported. A guarantee for Kevin, that's all. Not for me, for him."

"No guarantees. No deal."

"I'm going to ask one final time."

She cut him off. "Like I said, no deal. No guarantees."

Reznick ended the call as his mood began to darken, knowing they had to get the hell out of New York. He got back in the van and sped off.

"What did Martha say?" Trevelle asked.

"No deal."

"So, what do we do?"

"We need to find a place to hide out for a while. Out of the city."

Reznick sped over the Whitestone Bridge, the East River below. He drove through the Bronx and into the night, trying to figure out their next move.

Six

The early morning sun streamed through the windows of the beachfront cottage in Madison, Connecticut, bathing the inside in a beautiful tangerine glow.

Caroline Sullivan sat hunched over her computer, as she invariably did seven days a week, working to finally deliver her long-awaited book, a tome on America's national security threats in the twenty-first century. The more she learned about the ongoing threats from China, Russia, and Iran, among others, the more she feared for the country. Computer viruses. Psyops warfare waged online. Energy security. Robots. Drones. Asymmetric warfare through hacking economic and infrastructure facilities. The list went on and on. But despite America's spending, the threat level was increasing, and some of the spiraling hidden costs were allocated to future programs. If that wasn't enough, America owed an insane thirty-one trillion dollars and counting. The country's enemies were watching and waiting in the wings as America began to buckle under the strain.

She leaned back in her seat and bemoaned the mess all around her. Her desk was strewn with notepads and yellow Post-Its and excerpts of what she had already written. She cast a glance over typed interviews she had conducted with intelligence operatives, or retired analysts from think tanks, or politicians who had sat on intelligence committees. She grimaced at a collection of empty cups of coffee. The book was an all-consuming project. But it was also spiraling out of control, a bit like the national debt, becoming a bit of a monster.

She had already asked for two extensions over the last year. A third delay wasn't an option. It had to be delivered in three months. She was already two hundred thousand words in. She imagined at least sixty thousand words to go. It was a monumental task. She didn't want to think too much about it or she would never get any work done.

Her editor in New York, a sweet man, was getting antsy. He had called her two days earlier, wanting an update. He seemed partially placated with her progress. At least so far.

Sullivan took a few moments to appreciate the rest of her study. Framed journalism awards from the last fifteen years. Newspaper scoops for the *New York Times*. An Investigative Reporter of the Year award. She had been lauded for her tireless work on defense issues. She had broken numerous stories on foreign attempts to penetrate the National Security Agency's Fort Meade facility, penetration of FBI operations by foreign intelligence agencies, illegal operations by the CIA at home and abroad, and ongoing operations by Russia and China to infiltrate intelligence facilities and collect sensitive schematics of planes and drones being developed at secret defense facilities across America.

She loved her work. Maybe she loved it too much. She hadn't taken time to think of herself. She had no social life. She hadn't been into the city for months. But she had no time to slack now.

She spun in her chair to the windows facing the ocean in the distance. She loved the beach town. But occasionally, very occasionally, she still felt the pull of the big city.

The more she thought about it, the more she wondered if she needed to get back into Manhattan. The hustle and bustle, the distractions, the busyness, the cultural life she enjoyed. She was loathe to give up her family home, this idyllic retreat in an idyllic small New England town. She had made close friends who lived nearby.

Her phone rang, snapping her out of her daydreaming.

Sullivan picked up, expecting to hear the acerbic wit of her editor in Manhattan. "Yes, Caroline speaking."

"Caroline, I don't know if you remember me." The voice sounded familiar.

Sullivan couldn't place the voice. She wondered if it was a former colleague from the *Times*.

"It's Trevelle. Trevelle Williams."

"Ex-NSA Trevelle?"

"Ex-NSA Trevelle, right. How are you?"

"My God, it must've been nearly a year, right?"

"Listen, Caroline, I need some help."

Sullivan wondered what he meant. "What kind of help?"

"I'm in trouble."

"You?"

"Yeah, me."

"Who are you in trouble with? Do you need money?"

"No, I don't need money."

"What do you need?"

"I need a place to hide out for a few hours."

Sullivan's stomach knotted. "I don't understand . . . What've you done?"

"I need you to trust me. I trusted you with my confidence. Now I'm asking you to return the favor."

"I don't know how exactly I can help."

"Get me and my two friends out of sight. Just for a little while. Maybe a few hours."

"This is a little strange." Sullivan wondered what the hell Trevelle was talking about. "It depends. What did you do?"

"I know it's strange. It's actually more than strange. It's a bad situation. A few hours ago . . . Turn on the TV. Fox News."

"Why?"

"Just do it, Caroline."

Sullivan walked through to her den and picked up her remote control. Live footage showed a reporter in Lower Manhattan in front of a downtown bodega after a triple shooting in Chinatown. "OK, what does this have to do with you? You're not a killer."

"No, I'm not."

"Did you have something to do with this?"

"I don't want to elaborate on the phone."

"I'm not recording it, I assure you."

"There is more to this than meets the eye. A lot more."

"I'm going to need some more details."

A sigh. "Caroline, I'm desperate."

"Tell me what happened first. I need to know the big picture."

"Two of the people who were killed worked for the Chinese government. My friend killed them."

"Are you serious?"

"Deadly. Can you help us?"

"This doesn't sound like you, Trevelle."

"It wasn't me. But I am involved. Caroline, are you going to help?"

"I need answers first. Why did your friend kill them?"

"He was defending a guy from Hong Kong. A guy who was being threatened by these goons. My friend who shot the Chinese operatives is former CIA. He's the real deal. I will vouch for him any day."

Sullivan's journalistic instincts kicked in. "Tell me more."

"How much more do you need?"

44

"Tell me what you can."

"The man who pulled the trigger is a friend of mine, and we've worked together. He's a good guy. He's ex-CIA, ex-Delta."

"This is . . . a lot to take in."

Sullivan wondered if she should call the cops. That would be the right thing to do. Her mind raced, unsure, torn between different emotions.

"I need an answer, Caroline. It'll just be for a few hours."

Sullivan closed her eyes for a moment. "OK."

"Where are you?"

Sullivan gave her address in Madison.

Then the line went dead.

Seven

Madison was a place Reznick hadn't been before.

It was late morning when he turned the Ford van onto Neck Road, past beautiful colonial houses lining either side of the road. Then he turned onto Middle Beach Road. Past weather-beaten shingle-style houses overlooking the Long Island Sound.

The last house on the road, a beach cottage, sported a Stars and Stripes on the front porch, fluttering in the breeze.

Reznick glanced in the rearview mirror. "Is that it?"

Trevelle checked a map on his phone. "That's the address. Right at the end, she said."

"Can we really trust this woman? This is a big ask."

"I trust her. She has never betrayed my confidence."

Reznick reversed the Ford van into the driveway. "Fair enough. You want to talk to her first?"

Trevelle stepped out and knocked on the door. He stood and waited for a few moments. Then the door opened, and he disappeared inside.

Reznick peered in the rearview mirror at Kevin Chang. "Don't worry, son, we'll figure this out." But he could see the kid's eyes were filled with fear and apprehension. "Just hang in there. I think this is going to be fine."

"Can we trust her?"

"I guess we'll have to. We have to put our trust in someone."

Chang shook his head. "I can't believe the FBI didn't want to talk to me."

"They didn't say that. They do want to talk to you. And me. But they couldn't offer any guarantees that you wouldn't be deported."

"Thank you for what you're doing."

"Listen, let's just see how this goes."

The door opened, and Trevelle waved them both inside.

Reznick escorted Chang into the house. The woman who owned the home locked the door behind them. She showed them up to a huge attic furnished with two single beds and a sofa.

The woman smiled. She was very attractive, dressed in faded jeans, a white T-shirt, and sneakers. "Consider it your safe house. For a little while. I'll do what I can."

Reznick looked at Sullivan. "I appreciate this. It's very kind of you."

"And you're Reznick, I believe. Jon Reznick, right?"

"Correct."

Sullivan nodded. "I've made some sandwiches and soup for you guys. Down in the kitchen if you want some."

The three of them followed her back downstairs to a light-blue Shaker kitchen, walls decorated with black-and-white photos of the woman with political figures, writers, and journalists at award ceremonies.

Reznick noticed several professional black-and-white photos of a military man in uniform. A general.

"Take a load off," she said.

Reznick, Trevelle, and Kevin sat down at the table. On a white linen tablecloth she'd set an assortment of dishes and serving plates and a couple of large jugs of ice water with slices of lemon. "That's quite a spread," Reznick said.

"Thanks." She served up delicious bowls of piping hot lentil soup, coconut rice with blackened fish, and mango salsa garnish. She also served up plates of wild salmon sandwiches on rye bread.

The woman addressed her unexpected guests. "My name is Caroline Sullivan. I put in a few calls before you arrived. I now have a better idea of the situation that transpired. I would like to hear your side of the story. If that's OK."

Trevelle nudged Chang. "Caroline is a journalist. Don't be afraid. She can help you."

Chang nodded. "I think that's a good idea. I want to put on the record what happened. It might help."

"Great. Eat up first. You must be starving," Caroline said.

Reznick was floored by Sullivan's calm demeanor in light of what he had done. Trevelle and Chang loaded up their plates with rice and fish, devouring the sandwiches and the soup, famished. He dug in himself. It felt good to get some nutritious food after not eating for a day. "This is delicious."

Sullivan flushed. "It's whatever I had in the pantry."

"Seriously delicious."

Sullivan followed up the food with some fresh coffee and chocolates. "Coffee, Jon?"

"Absolutely."

Sullivan made small talk with them for the next half hour as they sat at the table. Then she cleared the dishes, helped by Trevelle.

Reznick looked across at Kevin Chang, who seemed distracted. "You OK?"

"I'm OK. Just new surroundings, getting used to it."

"You're good. Take it easy."

Sullivan held a copy of the *New York Post* with the photo of Amy Chang. "I learned this happened a few days ago. This is your sister?"

Chang closed his eyes and nodded. "Yes, ma'am."

"I'm guessing that there's a connection between her death and the killings of the Chinese diplomats in Chinatown?"

Chang nodded. "Amy was my sister. You are correct. And yes, her death connects to what happened yesterday at my friend's apartment. My sister feared for her life. She believed she was being followed."

"It's weird that this connection hasn't been picked up by the media."

"Maybe the information as to my identity hasn't been released," Chang said.

Sullivan nodded. "That's true; this doesn't mention you at all."

Reznick said, "The Feds will be keeping all this tight to their chests."

Sullivan nodded. "That's right."

Kevin sighed. "You see, this whole thing began when my sister was pushed to her death."

"It does make more sense now. The two separate incidents. The connection between the push and Kevin being threatened before the killings. The story in the *Post*, as it stands, just reads as a tragic piece of bad luck, after a spate of fatal pushes on the subway."

Chang shook his head. "Want to know the real story?"

Sullivan reached over for a legal pad and pen from her kitchen counter. She began to scribble a few shorthand notes. "You mind?"

"Please, I'd like you to hear our story."

"So, your sister was scared," Sullivan said. "She was being followed?"

"What happened to both of us is a pattern of surveillance and intimidation of dissidents from Hong Kong who live in America that culminates in cold-blooded killings."

Sullivan looked up and across the table at Trevelle. "What do you know as a friend of Kevin's?"

"Amy was my girlfriend."

"Oh my God, I'm so sorry."

"I can give you background on what happened. I wasn't in the room when Jon burst in. I was off to one side on the stairwell landing. When Jon took down the two people in the stairwell, I had moved into the room. I can tell you what I know and what I saw."

Sullivan turned her gaze to Reznick. "And Jon? What about you?"

"What about me?"

"I'd like to interview you. Get your thoughts on what transpired, in your own words."

Reznick shook his head. "I'll talk to you off the record. But nothing on the record. I will tell you what I know. And I'll help you. But no photos, no video of me whatsoever. Agreed?"

Sullivan scribbled some notes. "I got it. That would be really helpful. And you were the one who took them out?"

"Trevelle and Kevin can tell you what led up to it and how I got involved. But yeah, I did it. I killed all three."

"Categorically, you're not denying it was you?"

"Categorically, it was me. One hundred percent. I killed all three. Two diplomats and one Chinese private investigator from New York. I checked the IDs."

"Seriously?"

"As trained killers, that's what we do. We check to see if the people have any ID, wallet, whatever."

"Special forces, right?"

Reznick checked his watch. "I'll give you the full story. But first, I need to make a call. And I need some privacy."

"Not a problem."

Chang looked anxious. "Who are you calling, Jon?"

"I'm going to try and see if the FBI wants to cut a deal to keep you safe. They didn't want to last night. Maybe they've changed their minds today."

"I appreciate that, Jon."

"It's a long shot but worth trying."

Sullivan got up, and he followed her through the french doors that led out to her deck. She pointed across the sand dunes. "The path leads to the beach."

Reznick looked at Sullivan, amazed at how accommodating she was. "This is above and beyond what I expected."

"Just a temporary measure, Jon. I'm snowed under with work."

"Sure thing. We'll be out of your way in a few hours. You'll never know we were here."

Reznick headed across the wooden boardwalk and onto the beach. He walked down to the water's edge, small waves gently lapping the fine sand. He took out his phone and dialed Meyerstein's number. He had been reassured by Trevelle that his phone was wrapped up in cutting-edge military-grade encryption. Three years in advance of what was available. In time, maybe through a stroke of luck, the FBI or cops would eventually find them. Maybe through surveillance cameras out on the streets. Maybe through random police stops.

He wasn't stupid. He knew reaching out to the Feds or Meyerstein again posed risks. He had worked in high-risk situations all his life. Missions behind enemy lines in Iraq in the dead of night. He wasn't fazed by risk. But he believed that contacting the FBI was a risk worth taking. He knew they could offer a better level of protection and guarantee the security and safety of Kevin Chang. He was prepared to give himself up to allow it. He viewed it as a trade-off: Reznick for Chang's security and a guarantee he wouldn't be extradited. He thought it was a no-brainer.

Reznick waited a few moments for her to answer.

"Meyerstein," she said. Her voice sounded strained, which wasn't surprising. "Who's this?"

Reznick stared out at the calming blue waters. "Reznick. I'm sorry for calling again. But I want to do this deal. I want this to happen."

"Exactly what kind of deal?"

"The same deal I outlined last night."

"You are in no position to ask for any favors or any deal. Hand him over, Jon. And turn yourself in too. You're a fugitive. This is not going to end well."

"I can do all that, sure. I promise you that. But as I said earlier, I need a guarantee that he won't be handed over to ICE and deported to China. The kid is afraid for his life. He's a green card holder. Meet me halfway on this, Martha, and make this happen. Get O'Donoghue to sign off on it, and we're good."

Reznick walked farther along the beach, phone pressed tight to his ear.

"Where are you calling from? Let me know, and we can bring you all in safe and sound. Then we can talk."

Reznick sensed her hostility. It wasn't surprising. He peered up at the sky, a pristine blue, a few dark clouds visible on the far horizon. "I can help you if you can help this kid. And he is just a kid. A frightened kid."

"You're taking the law into your own hands, Jon, and not for the first time. This time it stops. It's over."

"Forget about me for a moment. Think about Kevin Chang. He's an innocent."

"But you're not! You killed two diplomats! Are you insane? This stops now. It's over!"

"You're not getting it. You're just not getting it at all."

"Getting what? What am I not getting?"

"You're not getting what I'm prepared to do to protect this kid."

A silence stretched between them.

Reznick sat down in the cold sand for a few minutes as he stared out at the big, blue sky. "I'm asking you as a favor . . . not for me. For Kevin. Please, I'm begging you. Try."

"I'm not in the business of doing deals with killers or their accomplices."

Reznick let the stillness wash over him.

"OK, here's what I'm prepared to consider. I'm going to think about this again. And I'll do what I can. How does that sound?"

"I need guarantees. Signed and sealed."

"You need to trust me. Trust that I'll do my best for Kevin. I'll do what I can."

"If it was just you, I would. But you're talking for the FBI. I don't trust them. Not one bit."

"What do you mean? Your daughter used to be a special agent herself. Did you not trust Lauren?"

"Enough bullshit. You'll be able to haul me in and let the Chinese consulate know you have the person responsible, just so long as Kevin is protected from those thugs in that regime. Take it or leave it."

"Goddamn it, I'm trying to cut you a break. We can work things out. But not if you act like this. You've gone rogue."

"That's rich coming from the FBI."

"What about Lauren?"

"What about her?"

"How do you think she'll feel when she learns that you're a fugitive?"

"What does Lauren have to do with this?"

"Have you thought about the impact this will have on her career at the Agency?"

Reznick was dumbstruck that Meyerstein would use emotional blackmail for her own means. "Are you serious? Her career? Are you threatening to derail my daughter's career at the Agency?"

"I just want you to see the big picture, that's all. All American intelligence agencies are interconnected."

Reznick wondered now if he had ever really known Martha Meyerstein. He had always thought when they worked together that there was a semblance of trust. A deep understanding of the other's concerns. A thread of common decency. A thread of humanity. But something along the way seemed to have eroded and finally destroyed that relationship.

Reznick sensed that Meyerstein was now finally cutting him loose. Except she wasn't saying it in so many words.

"Are you still there?"

"Yeah, I'm still here."

"Look, I'm sorry, I don't have the full story of what happened, it's true. I'm in the dark on some of this."

"I defended Kevin Chang and myself from those crazies."

"I believe you."

Reznick closed his eyes. It was a small validation of sorts. "Thank you."

"But we need this to stop. You need to turn yourself in. And Kevin."

"I can make that happen. But you know how these things work. With the FBI, it's all politics. DOJ. State Department. Beijing will be all over them, raising holy hell across diplomatic circles. And the Feds will cave on this."

"I hear what you're saying. I do. Listen, how about I get back in touch with the Director?"

"I could live with that."

"But I'm going to need time."

"You have twenty-four hours to deliver a deal. I've drawn a line in the sand. Do what you have to do."

Eight

The headlights bathed the deserted woodland park on the outskirts of Great Falls, Virginia.

James Bradley pulled up, switched off the ignition, and got out of his car, backpack in hand. He wore his usual running gear: hooded gray sweatshirt, pants, and Nike sneakers. He put down the backpack and began to stretch, making sure his quads and calves warmed up for at least five minutes. He never changed this routine, sure it had helped him stay free of injury. He took a few deep breaths of the cool night air. He loved his runs under the moonlight. He pulled on his small backpack, filled with emergency provisions, a first aid kit, and water. Then he headed off, down the trail and into the night.

Bradley pounded the dirt path as he began his session. He was a fifty-three-year-old running nut. Had been since his teens. In college, he had excelled. Gold medals for running. But he had never taken it up professionally. He went down a different career path. He got his master's, then a PhD in international relations. He joined the Army. He worked intelligence in Iraq. All over the Middle East. Then the CIA came calling. He became a highly valued senior analyst. But running was the one thing that was an outlet from his pressurized work environment. It gave him time to think. To clear his head. It made him feel good about himself.

Riverbend Park was a place he loved. He had settled in Great Falls twenty years earlier after joining the Agency. It was a beautiful small town, surrounded by thousands of acres of forests and ponds. But it also had beautiful hiking trails. He ran on the trails, no matter the weather. He felt free here. The endorphins kicked in. In the summer months, the place was swarming with people. He couldn't run without bumping into someone. But in the offseason, like it was now, he was in a little slice of heaven. The anglers he occasionally spotted also loved the pastoral serenity.

Bradley, more and more, just wanted peace. A place to forget. The life he had planned as a retired CIA operative should have been a breeze. But none of it had turned out like that.

He had fallen on hard times. His life had taken a downward spiral in the last few years, despite all his best efforts. On the surface, his life looked great. He lived in a large house in a delightful neighborhood of Great Falls. But his security consulting business was losing serious money. His neighbors, meanwhile, were oblivious. They had worked at the Agency with Bradley, attended his church, or worked in highly paid jobs in DC. He was always taught to put his best foot forward. Not to complain. And to work with a smile on his face. But his outward genial appearance masked the internal turmoil.

Bradley was facing financial ruin. He could see bankruptcy on the horizon. He couldn't face the ignominy. His head swam as he headed off down the river side. He stopped for a few minutes and did a few more stretching exercises. Then he set off on his nightly ten-mile run.

His friends at church thought he was weird for running alone at night. He didn't care. This was his time. A precious time. The moonlight illuminated the way, as it usually did. When it didn't, he ran with a headlamp. He preferred no lights. No distractions as he tried to figure out a way to salvage his dire financial situation. The same blight of bankruptcy had ruined his father forty years earlier when Bradley was a boy. He remembered the pain. The screaming matches between his parents during the inevitable family breakup. The poverty that had followed. He was haunted by the failure of his father. And now it was his turn. It was like a curse.

He ran on and on, pounding the hard ground. The musty smell of the water and fecund aroma of the trees and foliage filled his senses. It reminded him of running as a boy to escape his tormented father's mood swings as his own business went under. God, it was awful.

On and on he ran.

Bradley's mind flashed back to the moment his financial situation began to deteriorate three years earlier. His late mother had accrued insane amounts of medical bills. Two hundred and thirteen thousand dollars from enduring countless operations after being run over outside her retirement community in Florida by an alcoholic delivery driver. The driver was uninsured. She was insured. But the bills quickly outstripped her time-limited coverage. Bradley had picked up the tab. It was a big hit to take. And then he had his three children in college. That was killing him, as was his divorce settlement. He thought there was no way out. He had even contemplated taking his own life. But he couldn't face the oblivion.

Bradley ran until he got to the Riverbend Park boat ramp. He wondered if he should move abroad, maybe to Europe. He wondered if Dubai was a possibility. Tax-free, year-round sun, tens of thousands of American expats and businesses thriving.

His eyes wandered around the bucolic waterside setting. They fixed on a luminous yellow arrow marker alongside a luminous yellow triangle inscribed on a tree.

Bradley's senses switched on at that moment. This was it. They had finally made contact. They said they would. But now it was happening.

He jogged on for another mile until he got to a wooden footbridge. He spotted a luminous green circle marked on a tree, adjacent to the footbridge.

He kneeled and looked underneath the wooden bridge and spotted a black plastic bag tied with duct tape. He reached over and pulled the dripping bag toward him. It felt like a box was inside.

Bradley placed the bag and unknown contents inside his backpack, zipping it shut. He took a piece of yellow chalk out of his backpack pocket and chalked a yellow cross on the bark of a tall oak, his sign to tell them that the pickup had been completed. Then he headed back the route he had come on, finishing his night run through the dark, moonlit park.

Bradley returned to his car and quickly drove back home. He locked his door and headed to his study. He pulled the curtain shut and switched on his desk lamp.

He laid the black plastic bag on his desk, then ripped it open. Inside was an item wrapped in duct tape. He carefully peeled that off. Inside was an outdated, scratched Samsung Galaxy phone.

It's them. They want to talk.

Bradley turned on the phone. It came to life. A number appeared on his new phone. He called the unknown number.

It rang seven times before a voice answered.

"The weather is changeable," a man's voice said on the other end of the line. It was the coded phrase Bradley had been told to expect.

Bradley replied, "The forecast is mixed, so I hear."

"Good evening, sir. How are you?"

"I'm fine. Wondering what is required."

"We want to know the whereabouts of a man from Hong Kong. A criminal. Goes by the name Kevin Chang."

"Are the alphabet agencies involved in the search for this guy?"

"One hundred percent. NSA, CIA, and of course the FBI. Find out what they know. Even a nugget of information. We want to know anything they know. It might seem like nothing. But we want to know whatever it is."

Bradley already had the name *Kevin Chang* seared into his brain. "Got it."

"We'll be in touch. Your account in the British Virgin Islands has just been credited one hundred thousand American dollars. As we promised. So, you're up and running. We look forward to getting some fresh intel very soon."

Bradley closed his eyes with relief. "I'm much obliged."

"Don't let us down."

Nine

Just before midnight, Reznick headed back out onto the beach in Madison, needing time to clear his head. He had been cooped up inside since he'd made the call to Meyerstein. He needed to figure out his next move.

He should have anticipated Meyerstein taking a hard-line stance. He'd gotten them involved in a diplomatic crisis. You didn't have to be Henry Kissinger to know that.

He looked back at the lights in the house.

Sullivan stood on her deck, holding a mug of coffee, watching him. She waved and he acknowledged her.

He still didn't know if he could trust her. Journalists and writers used confidential sources. That was a given. Especially for investigative reporters working on sensitive stories. But if push came to shove, and under enough pressure, some journalists would cave on their principles. All it would take was a misplaced comment at a fancy cocktail party to an intelligence source, and his confidence could be breached.

Reznick's thoughts switched back Meyerstein. He could see that his fraught relationship with her was withering on the vine. It felt as if an unspoken trust and understanding between them had already eroded. The problem had been simmering for many months. Maybe the last year or so.

It began, or so it seemed to Reznick, very gradually. He sensed she no longer had his back. He felt a growing distance between them. It was almost imperceptible at the start. Maybe his trip to Switzerland, which had unearthed his wife's involvement as a CIA sleeper agent neutralizing Russian operatives had been the final straw for her. Maybe she had come to realize that his unorthodox involvement with FBI investigations was damaging her career. He had lost track of the times she had taken his side against the Director when he had crossed legal and ethical red lines. Maybe the relationship had simply run its course. Then came the rupture, caused by the killings in Chinatown.

Reznick headed back up the beach, doubts crowding his exhausted mind. Trevelle had vouched for Sullivan. He trusted her. Implicitly. It was all about judgment. Was Trevelle's judgment sound?

Sullivan gave a small friendly wave as Reznick approached. "Coffee?"

"Please, strong and black."

"I thought you were going to spend the night out there."

"Just clearing my head. Time to think. We've got to be heading out soon."

Sullivan headed back inside as Reznick followed behind her. He shut and locked the huge french doors that led out onto the beachfront deck. Then he pulled the curtains shut.

"You're very security conscious," she said. "I like it."

"Old habits."

Sullivan poured Reznick a cup of coffee. He pulled up a chair as they stared at each other across the table. "The boys are OK. They're upstairs."

"Getting some shut-eye, hopefully?"

"I hope so."

"We need to get going. I think we've overstayed our welcome."

Sullivan shrugged. "I'm not showing you guys the door . . . yet."

They sat in companionable silence.

"This is all very . . . out of left field. It's kind of thrown me. Freaked me out, actually, if I'm honest."

"Listen, we'll be out of your hair really soon, I promise. I don't want to cause you any trouble."

Sullivan curled her silky dark hair behind one ear.

"I've got a question for you," he said.

"Shoot."

"Why didn't you just call the cops on us? That would be the right and lawful thing to do, after all."

Sullivan shrugged. "My father always said to gather the facts the best you can. Then check, verify, and check again. That's what I did when I got the call from Trevelle. And what you've told me is interesting. I find it rather compelling that you went to Chinatown at the request of your friend. So, you were doing him a favor, right?"

"Right."

"Then it all went to shit, and you had to shoot the guy who was pointing a gun at Kevin and two others who had guns drawn on you as you tried to get out of there."

"Pretty much, yeah."

"So, you see, I've had time to check, verify, and check again. I also considered what Trevelle told me too."

"What did he say?"

"He said that late last night, you reached out to the FBI at a senior level. Said you would turn yourself in in exchange for a guarantee of Kevin's safety, that he wouldn't be extradited. And you did it again this afternoon."

"You got it."

"I also thought about what I would do if I was in your situation."

"And what would you do?"

Sullivan sipped her coffee. "Honestly? I don't know. What I do know is that what you're doing for Kevin is selfless."

"If the Chinese government gets its hands on him, he's dead. Make no mistake."

Sullivan nodded. "I agree. So, for all those reasons, I figure that putting you up here for a little while is a small sacrifice. But it has the added bonus for me that it allows me to get a front seat to Chinese methods of intimidation and tactics to threaten dissidents in America. And yes, in a selfish sort of way, it helps me too."

"Quid pro quo, and all that."

Sullivan laughed. "You can't beat a bit of Latin, right?"

"If you say so."

"Just to give you a heads-up, I've already had an initial interview with Trevelle and Kevin. This absolutely helps me write a fascinating, firsthand account of the events. Quite a crazy day you're having."

Reznick took a sip of the scalding hot coffee. "I could do without the aggravation. But it is what it is. Listen, I appreciate this hospitality. But I don't want to impose much longer, Caroline. We're not going to outstay our welcome."

Sullivan shrugged. "I would tell if you were."

"Straight talk works for me."

"Without trying to sound too mercenary—"

"You're a journalist, right?"

Sullivan laughed. "I hear you. It's not the most popular profession, I know. I'd really, really like to interview you at length. What transpired. What work you've been involved in."

Reznick felt himself grimace. "I don't know. Some of it is unpleasant. Some of it is classified."

"You said, correct me if I'm wrong, off the record would be fine."

"True."

"I don't give up sources for anyone. I give you my word."

Reznick didn't want to hang around much longer. He checked his watch. "It's three minutes after midnight. I think we've got to go. Maybe within the next half hour."

"How about you tell me what you know until they wake up."

"You do know we're fugitives?"

"I'm well aware of that, Jon." Sullivan reached over to a shelf in the kitchen and picked up a MacBook. She flipped it open. "Tell me what happened. Blow by blow."

"Off the record?"

"Strictly."

Reznick finished his coffee and spent the next twenty minutes going over the chain of events. The call from Trevelle, the trip to New York, then the triple shooting in Chinatown.

Sullivan typed quickly as he told the story, occasionally interrupting with further questions. Reznick reached into his pocket and pulled out the three IDs he had taken from the victims.

"Holy shit." Sullivan picked up her phone and took photos, front and back, of the IDs. She typed in the names of the victims and began to shake her head.

Reznick smiled at her. He could see close-up how beautiful she was. Her high cheekbones and soft, pale skin. The beautiful blue eyes, dark hair.

"Jon, I'm putting myself on the line for you guys, OK? Audio confirmation along with a contemporaneous verbatim note would please my editor and fact checkers."

"Well, you can use it as background, I guess. Deep background—whatever the hell you call it."

Sullivan tapped away as he spoke and saved the Word document. "So, I can't use your name if I'm asked by my editor?"

"Correct."

"What else can I say about you?"

"Ex-Delta operator, worked for the CIA under the supervision of the Special Activities Center. Clandestine, paramilitary, and covert operations the American government doesn't want to be associated with."

"Assassinations?"

"Now and again, yes. Actually, quite a lot."

Sullivan typed in his response. "And how do you feel about that?"

"It was my job. I served my country. Do with that what you will."

Sullivan tapped away furiously at the keyboard. "I don't know if I mentioned it, Jon, but I served too."

Reznick was surprised. "Yeah?"

"Graduated top of my class from the Army War College. I served for four years, military intelligence. And then I left."

Reznick was impressed. "Now that is interesting. Why did you leave?"

"I wanted to write. About geopolitics . . . and . . ."

"And?"

"I was in Afghanistan. I was sickened by what was happening to the country and to the Americans who served there. It was a mess. Twenty years!"

Reznick nodded, looking at her now in a different light. "So, you got a job at the *Times*?"

"Yeah. I stayed there for eight years. I'm on a leave of absence. I'm starting to wonder if it's more a leave of my senses!"

Reznick chuckled. "Are you ever going back?"

"To journalism? At this rate, I'll be lucky to finish the damn book I'm working on!"

Reznick cleared his throat. "Afghanistan, huh?"

"Kabul. Herat. Kandahar. Khost."

"Been to all those places too. Fucking awful."

"Not the best, that's for sure. I assume you were over there for a while."

Reznick nodded.

"How long for you?" she asked.

"Too damn long. A lot of al-Qaeda were already in Pakistan. No coincidence that's where they found Bin Laden. The fucker was there for years."

Sullivan nodded as she tapped away. "What do you know about the Saudi influence in Afghanistan and the general area?"

"I saw intel that pointed to us knowing the whereabouts of Bin Laden in the Waziristan region of Pakistan in 2005."

"We saw the same intel."

"I was shown the translated messages. Quite a few Delta guys were privy to that. We were on the ground."

Sullivan typed away. "Just making sure I'm getting this down."

"Some of that has been declassified now."

"A lot of it has not, I assure you." Sullivan leaned back in her seat as she saved the document to Dropbox. "Secure."

"You think?"

"Point taken."

Reznick looked at his watch before finishing his coffee.

"There's so much more I want to ask you, Trevelle, and Kevin. I'm going to need a lot more time."

"Time is something we don't have." He gestured at her computer. "You're writing a book?"

"Yes. It's partly about China's growing influence in America, right. I can't quite believe how, over the last twenty years, academia and corporations in America have been so badly compromised. I'm talking the top schools in the United States. China has been throwing around cash like confetti to countless universities and schools."

"What exactly does China get in return?"

"Access, among other things. Student exchanges. Soft power, able to use influence in seemingly benign ways. Cultural exchanges. And some of those students will have been approved by the Chinese Communist Party. Sleeper agents. Stealing technology, scientific papers, research projects—the tentacles run deep. It's not good."

"And what happened in New York? The three operatives?"

"A classic example of hard power, pure and simple."

Reznick grinned. "On my part or theirs?"

"Yeah, good one."

"When you say hard power, what exactly is that? I've got a rough idea."

"What I mean is that soft power could be Hollywood, US films showing American life, spreading our story far and wide. Hard power, by contrast, is when a country exerts its power through force. Military or economic. In this case, coercion at gunpoint. And in the case of Amy Chang, using the fear of being captured or killed to intimidate or silence opponents. But it's part of hundreds or maybe thousands of examples of hard power moves by the Chinese government at a micro level. Not the macro stuff."

"Meaning no war has been declared."

"Precisely. But they are on a war footing. These are hostile acts by Chinese operatives. That two diplomats are quite openly involved is shocking. Unprecedented. A quantum shift. You caught them red-handed strong-arming Kevin Chang."

Reznick chortled. "Red-handed, very good!"

Sullivan groaned. "You know what I mean."

"Relax."

"You mind me asking you a question?"

"Fire away, if you'll pardon the pun."

Sullivan grimaced, deep in thought. "How would you feel about me helping you?"

"I don't understand."

"I can help you, Kevin, and Trevelle."

"You already have."

"I have a place in Vermont. We can go there."

"You've done more than enough, Caroline."

"I can help you more."

Reznick shook his head. "We're very grateful. But I can't put you more at risk. Not a chance."

"I can decide what risks I take, Jon."

"I'm not saying you can't."

"It was my dad's old place, where I grew up. Now it's mine. We can stay there until you figure out the next move or get a guarantee that Kevin won't be extradited. It will buy you some time. Quid pro quo. I'll help you, and you can help me."

"How?"

"I need time myself for this book, to get more interviews with Kevin and Trevelle. And you too. This will bring a whole new dimension and dynamic to my book. Primary source material."

"This isn't in the plan I had imagined."

"You're not working to a plan, Jon. My place in Vermont is perfect. I have guns. I have food there, enough for a siege. We'll take the back roads."

Reznick contemplated the offer. He hadn't seen that coming. "This is real. And the consequences will be real."

"I hear what you're saying. I'm fine with that. What do you say? You're right; we'd need to move soon. While it's dark."

Reznick looked at her sparkling eyes and grinned. "You're crazy; you know that, right?"

Ten

The harsh morning light glinted off the glass towers of Lower Manhattan.

Meyerstein traced the skyline across to an apartment opposite the twenty-third floor of the FBI field office. A woman walked around her apartment. Meyerstein wondered what this woman did for a living. Was she a lawyer? A teacher? A cop? Maybe the woman was working from home. Maybe the woman had a day off, relaxing in her apartment. What she wouldn't give to have some free time. To spend some quality time with her children. Maybe a day or two just for herself. Maybe longer. Be herself. Get away from it all. She craved a new life. The peace. The quiet. The solitude.

Meyerstein felt a migraine developing fast. She closed her eyes as she tried to gather her thoughts. She hadn't slept a wink the previous night after her conversation with the Director. The Attorney General wanted her out?

Decades of loyal service to the FBI. And for what? The long, painful stretches away from home. Months at a time, at home and abroad. She wondered what all the sacrifice had been for. The loneliness since her husband had brutally left her still hurt. It hadn't been easy on her kids. They put on brave faces. But they didn't talk about it much. Maybe that was her fault. Only her immersion and love of her job had been the glue that got her through it. Upon reflection, it wasn't just that. None of that was the cause of her feelings of emptiness.

There was also the Jon Reznick component in her life, professionally and personally. She had grown increasingly close to the man since their first encounter. Reznick had then been tasked with assassinating a man who had been deemed a real and present danger to US national security. The order had come through a rogue handler, a man Reznick only knew as Maddox, but it transpired that the handler was working for the Pakistani intelligence services. Reznick was thorough, and he discovered the true identity of the man, an American scientist, and protected the man until the FBI made contact.

That was the old Jon Reznick she knew. He had put himself on the line for the scientist despite being tasked with the assassination. Just as he had put himself on the line for the FBI, time after time. He was wild. He didn't enjoy authority. But he invariably had impeccable judgment and would do the right thing, sometimes using unorthodox and occasionally illegal methods. Truth was, he was a law unto himself. It hadn't been a problem before. Until now. Now all that loyalty had blown up in her face. Her loyalty to him seemed to count for nothing.

Meyerstein had grown to understand that he needed space to operate in his world. She had allowed him leeway since she wanted to learn to trust him. But as the years had gone by, she had belatedly begun to realize that his modus operandi was completely at odds with her role in a law enforcement agency. No matter how she framed his latest methods, Reznick had crossed a red line.

Meyerstein had known all along that Reznick crossed boundaries. In the past, she had tried to rationalize his actions when she spoke with the Director. She told him about Reznick's military code of honor, code of war, and no-holds-barred way of dealing with sensitive and dangerous classified issues. He dealt with things using pure force. Power. Menace. By killing whoever the hell got in his way. At least that's how it seemed. But this was, even by his standards, untenable.

The more she thought about the situation and how she was literally in the final days of her career, the more she despaired. For her future. For what was going to happen to Reznick. What had all the sacrifices over the years been for? Was it worth it, the time spent away from home? The years of penance. But she hadn't had any choice in the matter.

Besides, she was the main breadwinner in her family. The only breadwinner. She was a single mother. Her kids needed a good college education. She loved her smart kids now trying to make their way in Ivy League universities. Harvard and Brown. The tuition was crazy. Her husband paid his share. But she was reliant on her job. They needed health care. A career in the highest echelons of the FBI was well compensated. She had her pension. She would get by. But she wanted to work. She needed to work. That was her life.

Meyerstein wondered if Reznick knew the true cost to her of his violent actions. She knew that concern would intrude on his zero-sum-game methods. One side wins, the other loses. The end justifies the means. Meyerstein herself was responsible for giving him such access to the FBI over the years. She had facilitated his introduction to her world of sensitive and highly classified investigations. She had called on his experience. His skill set. And it had paid handsome rewards. She had received praise for her work. Countless investigations had succeeded because Reznick crossed boundaries. But as for the rest of the FBI, friends and colleagues of Meyerstein's, they privately abhorred his free rein.

In hindsight, they were right. How had she allowed herself to be put in this position? Why had she allowed it to get so crazy? It had paid off in the vast majority of investigations. But the blowback on this investigation was devastating.

The best she could do was to try and clear this up. But first she needed to find Reznick, Chang, and Williams. The FBI needed to bring them in. The question was how.

She checked her watch. A little over five minutes until the first meeting of the day, the morning update for the New York field office on the killings. It wouldn't be pretty. She headed into the private bathroom adjacent to her office, freshened up her makeup. She applied a little concealer to hide the dark shadows under her eyes. But there was nothing that could solve the bloodshot eyes from lack of sleep.

Meyerstein straightened herself up and headed out of the office, down a corridor, and into the meeting room. It had already begun, despite her arriving one minute early. "What's the latest?" she snapped as she took her seat at the table. Analysts, FBI counterterrorism experts, Homeland Security analysts, and four young special agents all sat scrupulously taking notes.

Don Laslow, Special Agent in Charge, picked up a remote and turned on the huge screen. "We'll get you up to speed, Martha," he said in his patronizing voice. He clicked as a succession of grisly forensic photographs of a woman sprawled on a subway line appeared in high definition. "The remains of one Amy Chang, green card holder from Hong Kong." He pressed the remote, and it showed Homeland Security passport photos of Amy. "This is her arriving at JFK. Bright girl, loved New York, worked tremendously hard with sections of the Chinese and Hong Kong communities that have settled across New York."

Meyerstein studied the photos. "The push happened in Times Square. What about the footage? MTA had no cameras down there?"

"They did, but they weren't working. Electrical failure apparently knocked out the surveillance cameras at that station. They'd been out for the previous ten days."

"How very convenient. So, no surveillance footage of the moment she was pushed? What about the subway cars. Don't they have cameras?"

"The Metropolitan Transport Authority is rolling out a program of installing two surveillance cameras in each subway car. But there were none on this particular train. According to them, the program isn't scheduled to be completely installed for another eighteen months. Minimum."

Meyerstein pointed to the screen. "What about phone footage on the platform?"

"The NYPD is gathering it. One or two were filming. But it doesn't show the attack. Just some goofball lawyer ragging on about panhandlers on the subway or something. And an NYU student influencer showing a typical day for her, or something. But they haven't found anything that will find the killer."

"So, just to be clear, Don, you believe this was a push?"

"No question; according to the train driver, it was as if she got a sharp push in the back and was flung forward. She was pushed. But there have been nineteen fatal subway pushes in the last year alone. It was higher last year."

"Are we sure this is random?"

Laslow looked around the table and shrugged. "That's the question. We don't know for sure, that's the honest answer. But ninety-nine times out of one hundred, it's a stranger pushing a random man or woman."

"What if it wasn't random?"

"The Chinese connection?"

"She was a dissident. She worked with people who have been threatened or coerced by people working for the Chinese government."

Ryan Dalton of Homeland Security interjected, "We absolutely cannot rule that out. In my opinion."

Laslow grimaced. "I don't know. It's a stretch. They wouldn't kill in such a crude manner. Subtle coercive pressure is more their style."

Meyerstein said, "What if the Chinese operatives are getting more aggressive?"

"It's a possibility," Laslow conceded.

"Bring up the forensic photos of the murder scene on Forsyth Street," Meyerstein requested.

Laslow pressed the remote control. The screen showed the first victim, face bloodied, lying twisted on a bare wooden floor. "This is in the living room. Chinese diplomat in the fourth-floor walk-up."

He pressed the remote control again. "This is on the stairs leading to the apartment. If you look closely, you'll see the guns still in the hands of both diplomats after they were killed as well as the private eye," Laslow said. "This is significant. It indicates that they had headed to that address where we believe Kevin Chang was hiding out. Maybe they were downstairs and responding when they heard the gunshots upstairs from Reznick. Anyway, the apartment is registered and belongs to John Lee, a second cousin of Kevin Chang."

Meyerstein shook her head. "What's he saying?"

"He's terrified. Not saying a word."

Laslow pressed the remote again. The huge screen was filled with a grainy still image of three men. She recognized all three. "Kevin Chang is in the middle. Trevelle Williams is on the right of the screen, and then the gentleman we have all heard of too many times to mention, Jon Reznick. His daughter worked here in this field office until seventy-two hours ago."

Meyerstein closed her eyes.

Laslow looked straight at Meyerstein. "You know Jon Reznick quite well, don't you, Assistant Director?"

"He has worked on several classified investigations with my team over the years. I can only assume this is a case of self-defense."

"Well, we don't know that. What we do know is that the bullets are from a 9mm Beretta. We know that Reznick has a 9mm Beretta registered in his name. The blood of these three is on his hands."

Meyerstein shook her head. "We need to find Reznick first, and then the other two."

"Has he been in touch?" Laslow asked.

"Twice."

Laslow nodded but remained silent.

"Once from a pay phone in Queens and once from a phone whose GPS we couldn't determine, despite extensive efforts from the NSA."

"The NSA couldn't pinpoint Reznick?"

Meyerstein shook her head.

"What were you talking to him about?"

"He was talking to me. He wants to cut a deal. Guarantee that Kevin Chang is not deported or extradited. I said no, but to buy time I said I'd see what I could do."

Laslow nodded. "I've been exploring that option, but it's no deal from the State Department. Which is tricky."

"Indeed."

Laslow cleared his throat. He took a further fifteen minutes to show the last sightings of Reznick at the pay phone and the vehicle crossing the bridge. He froze the image. "The last image of Reznick before he, Chang, and Trevelle disappeared."

"Any leads on the vehicle?"

"It's gone cold."

"So, where the hell is he?"

"We called in a specialist team from the NSA, but since Trevelle used to work for them, any electronic communications will be wrapped up in the most advanced military-grade encryption. It pings from every phone tower from Europe to New Zealand to Nebraska and back."

"We're flying blind?" Meyerstein sighed.

Laslow nodded. "We are flying blind."

"Here's the thing," Meyerstein said. "Reznick has reached out to me twice. The one thing we've got going for us is that channel of communication. I'm wondering if we need to reach out to him. Or at least show that we're trying to reach out."

"Worth considering. You think he'll be interested?"

"I believe he will. As you said, I've known Jon for quite a while."

Laslow glowered. "I agree. Listen, I know this isn't easy for you, Martha. And I appreciate your candor."

Meyerstein sat impassively, feeling all eyes on her.

"So, let me get this straight. Reznick is simply looking for guarantees that Kevin Chang will be protected and not extradited to China?"

"Pretty much. Said he'd hand himself in if we agreed to that."

"I could live with that, but we don't have approval."

"I told him that. Twice. What if he comes back a third time? Do we say no again?"

"What do you suggest, Martha?"

"If he calls me again, we need to have a plan in place. We need to be receptive to what he's saying, or at least appear to be receptive."

Laslow smirked. "You're talking about setting a trap?"

Eleven

Caroline Sullivan drove fast as they headed through a rural part of western Vermont.

In the passenger seat, Reznick checked his watch. Trevelle and Chang slept in the back. It was just after five a.m. and they were only a few miles from Bennington College.

Sullivan glanced in her rearview mirror.

"How long till we get to your place?"

"Ten more minutes."

"Nice part of the world," he said.

"Yeah, I love it up here."

Sullivan drove for another few minutes until she turned up a dirt road.

"We here?" Reznick said.

"This is it," Sullivan said breezily. "Middle of nowhere, no surveillance cameras in sight."

"You might not believe me, but I actually know this area quite well."

"You do?"

Reznick nodded. "Been a few years. But it never changes."

"Did you have a place up here?"

"Nope. My daughter, Lauren, she went to Bennington College."

"No kidding. I did too. Did your daughter like it?"

"She loved it. Not so much when I showed up on the weekend."

Sullivan laughed. "Yeah, I get it." The headlights bathed the dirt driveway, which was fringed by large oaks and pines, as she headed toward a large, imposing house in the distance.

Reznick nudged Trevelle and Kevin awake. "We're here."

Trevelle peered through his disheveled hair as Kevin looked wary.

Reznick got out and helped Caroline with the bags of supplies she had packed. He followed her into the house.

Caroline switched on the lights. A dark oak hallway led into the kitchen. She put on the recessed lighting in the dark-blue Shaker-style kitchen overlooking a walled garden.

"I thought your place in Madison was cool, but this is nice."

"You like it?"

"Yeah, just a little."

Sullivan beamed with pride. "Actually, it was my parents' place. I grew up here. But I've added my personal touch to it over the last few years." She put the bags down on the kitchen table, then waited until Trevelle and Kevin were inside. "How about I show you boys to your rooms. There's a small cottage on the other side of the house."

Kevin cleared his throat. "You're very kind, Caroline. I'm overwhelmed."

Sullivan blushed and tucked some hair behind her ears, seeming slightly embarrassed at the praise. "Yeah, well, you caught me on a good day. What can I say?"

Reznick appreciated the self-deprecation. He watched as she led the way, making small talk with Chang and Trevelle as they went out through the kitchen and down a lit path to the cottage. He decided to nose around. In a wood-paneled study he found a wooden desk, an antique lamp, and walls full of weapons. Rifles, classic Winchesters, military sniper rifles. Black-and-white photos of Sullivan on her graduation day with her proud parents at Bennington. Blue bloods. He should know. He married one.

A few minutes later, Sullivan breezed into the room. "Ah, there you are. Kevin and Trevelle are in the cottage. It's separate from the main house but part of the property. Fifty yards away. It will give you all a bit more privacy."

"This is all very, very kind of you. Don't know what to say."

"It's certainly not a typical day, but I'm glad I can help. At least for now."

Reznick sighed. "Aren't you worried about what might happen?"

"What do you mean?"

"I mean, if we're found here, you would go to jail for knowingly hiding a fugitive from law enforcement. I assume you know that."

"I do know that. Here's the thing, Jon. My father was strong on principles. He always used to say, no matter what, do the right thing for the right reasons. Fuck the consequences. I'm sticking to that."

Reznick raised an eyebrow. "Sounds like my kind of guy."

"Very similar. I'll cross that bridge if and when it arises. Besides, real journalism should be about holding power accountable. This gives me a way of doing that. Unorthodox, sure. But I want to do a deep dive into all of this. We might be the first or among the first to witness this more assertive Chinese brand of diplomacy. I'm not defending you. You killed people. But I believe you had your reasons."

"I believe it was self-defense."

"I know a few lawyers. So, you would have to prove that you were confronted with an unprovoked attack. Threat of injury or death has to be imminent. And the degree of force has to be reasonable. And there has to be objectively reasonable fear that you or someone else was in mortal danger."

"You figure I meet those criteria?"

"Most certainly. But proving it is another thing."

"Good point."

"Listen, I'm involved because I believe it was the right thing. But also, I'm afraid this is the sort of story that doesn't usually see the light of day unless it's in a palatable format."

"What do you mean?"

"I mean by the time the FBI has presented the story, the true sequence of events can get clouded. Call it public relations journalism, whatever, but for an investigative reporter to get primary sources for such an incident is incredibly rare. From my perspective, this story is priceless, showing the growing and malignant influence of China in the West."

"And yet you could be arrested and put in jail."

"I know all that. But while it might be ethically unsound in some eyes, people like me can be protected so they can do their job to the best of their ability, not having to give up sources. Media shield laws. Bottom line? If I'm caught with you guys, I would refuse to reveal the sources of the information. Neither would I discuss what transpired between us, and I would rather go to jail for contempt before I testified about this."

"That's pretty hard-core, Caroline."

"Some things are worth fighting for."

Reznick looked around the study again. "Hope you don't mind, just admiring this lovely study."

"It was my father's. He was a gun nut. I am too."

Reznick saw something new in her. He beamed, "Is that right?"

"Oh yeah."

"Interesting." His gaze wandered around the rest of the study, back to the photo on graduation day. Sullivan had a Goth hairstyle, heavy white makeup. "I'm assuming this is before you joined the military."

Sullivan blushed. "I don't know what I was thinking then. It was a long time ago."

"It's nice."

"That haircut?"

"No, the photo of proud parents and their daughter on graduation. I felt exactly the same when Lauren graduated from Bennington."

"I felt comfortable there. It felt like home since I lived so close anyway."

"Do you use this place much?"

"I usually come up here when I'm doing intensive research. Need a place to cut off from everything for a week or two, usually in the depths of winter. I get snowed in."

"I thought your place in Madison, the beach house, was perfect for that."

"It is. For writing. Up here, I can be left alone. Phone coverage is spotty at best. And that's good for peace and quiet. You hungry?"

"Starving."

"That makes two of us. I'll go and get some breakfast started and make some food for you and your friends."

Reznick laughed softly.

"What's so funny?"

"Just the risks you're taking with us."

"Maybe I'm getting more reckless as I get older."

Reznick stayed quiet.

"You think I'm going to sell you out? Is that what's on your mind?"

Reznick realized how perceptive she was at reading people. "In my line of work, you learn to trust people. But only a very select group of people."

"Can you trust me?"

He shrugged. "Trevelle has put his faith in you. That's good enough for me."

"Just so you know, I'm a pretty old-fashioned girl at heart."

"Is that so?"

"I believe in the American way. The First Amendment of the Constitution is all about individual freedoms. That's important in my line of work. Freedom of speech, the free exchange of ideas. And that's what Kevin Chang is trying to exercise in a free country, right?"

"Right."

"So, we should defend people in this country who want to be free of tyranny."

"That's the way I see it too."

Sullivan tucked some hair behind her ear. "Now that we're on the same page, I need to get organized. Make yourself at home."

Reznick headed back out of the house, through a side door, and down a sheltered path to the cottage, away from the main house. He gave a sharp knock and went inside.

Chang was curled under a thick duvet on a single bed.

Trevelle sat in a chair, tapping away at his MacBook, AirPods in. He looked up and took out his AirPods. "I gave him a couple of Valiums. He needs to sleep. He's in shock."

Reznick nodded. "What about you?"

"I feel like swallowing the whole bottle."

"Don't talk like that."

"I feel empty. I'm heartbroken, Jon. Amy is dead."

Reznick sat down beside him. "I'm so sorry for what happened to her. She sounded like a lovely girl."

"She was. Super smart. Real funny too. I've never lost anyone so close. I feel like I'm losing my mind. Literally, going fucking crazy. You know what I mean?"

Reznick nodded. He knew better than a lot of people. The suffering that comes from loss. The loss of blood brothers on the battlefield. The arena. But also his devastating loss for more than twenty years, believing his wife had died on 9/11. Her bizarre disappearance, facilitated and conceived by the CIA, then her reemerging. But in a way, Reznick was lucky. His loss was temporary. Trevelle, by contrast, had lost his girlfriend in the most destructive, violent, and horrific way imaginable. The blink-of-an-eye disintegration of a young man's hopes and dreams. "When I lost, or rather when I thought I lost Elisabeth, no one could reach me. I didn't want to speak to anyone. I disappeared into myself. I became haunted by the events. I know what you're going through. I became defined, for a while, by my loss. You? I can sort of imagine the emptiness inside you. But only you can go through it. I wish I could say or do something to make you feel a little better. But that's not how it works. I want you to know that I'm here for you. It's a small consolation, I know. I'm here for you. Right here. Flesh and blood."

Trevelle scrunched up his eyes. "I feel . . . I feel as if I'm drowning. I feel panicky. Alone. Really, really alone. She's not going to call me. No more texts. No more funny little memes. It's all gone."

"It's funny, isn't it? It's the little things."

"I remember her perfume. It's still on one of my shirts. I can smell her."

"I know it's not much, but you will come to cherish the memories you had with Amy. The good times together."

Trevelle nodded.

"Hold those memories close to your heart. They will be with you forever, even if she's not."

"You know the funny thing?"

"What?"

"She was the one. I knew it the first time I met her. The absolute first time."

"Really?"

"I've never been great with the whole relationship commitment thing. Maybe too much of a geek. But she got me. She really did."

"I admire the fact that despite losing Amy, you're not forgetting Kevin in all this. It's tough what he's going through too. But it's nice you're there for him."

Trevelle nodded, closing his eyes as if lost in thought.

"You had a sacred thing with Amy, man. You had a girl you loved and she loved you. Maybe for a short time. But you had it. Just for a moment."

"It's going to be impossible to try and move forward from this."

"You will. Trust me. Dark days come to us all. The random nature of it all. It's a crapshoot. But we learn to cope. Day by day. You'll beat yourself up too, about why you weren't there with her when she was pushed."

"I think about that."

"It's natural. I often look back and wonder why I came out alive after fighting for days in Fallujah when the guy next to me got a bullet in the head. It's a way of making sense of it all. It's sad, I know. Gut-wrenching. But I promise, Trevelle, it will pass. It won't be easy. You won't forget what happened. How could you? The pain will, one day, not be so unbearable."

"I know it will. Listen to me. I'm sorry, again."

"For what?"

"For everything . . . this whole thing has nothing to do with you."

"Don't sweat it. This is Jon Reznick you're talking to. Look, you're in a safe place. I'm here. We are going to figure this out."

"You like Caroline?"

"Yeah, I like her a lot . . . She's got a lot of guts to do what she's doing."

Trevelle rubbed his eyes with his hands. "I just want this to be over. It's a nightmare."

"I know . . . I intend to try and resolve this in any way I can. Might be a long shot. But I'm not giving up yet."

"I thought you said Martha wasn't interested in striking a deal."

"Apparently not . . . but I'm not finished. I'll do whatever it takes to get a guarantee for his safety. And yours."

"So, what next?"

"We're going to hide out here for a little while. I figure this is as safe as we can get under the circumstances."

"Do you really trust her?"

Reznick thought about that for a few moments. "I do. I guess there are no guarantees. But, yeah, I do trust her."

"I've been a source of hers for years. Since I left the NSA. Nothing that can compromise national security. But steering her on the extent of surveillance on ordinary citizens. That's what concerns her."

Trevelle shut his MacBook and scrunched up his eyes. He began to sob again. "Amy had her whole fucking life ahead of her. Our life. She just wanted to be free."

"We're going to get through this. You will get through this."

"Amy's not coming back. She's dead."

"We owe it to her, to her memory, to make sure Kevin is safe. That's what concerns me now."

"What about the consequences for you, Jon?"

"I'll deal with any consequences that come my way."

Trevelle dabbed his eyes. "It's shocking to see killing firsthand. It's horrible."

"I understand. It's tough. But we need to be alert. We need to be ready to move at short notice."

"We can't keep running forever. They'll eventually find us."

"Eventually, yeah."

Trevelle shut his eyes for a few moments. "I don't know if I can do this, Jon."

"Do what?"

"Deal with this. I can't seem to get my head straight."

Reznick kneeled beside him and wrapped an arm around him. "We roll with the hand we're dealt. I'm not going to bail on you. But we need to stay strong. Not easy, but we have to."

"I'll try."

"Get some sleep. You'll feel better."

"I'll try, Jon."

Reznick found Sullivan in the kitchen frying eggs, making toast and pancakes. "You don't ever stop, do you?"

"Sometimes it feels like that. I like cooking. I'll have you fed in a little while."

Within an hour, all four of them—including a drowsy Kevin and Trevelle—sat around the kitchen table, digging into fried eggs, wild mushrooms, hot black coffee, and thick homemade pancakes drenched in maple syrup.

Reznick ate up and reached across to Kevin. "How you doing?"

"Drowsy. Overwhelmed. With what's happened. But also touched. Touched by your bravery. And Caroline's kindness. It's too much."

Caroline ate a slice of toast with a bit of egg hanging off it. "Trevelle said you were part of the Umbrella Movement in Hong Kong."

Reznick interrupted. "Sorry, the what movement?"

"Umbrella Movement," Trevelle supplied.

"What's that?"

Chang set down his fork. "It was the name given to the political movement involved in the Hong Kong democracy demonstrations in 2014."

"I see."

"That was the reason I had to flee Hong Kong, and I ended up in America. I thought I had left all that behind."

"You mind me asking what you were campaigning for? I mean what were the Umbrella Movement's aims?"

"Transparent elections."

"Not a bad idea," Reznick observed wryly.

"So, we had a seventy-nine-day occupation of the city," Chang said. "Maybe we were idealists. I don't know. We were very young. Early twenties. There was brutal repression, and I could see how it was all going to end. Friends I know were kidnapped in the middle of the night and disappeared. Plainclothes police watched us day and night. It was terrifying."

Kevin Chang went on, more animated than Reznick had ever seen him, about how he and his sister had escaped Hong Kong on a fishing boat. The fear, the sadness, leaving behind friends and relatives, all at the mercy of China's repressive state.

After breakfast, as the first light bathed the kitchen, everyone went their separate ways. Reznick showered and freshened up. He headed downstairs and sat as Caroline began to interview Kevin and Trevelle. They covered the days leading up to Amy's death and the hours leading up to Kevin trying to escape the clutches of the Chinese state in New York.

Reznick listened, glad that Kevin was at least compos mentis and Trevelle seemed not to be as anxious. The morning passed. They stopped for a light lunch after one. Then the exhaustive interviews of Kevin and Trevelle dragged into the evening. When it was all over, Trevelle and Kevin retired once again to the cottage for some much-needed sleep.

Reznick had taken a few Dexedrine and was wide awake. He was amazed that Sullivan didn't seem tired, maybe running on adrenaline.

Sullivan opened a bottle of red wine and poured herself a glass. "I think I need this. You want to join me?"

"You got any Scotch?"

"A single malt. My father's favorite. Laphroaig."

"Set it up."

Sullivan opened a fancy liquor cabinet beside the bookcase and poured a measure of Scotch. She handed him the glass. "So, what's your next move, Jon?"

"Me?"

"I'm assuming there is a next move. At least you're thinking about your next move."

"I've tried to talk to the FBI twice. I believe that's the only way to properly guarantee Kevin's safety. I need to get them to give me some assurances."

"I think that's a good idea."

"Just a simple agreement saying that Kevin won't be handed over to the Chinese government. That's a red line for me. And Kevin too."

Sullivan nodded.

"The problem is," Reznick said, "I don't detect a willingness to compromise from Assistant Director Meyerstein."

"Do you know her well?"

"Martha? I do. Very well. But I'm starting to wonder if my optimism for a deal is misplaced."

"What makes you say that?"

"I sense she's not up for a give-and-take. I think she sees this as a hand-yourself-in-and-shut-up sort of scenario. I've told her I'm prepared to give myself up to secure the guarantee."

"You think she's going to play hardball if you ask her a third time?"

"I *know* she's going to play hardball." Reznick took a sip of the single malt. The liquor warmed his belly. "That's nice."

"My dad swore by the stuff."

"I know a lot of people who swear after drinking this stuff."

Sullivan sipped some wine. "So, you've worked with the FBI in the past?"

"I don't want to get into details, and this is off-the-record background, without my name attached in any way. You know the drill."

"You have my word."

"So, yeah, sensitive cases. Classified, a lot of it."

"So, we're talking top secret, right?"

"Pretty much."

"How did you start working with them?"

"With the Feds?"

Caroline nodded.

Reznick wondered how much he could or should divulge. "Let me just say before we get started that I used to work on some interesting black-ops stuff for the CIA. So, I know a bit about the world of intelligence, disinformation, covert operations, assassinations—all that. A contractor, sort of."

"That's pretty heavy duty."

"Anyway, on this occasion, I was given an assignment. The assignment was to kill a particular person. This person was on American soil. Which was pretty unusual. But what made it unique, in my experience, was that it was an American. Except I didn't know it at the time. I learned that. And that was a bit of a red flag."

"What happened?"

"What happened was that my handler, a very senior ex-CIA operative, a man I knew only as Maddox, had gone rogue. Flipped to Pakistani intelligence. His real name was Vince Brewling, and he ended up running a law firm in Miami. This law firm was pulling the strings for operatives to carry out hits authorized by Pakistani intelligence. It was pretty brilliant, actually. Anyway, they were contracted by foreign elements, rogue states. And that seemed to work. But it went south for them when, unbeknownst to me, I was contracted to kill an American scientist."

"And the client?"

"The client was a foreign government."

"Anything else?"

"Inter-Services Intelligence, Pakistan. They were running the operation to kill the American scientist, as this scientist was, I believe, if I remember correctly, a sleeper agent working for the Pakistanis in a US bio lab. Scott Caan. I think the original spelling of his name was K-H-A-N. Very elaborate."

"So, you didn't kill the scientist?"

"No, I did not. The details I had been given, an elaborate fake identity of the man I was sent to kill, were bullshit. I had to inter-rogate the scientist, find out who the hell he really was. But it was clear that it had all been set up. I was being used. So, I tried to figure it all out and keep the guy safe until I could hand him over to the FBI. And that's when I first got introduced to Assistant Director Martha Meyerstein."

Sullivan swirled her wine. "Crazy stuff."

"You don't know the half of it."

"That's shocking."

"It absolutely is."

"Do you mind if I take some notes on what you've just said?"

Reznick sighed. "Nonattributable?"

"Sure."

"Why not. Fuck it."

Sullivan reached over to a bookcase and picked up a notepad and pen. She scribbled down the details. "Brewling, right?"

"Vince Brewling. He's dead. He was neutralized in Pakistan. But he was ex-CIA before he went rogue."

Sullivan captured the details Reznick had divulged. "That's outrageous."

"Yup. The Agency has some secrets that will never see the light of day."

"Maybe they don't think the American public is ready to know what they get up to our behalf."

"Secrecy is one thing. That's a given in intelligence matters. But the problem is that it allows malignant influences like Brewling to flourish and exploit the system from within. He was bad to the bone."

"Money?"

"Precisely. Perhaps hundreds of millions, I don't know."

Sullivan put down the notepad and pen on the table in front of her. She picked up her glass and took another sip of her wine. "Tell me about you and Martha Meyerstein. It seems like you have an understanding, right?"

"We did. At that time, yeah. I guess that's right. But what happened down in Chinatown . . . I guess that was over the line for her."

"There's only so many times she can turn a blind eye."

Reznick shrugged.

"So, what do you propose to do?"

"That's a tough one. I still believe, despite getting knocked back twice, that she holds the key."

"Are you going to reach out to her again?"

"Third and final time."

"Where is she?"

"Trevelle said she's been working out of the FBI's New York field office. But he learned that she's staying nearby at a hotel in Lower Manhattan."

"How does he know this stuff?"

"Don't ask. So, I'm thinking I might head back to New York and speak to her face-to-face."

"At the hotel?"

"I don't know yet. Maybe." Reznick took a drink of the single malt, the warmth burning his throat and stomach. "Might be a bit risky if she has an FBI security detail near her. But it needs to be face-to-face. One final time."

"That poses an inherent risk to you."

"I'm aware of that."

"You think you can trust her?"

"I have to. Besides, I think she'll be under enormous pressure to bring in not only me but Kevin too. I can deal with the consequences. I'll roll with it. Whatever they throw at me. But it would all be for nothing if Kevin is extradited."

"Do you think she'll go for it?"

Reznick shrugged. "We can try."

"What about Trevelle and Kevin?"

"They need to lie low."

"You want them to stay here?"

"That's your call."

"It's OK with me. The place is perfect. I'm here. I'm not going anywhere."

"Usually, I would only be happy entrusting their safety to a Delta friend, someone like that."

"Sure."

"I'm entrusting you with their safety and safekeeping. Do you really understand the magnitude of that commitment?"

"Very much, Jon. Here's the deal. I give you my word I will look after them. And you can meet up with this friend of yours. But I have one condition of my own."

"And what's that?"

"When this is all over, I want to interview you. At length."

"I can live with that."

"Is that a promise?"

"That's a promise."

"Then I will look after them. How are you going to travel to New York without the cops or Feds finding you?"

"I'm not sure."

"Can I make a suggestion?"

"Shoot."

"In the barn out back, my father had an old Moto Guzzi still registered to a friend of a military friend of his. You could use that. The ownership, technically, is the friend of the friend."

"So, if I'm stopped, there would be no trace back to you. Smart."

Sullivan gave a sheepish grin. "I have my moments."

Reznick finished his Scotch, put down his glass on the table, and picked up the pad and pen. He wrote down the address of Sam Ripley, a former Black Hawk chopper pilot. Ripley had worked with Reznick and Delta Force on numerous top secret missions. He tore off the scrap of paper with the address and handed it to Sullivan. "If I'm not back in forty-eight hours, you head there."

Twelve

The sun peeked through the trees on the eastern side Caroline's house in Vermont.

It felt like she had taken leave of her senses. The question was why. She had been full of bravura when she was speaking to Jon Reznick the previous afternoon and evening. She could see how huge the story was. And to get a raw, primary account of the events that transpired in Chinatown would enhance her book unbelievably. Reznick was useful to her. But the risks she was taking were huge and so, so out of character.

She wondered if there had been a return of what her mother once termed an "episode." As a young woman, she had been diagnosed with bipolar disorder. It had started at Bennington. Some referred to it at the time as manic depression. Sullivan would spend days, sometimes weeks, in her bed or locked in her room. She loved college life. But the stress mounted, month after month, and it took a major toll on her mental health. She had to take a year away and return the following year to start again. She began a course of antipsychotic medication, and this had stabilized her mood.

Was this now a manifestation of her terrifying highs and crippling lows returning with a vengeance? She had learned to live a simple life, shunning the social scene if she could. She preferred her own company, the silence of her beachfront home. The stillness. But had the out-of-the-blue events upended her world, possibly sparking a manic episode? Her world had been turned upside down. And she had allowed it.

Sullivan had barely slept that night. She woke when Reznick left the house in the dead of night. She watched from a rear window as he wheeled the old bike out of the barn. He kneeled and checked the bike for a few minutes. Then he pulled on the crash helmet, the same one her late father had worn on road trips around the rural roads of Vermont.

Reznick switched on the bike's headlights, illuminating the dark driveway in front of the house. He revved up the bike for a few moments, then edged off into the darkness, alone.

She wondered when he would be back. Her mind began to work overtime, whirring and spinning out of control, imaging scenarios if Reznick didn't or couldn't return. She felt the old fears and insecurities returning. My God, had she lost her mind?

Reznick was a fugitive, wanted by the FBI. He had killed three people in Chinatown. He had blood on his hands and not for the first time. But still, knowing all this, she had sheltered him, Chang, and Trevelle. The consequences for her would be huge if she was caught. She would be fired by the *Times*. Fired by her publisher. And put on trial.

The more she thought about it, the more she wondered if she shouldn't just cut her losses. She could let the FBI know what had happened, admit she had made a mistake, and be done with it. It was a fleeting thought. It would be a terrible betrayal. A betrayal of not only Reznick but Chang and Trevelle as well. And what if Reznick was right, and Kevin Chang was handed over to the Chinese government? What then? She would be solely responsible. How would she feel then?

She closed her eyes for a few moments and did some deep breathing exercises. *Quiet your mind, Caroline. Quiet your mind.*

But she couldn't. Her thoughts began to run out of control, fear washing over her, getting its claws into her.

Her phone rang, and she nearly jumped out of her skin.

Sullivan checked the caller ID. She immediately recognized the number, and her heart sank.

"Caroline, it's Bert." Her editor in New York. "How are you?"

"I'm good. How are you?"

"Not bad. So, I just thought I'd give you an early call before a succession of meetings this morning. I'm not disturbing you, I hope."

"Not at all. It's nice to hear from you."

"So, you working hard at the beach?"

Sullivan felt herself grimace. "Yeah, I'm getting there."

"The deadline is fast approaching, Caroline. This needs to happen."

"I'm on it."

"Listen, you know I don't like bothering you unnecessarily, but I was hoping I could swing by your place in Madison this afternoon. I have some rather extensive notes on the first half of the book. Quite extensive."

"I see."

"Listen, if you're worried I'll take up too much of your time, forget it. One hour and I'll leave you to it. I was hoping to stay with my brother-in-law, who lives nearby."

"Oh, I didn't know." Sullivan's mind raced as she tried to think of excuses. Her editor wasn't a man to be put off by vague excuses. He was very assertive. "I'd love that, Bert. But I can't today, sorry. Maybe another time."

"Why the hell not?"

"It's complicated."

"I just spoke to Harry, our esteemed publisher, as he keeps reminding me, who has told me confidentially that he is inclined to dump your book."

"What?"

"It's crazy, I know. Harry says it's more hassle than it's worth. And besides, it's so far behind schedule. That's what he said to me. This is serious."

"Why don't you email me the notes?"

"Ordinarily I would. But that won't cut it with Harry. Besides, I know what you're like."

"What does that mean?"

"It means I will not email the notes just for you to ignore them. I need to go over these points—and there are a lot of them—face-to-face. It's stuff that's best conveyed in person. I'm sorry to come down hard on you, but this comes from the top."

"Bert, this is not what I expect of our working relationship."

"And there's the small matter of the two-hundred-thousand-dollar advance you received."

"Bert, this is intolerable. You know I work in private for weeks at a time."

A sigh. "I'm sorry to come at you with this bullshit. I love your work. We all do. But Harry is talking numbers. He's been looking again at the P&L for your title. The numbers aren't adding up, he said."

"What kind of numbers?"

"He's talking about slashing budgets, cutting the size of my list, cutting everybody's list. To the bone."

Sullivan closed her eyes for a moment. "Listen, I'll call my agent."

"I just got off the phone with Nicole."

"You did?"

"Of course."

"What did she say?"

"Nicole said it might be better coming from me. Straight from the horse's mouth, so to speak."

Sullivan was reluctant to say that she wasn't at her beach house in Madison. He would want to know where she was. But she couldn't tell him she had a place in Vermont. He didn't know about that. She figured that if she told Bert, he would catch a flight up. Maybe even drive all the way there.

"Caroline, I'm headed up to Madison anyway. It'll only be an hour, two hours tops. And I'll head back to see my sister and my brother-in-law at night. Can't get easier than that. And it will get your book back on track."

"I've got other stuff as well my writing."

"Is there a problem I need to know about, Caroline? If there is, it is imperative that I know. Further delays are not an option. And Harry is looking for an update from me tonight by ten o'clock at the latest. I don't want to give him bad news. He doesn't like bad news."

Sullivan closed her eyes for a few moments as she tried to think up a good excuse for why he couldn't come to her house in Madison. "Bert, I'm going to level with you . . . I have some personal issues I'm working through."

"Ex-husband kind of personal issues?"

"I'd rather not talk about it. I will get this right. But I need more space. Besides, the story is growing wings."

"What kind of wings?"

Sullivan wondered how much she could divulge to buy her some precious time. "I have some inside intel which will greatly enhance my book."

"What kind?"

Sullivan grimaced. She wondered if she should share information on the gunning down of the two Chinese diplomats and the fatal pushing of Amy Chang. She checked herself at the last minute. "I believe there is another chapter which is currently unfolding. And it is pertinent to my book."

"Give me details."

"I have, very, very recently, gained knowledge of and access to a Chinese operation in the US. This is a fluid situation."

"That's great. That is really good. Let's get on with that. But I need to see you this afternoon."

Sullivan was in a bind. She couldn't and wouldn't leave Trevelle and Kevin Chang. She had given Reznick her word. She wondered if there was another way.

"Anyway, I'll be swinging by this afternoon, Caroline."

Sullivan realized that he would notice that her car wasn't there, parked in her driveway. She heard a yawn behind her and saw Trevelle walking into her study. "Bert, I've got to go. Drop it off if you like if I'm not around. And we'll talk soon."

Thirteen

Reznick prowled the Lower East Side, riding the old Moto Guzzi. He had ridden through the night. He had stopped and filled up once in rural Connecticut before he headed down through the Bronx and along the FDR into Lower Manhattan. The sun had started its ascent as he turned along Delancey and then west through Soho until he found what he was looking for. A parking garage, a handful of other vehicles parked there. He rode up to the roof and braked hard.

Reznick switched off the engine, flicked up his visor, and called Trevelle.

"Hey, man, you OK?" answered a croaky voice.

"I'm fine. Glad you're awake."

"Lot on my mind."

"I know . . . How are you holding up?"

"I'm OK. Well, I'm not. I'm pretty devastated. But I'm trying to stay strong for Kevin."

"Listen, I need some help."

"Sure thing."

"Martha Meyerstein . . . can you pinpoint where she is at this precise moment?"

"Gimme a few minutes . . . Caroline sends her best wishes."

"Tell her I'll be back and hopefully out of her hair in no time."

"Will do . . . OK. Martha Meyerstein's phone is showing she is at the Conrad Hotel, downtown Manhattan. You're not far from her. You going over there?"

"I thought about that."

"But?"

"Maybe not a good idea. Security, Feds hanging around."

"Fair. Yeah, so she's checked into a fourth-floor room. I can give you her direct landline for the room."

"I'll use her phone. More secure, right?"

"Got it. Take care, man."

Reznick knew the Conrad Hotel was close to Battery Park, adjacent to the Hudson on the West Side. He checked his phone and saw a parking garage close to the Battery Park City Esplanade. He turned around and headed back down the parking ramp, paid the $4.50 parking charge in cash, and rode out onto the street. He negotiated a few near-gridlocked downtown streets snarled with traffic.

He rode into the parking garage at River Terrace in Battery Park and up three levels. He pulled up and turned off the bike's ignition. He flicked open the visor and called Meyerstein.

The germ of an idea had begun to form. He wondered if she would listen to him or hang up. It rang for thirty seconds before she answered.

"Meyerstein speaking." Her voice sounded strained, tired.

"Don't hang up, Martha."

"Jon?"

"Yes, it's me."

Meyerstein cleared her throat. "Where the hell are you? This has gone on too long. It has to end. Now."

Reznick got off the bike, keeping the helmet on. "Are you finished?"

"Where are you?"

"Never mind. This is the third and final time I'm going to reach out to you. There won't be any more calls."

"Are you giving me an ultimatum?"

"I'm giving you a chance to speak to me."

Meyerstein was quiet for a few moments as if trying to figure out her next move. "Where are you?"

"Do you want to talk?"

"What are your conditions?"

"No conditions. No strings. I want to talk. Just me and you. Face-to-face."

"I'm in New York. You would have to come into the city."

"I'm already here."

"In New York?"

"You want to talk or not?"

"I'll talk."

"No conditions."

"Where do you want to meet? I guess you don't want to talk at the field office."

"Correct."

"Where do you want to go?"

"I want you to walk along Battery Park City Esplanade and head north."

"I know it well."

"You need to be alone. On foot. You got that?"

"Where will you be?"

"Just be there. I'll find you."

"When?"

"Fifteen minutes. If you don't turn up, I'm gone."

"Anything else?"

"Come alone. Can I trust you?"

"I hope so."

Reznick saw Meyerstein alone amid the crowds as she walked the Esplanade. He had picked her out among the joggers, strollers, walkers, and cyclists. Well-heeled mothers pushing expensive strollers, talking into their phones. People chatting on park benches. But all the time he focused on Meyerstein.

Her hands were pushed deep into the pockets of her overcoat, a scarf covering her mouth and neck. She was wrapped up against the cold wind whipping across the Hudson. Reznick stood poised as she approached.

Meyerstein glanced around. "This is a bit irregular, even for you, Jon."

"I'm glad you showed up."

"Let's walk and talk."

They walked on.

Reznick stared straight ahead. "How are you?"

"Me? Not so good."

Reznick indicated for them to head into Rockefeller Park. "This OK for you here?"

"I like it here."

"Me too. Lauren loved it also. She liked the space. The light. Said it had a different feel from the rest of New York."

Meyerstein nodded but stayed silent.

"Listen, I want us to reach a mutually acceptable outcome," he said. "I've asked you for this guarantee already. This is the third and final time I'm going to talk."

"I'm listening."

"I'm going to hand myself over. But I want to have a guarantee in place for Kevin Chang. I think it's the least he deserves."

"You need to turn yourself in without any conditions or obligations. What don't you understand about that? You need to accept that you gunned down three people."

"I was protecting Kevin Chang."

"You'll have to explain that in court."

"I had no option."

"So, that's OK, then, huh?"

"No, it's not OK. I want to turn myself in, but I want something in return. Please give me something."

"Jon, I'm begging you, please turn yourself in to the FBI. Then we can talk. And I promise, we will listen to what you're saying. We can arrange something. Trust me."

"Trust is a two-way street."

"For the love of God, Jon. Accept responsibility!"

"Martha, I'll face whatever consequences come my way. I've told you that twice already. But I'm not prepared to sell out Kevin Chang to save my own skin. He has risked his life to get to this country. His sister was pushed to her death. He believes she was murdered."

"There is no proof that it was a targeted killing."

"You need to do some more homework."

Meyerstein stopped and shook her head. "You're killing me, Jon."

"I want one goddamn thing, Martha. I know how these things work. The pressure from the Chinese government will be overwhelming. The State Department will be calling the shots. They'll force your hand. As will the Department of Justice."

"That's why what you're asking for is not feasible."

"That's it, then."

"Not possible in this atmosphere. I don't even understand why you were there in the first place."

"I got on board because Trevelle's girlfriend, Amy, was murdered a few days ago. In the Times Square subway station. Then the heavies appeared at Kevin's door. Connect the dots. There's a direct connection."

"There is no evidence that Amy Chang's tragic death was a targeted killing."

"Do you have proof that it wasn't? I'm telling you, she believed she was being followed. She was scared something was going to happen to her. She sensed it."

"Is it possible she took her own life, Jon?"

"No evidence of that either."

"We could go around in circles forever."

"Here's what I know. China is getting more assertive in its operations in America."

"I know that."

"Then you also know full well that China is operating unofficial police stations in the city."

She brushed it aside. "This is not the time and place to discuss such things."

"Masquerading as little businesses operated by Chinese, living in America, loyal to Beijing. They run fronts across the country. How was that allowed to go on?"

"We're well aware of this."

"Really?"

"Yes, really."

"And get this, their number one target is dissidents. Kevin Chang and his sister are dissidents. They tried to resist China's crackdown on their free speech and freedoms in Hong Kong."

Meyerstein shook her head as if not wanting to listen or believe what he was saying.

"This is deflection. This is not about Kevin or Amy Chang. This is about you, Jon Reznick, killing, in cold blood, two diplomats from the People's Republic of China. The Vienna Convention on Diplomatic Relations is an international treaty."

"Great, so you're going to give me a lecture on international diplomacy now?"

"The host country must protect accredited diplomats, their families, and their property while in the United States, at all times. It doesn't get any more serious than that."

"What about Kevin's rights under international law? I'm no expert, but don't we offer asylum for political dissidents?"

Meyerstein was silent.

"You know that's true, Martha."

"I accept that."

"So, why don't you give me your word that a guarantee will be in place for him, he will be offered asylum, and I will turn myself in?"

"This is getting us nowhere. I'm asking you to see sense. I will do my best to ensure that Kevin is offered the maximum protections under the law. But I can't offer the unconditional guarantees that you're looking for. That's the best I can do. I want to help, Jon."

"Do you really?"

Meyerstein stopped walking. She turned away from him and stared over the water. "I don't have to come up with a deal. I'm sorry, Jon, but you're not giving me any options."

Reznick was focused on pressing the point for as long as it took. "Consider this. If you can get a guarantee for Kevin Chang, the FBI would be able to utilize him for intelligence gathering purposes too. Now and in the future. He could be a valuable asset. He's super bright."

"Where is he being kept?"

"I can't say where he is."

"You're putting your life on the line for a kid you don't even know. You don't know what he's wanted for in Hong Kong."

"He's wanted for sedition. He didn't want to live in a police state. Besides, I wouldn't believe one word coming from the Chinese government. The end justifies the means in their world. It's their way or death."

Meyerstein strode away down the Esplanade.

"Where the hell are you going? Is that it? Are we done?"

Meyerstein kept on walking.

Reznick realized then that men with FBI SWAT vests were approaching across the park, guns and rifles drawn.

"Hands in the air, Reznick!"

It had been a setup all along.

Fourteen

James Bradley sat on a park bench in Leesburg, Virginia, reading a copy of that day's *Washington Post*, as per his instructions. He had been waiting for twenty minutes already, making sure he wasn't going to be late. He hated tardiness. Had all his life. He observed the tiny, neat park nestled in the beautiful town. He liked the area. Cool bars, restaurants, cafés, and microbreweries gave the historic town a nice vibe. He had at one point considered buying a property here. Maybe he would if his situation improved over the coming months. He was an optimist if nothing else.

An Asian woman wearing over-the-ear headphones entered the park from South King Street. Backpack slung over her shoulder, she seemed miles away, as if lost in her own world. He instinctively knew that this was her. He had never met the woman. But he had been reassured by his handler that she was the best there was. Smart, cool under pressure, and always delivered results.

The woman walked past him, not even giving him a glance.

Bradley watched, transfixed, as she strolled carefree through the park. She walked on for a hundred yards or more. Then she kneeled down and tied her shoelaces.

She checked her watch, stood up, and walked straight back along the path toward him. She pulled a phone out of her pocket and appeared to be taking a call. But no sooner had she taken the call than it ended.

The woman put her phone away and sat down beside him.

Bradley felt a few butterflies in his stomach. He turned and smiled at her. But she didn't let on, oblivious to his presence. She opened her backpack and pulled a sandwich out of a Tupperware container. She carefully placed the backpack at her feet and took a large bite of the sandwich. Then she took off her headphones.

"This is my first time in Leesburg," she said, staring straight ahead. The code words had been spoken. She took another bite of her sandwich.

Bradley responded as he had been instructed. "I'm from around here."

The woman cleared her throat. "I take it you have no electronic devices of any sort on your person."

"Correct. Do you need to check?"

"No."

Bradley assumed she would have a phone jammer or blocker of some sort in her pockets just in case, allowing her to disable any device within ten or twenty yards.

"So, what can you tell me about Kevin Chang?"

Bradley took a few moments to compose himself. "My sources in two separate intelligence agencies have confirmed that he is most likely in Connecticut, upstate New York, or Vermont. That's all they know."

"So, they don't know where he is."

"Correct."

"That is most unusual that the FBI or police have not been able to pinpoint where Kevin is."

"I might have the answer why. I'd like to give a name to you that has come up in various conversations I've had over the last day or two. A name that I believe is priceless for you."

The woman took a bite of her sandwich and stared straight ahead. "A name?"

"Jon Reznick. J-O-N. R-E-Z-N-I-C-K."

The woman nodded as she wiped her mouth with a napkin. She carefully put the half-eaten sandwich into the plastic Tupperware and shut the lid. She took a notepad and pencil out of her coat. She scribbled the name down. She showed it to Bradley. "Like this?"

Bradley checked the spelling. "Correct. You're not going to believe this guy's background and his links with American intelligence agencies."

"I'm intrigued."

"You should be. He's the reason Kevin Chang is still on the run."

"What else can you tell me about this man?"

"This guy is highly dangerous. A stone-cold killer. The cops, Feds, everyone is looking for him. He's the guy who killed two of your people."

"Three."

"I was told it was two consular officials and a private investigator."

"The investigator is one of our team too."

"Got it."

"Tell me what the FBI knows."

"I got an update about an hour ago. Here's how it went down. Reznick went to New York. He met up with a guy called Trevelle Williams, ex-NSA. They then headed to the room where Kevin Chang was hiding on Forsyth Street."

"Can you tell me his skill set?"

"He has what I'd call a black-ops, off-the-books approach to problem solving. He has worked on numerous highly classified investigations with the FBI. But it's based on a relationship with one woman."

"Name?"

"Assistant Director Martha Meyerstein."

The woman scribbled down the details and names.

"And now I've been told that Meyerstein herself is taking an active part in this hunt for Reznick, working alongside an FBI joint task force in New York, the US Marshals, NYPD—everyone is after this guy."

"So, Reznick, who killed three of our people, works for the FBI? And the woman he reported to is the one who is leading the investigation?"

Bradley nodded.

"Interesting. Duly noted."

"The assumption is that Reznick has gone on the run with Williams and Kevin Chang. I'm hearing that Reznick is concerned that Chang will be deported back to Hong Kong. They're saying Chang is a political dissident."

"So, this Jon Reznick guy has acquired a conscience?"

"He wants to make sure Chang isn't deported back to the old country."

The woman stared straight ahead. "Chang is not a dewy-eyed innocent. He is no political dissident. He is wanted for crimes against the state. He needs to face justice."

"You're not going to get any arguments from me. Forensics shows the bullets that killed your people are from a 9mm Beretta. Reznick uses this gun."

"Beretta 9mm?"

"His favorite weapon. But there are millions of such weapons across the United States. There is no footage of him killing any of the three. But there is surveillance footage showing Reznick, Williams, and Chang leaving the apartment building after the shootings."

"That's all very compelling. But unfortunately, it doesn't take us any further forward with regard to locating Chang or Reznick."

"Maybe not," Bradley drawled, "but I have managed to unearth a rather more interesting aspect about Jon Reznick and Meyerstein."

"Give me whatever you can."

Bradley shifted on the park bench, leaning in closer as he whispered, "I've heard an FBI source say that Assistant Director Meyerstein's relationship with Reznick may not be simply platonic."

"What?"

"Wild, huh?"

The woman sighed long and hard. "Your source?"

"Within the FBI."

The woman wrote down more notes, underlining the name Reznick again. "So, he has access to the FBI through Meyerstein. And she is investigating this case. Could this be a conflict of interest?"

Bradley nodded. "You better believe it."

"That is most interesting."

"One final thing."

"Yes?"

"It doesn't end there."

The woman sat in silence.

"Reznick has a daughter. Her name is Lauren. Lauren Reznick."

The woman shrugged. "So?"

"So . . . Lauren Reznick worked for the FBI too until recently."

"This is excellent. Thank you."

"Need anything else?"

The woman shook her head. "Check your bank account when you get home. It'll show that your account has been credited."

"Do you mind me asking by how much?"

"Fifty thousand dollars. But I have the authority to add any bonus I see fit. What you have given me appears to be superior intelligence. I'm impressed."

"Thank you."

"If this is deployed correctly, this information could cause exceptionally grave damage to American intelligence. Do you understand?"

"I'm well aware of that. Besides, I'm past caring."

"We deeply appreciate what you're doing."

"Are we done?"

"I'll be in touch."

Fifteen

The gray walls of the interrogation room seemed to be closing in.

Reznick sat, arms folded, drained. He had endured hours and hours of questions from a succession of FBI agents. He knew the repeated questions from different faces was a good way to disorient and overwhelm the suspect. It was no big deal. In fact, it was child's play for him. But all the same, he felt numb as they fired off question after question.

The more he thought about it, the more he realized it was more than that. His main bone of contention was Meyerstein's betrayal. He hadn't seen that coming. He had assumed they were operating on a basis of absolute trust. But that had turned out to be a false assumption. He thought that he would show up in New York, and they would have a candid talk. Then he would disappear as if he had never been there. Maybe it was a dumb move on his part.

He had been set up. His conversation with her had been covertly recorded. Maybe a mic on her brooch. But whatever way it had gone, they'd had a full and frank confession saying that he was responsible.

It was cold. And he had been well and truly suckered.

Reznick was done chatting with the Bureau. It was over. He stared at the two FBI special agents on the other side of the table: a middle-aged guy taking notes and a thirtysomething female agent asking the questions.

"We've got all the time in the world, Jon," she said. "Three hours, ten hours, whatever it takes. You will talk to us. Eventually." She looked at her watch. "I make it five hours and twenty minutes that you've been here. Just tell us where Kevin Chang and your buddy Trevelle are, and we'll be out of your face."

Reznick glared at her. This could have been his daughter a few months back asking the tough, searching questions. He hadn't been disrespectful. He hadn't been argumentative. He hadn't raised his voice to either of them. Fat lot of good it did him. Instead, he just sat, zoning out.

His thoughts turned to Kevin Chang and Trevelle. He wondered how they were at that moment. Was Caroline looking after them as she had promised? He wondered for a fleeting moment if his trust in her was misplaced as well. He couldn't say for sure. But he sensed she was genuine. At least he hoped she was genuine.

"Do you want me to play the taped conversation again? You know, just to jog your memory?"

Reznick had incriminated himself. They had him right where they wanted him. He could argue semantics in court about privacy. He could, hypothetically, argue that the FBI had been conducting illegal electronic taping without his consent. They would argue it was in the interests of national security. The best thing he could do under the circumstances was say nothing. The problem was that he was worried that Kevin Chang's location would be tracked down by the FBI or the NSA. He just hoped that Trevelle's advanced military encryption of electronic devices was really ahead of the game.

"You did it," the female agent said, smiling. "You said it yourself. It's all there on the tape. It's as good as a confession. You may as well try and look after number one, instead of watching out for

Kevin Chang's interests. What about your interests, Jon? And your daughter? I believe she's working overseas."

Reznick sat in silence and stared back at the agent. He wasn't going to rise to the bait.

"What about the consequences of your actions?" she said. "The way it stands, unless you play ball and tell your side of the story, or at least tell us where Chang is, here in this interview room, we're going to have no choice. You'll be looking at substantial prison time. Decades. But if you decide to use your head and think logically and begin to cooperate, then we can come up with some sort of deal. You like playing hardball? Trust me, I play hardball all the time."

Reznick shifted in his seat. Her voice was as annoying as her phony tough-guy persona.

The male agent stopped scribbling notes. "I've looked over your file. It's impressive. You're a veteran. A military man. I'm ex-Marine myself."

Reznick nodded.

"I respect the military. I respect veterans. Not easy. But I know that your work in Delta, CIA, and the FBI makes me want to offer a special one-time deal. We'll do our best to ensure that Kevin Chang stays on American soil . . . I know that's an issue for you . . . and we can cut a deal for Trevelle, who'll see no charges. But for you, the deal is straightforward. You tell us where Kevin Chang is, and you can be offered an immunity from prosecution waiver. This comes from the highest levels of the FBI. No trial, no anything. We can make this work for you."

Reznick sat quietly, waiting for the punch line.

"So, for no trial, no anything, all you need to do is hand over Chang. We're giving you a choice. It's you or him."

Reznick stared at the agent long and hard. He couldn't believe a word they were saying. It was bullshit. It wasn't up to the FBI to decide if he would stand trial or not. It would be the Department of Justice's decision.

"The smart move is to look after number one. You don't know Kevin Chang. I guarantee that deal is the best we can give. And we can deal with any fallout. We'll deal with the Chinese government."

Reznick looked past the agent at the mirror on the far wall. Were there cameras on the other side secretly filming? The Feds didn't formally record interviews. Was this their covert way of doing it? No other law enforcement agency in the world in the twenty-first century considered notes taken by special agents during interviews as reliable. It was the agent's word against yours. And it also gave them plausible deniability if it was claimed they had offered a deal or anything else. It was a relic of the Hoover era. Maybe the Hoover era of illegal surveillance had never gone away.

The female agent shrugged and feigned a bit of boredom. "Your choice. Make the deal, and we can navigate this without you facing a trial and jail time. It's a take-it-or-leave-it sort of offer." She reached into a briefcase at her feet and pulled out a typed document, waiting for his signature. She placed it in front of him with a pen. "Your signature, and we can all move on."

Reznick folded his arms and remained in a stony silence.

"Sign it, tell us where Chang is, and we're good to go."

The male agent cleared his throat, betraying a sense of nervousness. "You'd be off the hook, plain and simple. If I was in your position, I would bite my hand off for this deal. It's been cleared by the Department of Justice at the highest level. They're looking at the big picture. This is the moment when you can put this whole episode behind you."

Reznick sat, impassive.

The female agent blinked a few times. "This is time-sensitive, Jon, just so you know. We are authorized to say that this deal is on the table now, but when we walk out the door in five minutes, if it's not signed, the deal is off. Best move for you?" She pointed to the space for his signature on the document. "Do the right thing for you, Jon. Think of you. And you're free to go. No trial. No consequences. And we'll look after Kevin."

The male agent interjected, "Just do it, Jon. Sign it and we're out of your life."

Reznick said nothing.

The female agent got to her feet and glanced down at him. "You're on the clock, Jon. Have we got a deal?"

Reznick shook his head and picked up the pen. He scrawled in bold letters on the document the words, *NO FUCKING DEAL*.

Sixteen

Meyerstein watched Reznick through the glass, tears spilling down her face. She was devastated. She'd misread him; he would not compromise. She had assumed his response would be rational. She assumed he would act as most people act, in their own best interests. But she had thought wrong.

She had been absolutely convinced when she made the snap decision to wear the surveillance mic on her brooch that it had been the right call. She assumed he would bend to her will. But she was heartbroken by how little she knew him. She had burned any chance of Reznick wanting to see her again. Maybe that's what hurt her the most.

Meyerstein thought that crafting a bespoke deal to allow Reznick to go free in return for Chang being handed over would convince him. She wanted Reznick to go free. Not because he wasn't guilty. He was guilty of a triple homicide. He had said so on the recording. But the whole investigation had ultimately backfired on her so spectacularly that it was difficult to stomach.

Getting the go-ahead on the deal had used up what little political capital Meyerstein had with O'Donoghue and the Attorney General. She didn't think O'Donoghue or the Department of

Justice would go for it. But they had, assuming the deal could mean Chang would be back in a secure place. The plan had failed.

She figured, perhaps naïvely, that Reznick would see the devastating personal consequences if he didn't give up Kevin Chang, a total stranger. Did he even know or care what he was doing?

Reznick's face was impassive. She couldn't read him. He stared back through the glass. She wondered if he knew she was on the other side.

She could see his bitterness. The anger etched on his handsome, lean features. She didn't want their relationship to end like this.

Reznick sat, unbowed. Defiant. No compromise. Her mind began to imagine if this played out as she knew it would: Reznick on trial. The secrets of the special relationship between a trained American assassin and the FBI, not to mention Meyerstein herself, would be laid bare for all the world to see. The fallout would be brutal.

After today, Reznick wouldn't break or change his mind. Personal honor. Sacrifice. That was Reznick. The American way. A portrait of a man unable to be swayed. Cussedness. A man who would rather die than sell out his principles. His values were old-fashioned. No quarter given.

Meyerstein quietly left the side room. She walked back to her office, shut the door, and slumped down in the leather chair.

Maybe she should start up her own consulting firm. Maybe lecture. Who knows, maybe she would write her memoir. But she knew it would end up being heavily redacted before it was published. Still, the thought of a future without the FBI was starting to resonate with her.

The biggest draw would be spending more time with her family. It would be nice not traveling here, there, and everywhere at the drop of a hat. Maybe it was time to get off the treadmill she had been on for decades, since she graduated from Quantico.

Her desk phone rang, snapping her out of her warm thoughts.

It might be the Attorney General wanting to speak to her, demanding an explanation. Maybe it was the FBI Director himself telling her she had to clear out her desk that day and return to Washington.

Her stomach knotted with tension as she picked up the phone.

"Sorry to bother you, ma'am. It's Malia in reception."

"What is it?"

"You have visitors."

Meyerstein checked her watch and flicked through her diary. "I don't have any meetings for another hour. Are you sure?"

"Ma'am, we have the Chinese consul general, a defense attaché, and an executive assistant here to see you."

"This is most irregular. They are not on my calendar."

"They've passed the security screening. And they would like to speak to you. Do you want me to send them away?"

Meyerstein sighed. It was the last thing she needed. "Send them in, and make sure they are definitely not carrying phones, guns, or whatever."

"Already done that, ma'am."

"Make sure they are accompanied by two security guards into my office."

"Thank you, ma'am. Sending them your way."

Meyerstein opened her handbag, took out her mirror, and carefully reapplied her makeup. She put her belongings in a drawer.

A loud knock at the door nearly made her jump.

"Yes, enter."

The door opened, and a huge security guard stuck his head in the door. "Three officials for you, ma'am. You OK to see them? I haven't got them in the daily log."

Meyerstein stood up. "Absolutely. Show them in."

The three officials walked in, each giving a small, courteous bow before standing before her desk.

Meyerstein shook hands individually with them as they exchanged brisk introductions. Meyerstein recognized the name Robert Chow. He was the consul general who had phoned her a few days ago, demanding answers. "Take a seat," she said.

Chow sat down first. The executive assistant pulled out a notepad and pen.

Meyerstein sat back down. "Mr. Chow, this is a bit irregular if you don't mind me saying. I can usually arrange to see you at a predetermined time and place in Washington if you like."

"I would like to raise directly with you an issue of mutual concern."

"I'm sorry, I don't follow."

"Martha Meyerstein, don't take me for a fool."

"I beg your pardon; no one is taking you for a fool. Let's get one thing straight from the start. You address me as Assistant Director. Do you understand?"

The consul general stared back at her with nothing but contempt and hatred in his eyes, then gave an exaggerated nod of his head. "Forgive me, this issue has affected everyone at the consulate. Two of our most beloved colleagues have been gunned down here in New York City."

Meyerstein glanced at the executive assistant, who was taking notes in what looked like Mandarin. "I believe this is an ongoing investigation, and I can't divulge anything further at this stage."

The defense attaché, a woman, also began taking notes.

The consul general shook his head, his face like stone. "That indicates that you are no further forward with your inquiries or the FBI is being economical with the truth. Not for the first time, I might add."

Meyerstein remained calm, hands clasped on her desk. She couldn't believe she was getting a lecture on ethics from a Chinese diplomat. But she decided to hold her tongue.

"Would you like me to talk about Kevin Chang, a political terrorist in Hong Kong?" Chow said.

Meyerstein leaned back.

"We have evidence he firebombed both the police and army personnel several years ago during violent upheaval. A CIA-backed and organized attempt at insurrection. And we want to say, categorically, that the United States is harboring a known terrorist."

"I can't comment on that; I'm sure you'll understand."

"Meanwhile, two of my staff—both trusted, loyal, law-abiding Chinese citizens and hard-working with devoted families—lost their lives. Their crime? They wanted to encourage Kevin to face trial in our country. My staff was ambushed and killed in an FBI operation. A kill operation to protect a man who was spying for America."

"Quite a tale you're weaving."

"Assistant Director, this is no tale. Quite the opposite. I trust you are aware of the Vienna Convention on Diplomatic Relations of 1961. Diplomats and their families working abroad are protected by international law."

"I'm well aware of the law. I would like to convey my condolences on behalf of myself and the Bureau on the loss of your colleagues."

"Thank you for that. However, kind words do not take us any further forward. This matter has been referred to the highest levels of the American government. It will be debated at the Security Council within the next month."

Meyerstein hadn't been briefed about that. "What?"

"Assistant Director, be aware, the wheels are in motion. We will hold the people responsible for their crimes against the staff and officials of the People's Republic of China."

"We don't discuss investigations. As I said, matters are ongoing. That's all we have to say. And that's our final word."

"Are you sure about that?"

Meyerstein felt his piercing eyes on her. "Quite sure."

"Assistant Director, let me put my cards on the table. Do you know I've been in touch with the Attorney General? We have information from a credible source that says that a man, Jon Reznick, reported directly to you, Assistant Director, when you were based in the Hoover building. He worked within the highest echelons of American intelligence. He had access. You *gave* him access. He is guilty of murdering Chinese citizens."

Meyerstein felt sick, although she tried to mask her emotions. She duly noted the comments, knowing all this was another nail in her coffin.

"Was he sent by the FBI or by the CIA to kill our people and protect a terrorist?"

"That is an outrageous accusation."

"Is it?"

Meyerstein felt suddenly very alone and vulnerable.

"It turns out you know the man very well. The assassin. Not only professionally but personally. You had an affair with him."

Seventeen

A shard of light peeked through the blinds.

Reznick yawned as a new day began. He sat alone in the locked interrogation room, leaning back in his chair. He figured he had been in FBI custody for nearly twenty-four hours. The questions had gone on until four in the morning. But he hadn't issued a word since he had told them *no fucking deal*. The two Feds had never let up, keeping up the questioning. On and on, through the night. But for Reznick, it was easy to zone out. His mind drifted off as the agents raised their voices. He knew they were trying to unnerve him. Needle him to respond. Maybe they wanted him to lash out. But he did none of that.

Reznick stifled another yawn and stared at his reflection in the mirror. He had a sickly pallor and was unshaven. The dark shadows grew under his eyes. He wondered if, at that moment, on the other side of the mirror, he was still being watched.

Suddenly a sharp knock at the door, then a lock turned.

Meyerstein walked in briskly as the door was locked behind her on the other side. She stood a few yards from him. A blank look, as if they'd never met before. "You're free to go."

Reznick sat up straight in his seat. "Why?"

"We don't have to give reasons."

"So, I can just walk out?"

"You will be escorted down to the lobby, and you will be free to go."

Reznick stretched for a few moments. He sensed they were still fucking with him. "That's quite a turnaround. One minute it's entrapment; the next morning, you're free to go."

"You can hang around here if you wish and discuss this further."

Reznick got to his feet. "Just like that, I'm free to go."

"Just like that."

"You Feds really do make stuff up as you go along, don't you?"

"Enough! Who the hell do you think you're talking to?"

"I'm talking to the woman I thought I could trust."

Meyerstein's face flushed red.

"Guess I was wrong. You're a piece of work."

"You're free to go."

"You mind me asking why? I was accused of killing three people. Am I being charged?"

"We're done. I tried to help you."

Martha rapped hard on the door until it was unlocked. A couple of burly, fresh-faced special agents came in and escorted Reznick down to the lobby.

Reznick walked out into the harsh morning light on Worth Street. He took a few moments to get his bearings. It had slowly begun to dawn on him that the FBI might have released him without charge hoping he would lead them to Kevin Chang. It was a high-risk strategy. He wondered if he was just exhausted and more than a bit paranoid after being interrogated throughout the day and night. But he could imagine that if he was released, he would be off guard and could be tracked and monitored as he left New York. It would be a complex operation. Thousands of surveillance cameras dotted around the city, especially peppering roads, subways, and transport hubs. He needed to be careful. Very careful.

He crossed Broadway as he headed west to Tribeca, doubling back on himself. Then he walked east, then turned north, as he took a long, circuitous route to get to the motorcycle.

He walked along Warren and past the Battery Park City soccer fields until he got to the parking garage.

Reznick headed up a flight of stairs and looked around the parking garage. A few empty cars. Maybe he was just being paranoid. He looked around until he saw that the bike was still there, the helmet still locked onto the front wheel.

So, there were two ways he could be trailed, theoretically.

He stood and took a good, long look at the bike. It all looked like he had left it. What if the FBI had simply covertly inserted a GPS tracker on the bike?

The more he thought about that, the more he realized that would make perfect sense. A skilled FBI tech expert could have done the work as Reznick was being held throughout the day and night.

He kneeled down and examined the bike visually. He reached underneath the seat, then the engine, to feel for any magnetic trackers. But after a few minutes he realized there were none.

He unzipped the leather panier and pulled out a small tool kit. He opened it up and took out a couple of screwdrivers. He unscrewed the seat top to get access to the battery. He carefully lifted off the seat and scanned the wires and metal in and around the battery. He thought there might be a couple of rubber insulation wires that seemed extraneous. Newer insulated.

Reznick reached for the second screwdriver and began to unscrew the rear seat used for passengers. He pried it off and looked closely at the underside of the tail section. *And there it was.* The same new rubber insulation below the rear seat, two wires attached to a brand-new three-inch- by-one-inch GPS tracker. A professional job. He knew for sure this was the Feds. Not a quick metallic tracker that a private investigator might attach to the underside of a motorbike or a car. But concealed, out of sight. Very, very clever. Discreet.

Reznick's natural reaction was to rip it out and throw it in a trash can. He didn't want them to remotely track him. But if he did dismantle the tracker, that would also put the FBI on alert. They would know for sure that the device had been found and disabled. If a physical tail and electronic tracker's GPS position didn't match, they would figure out very quickly that he had thrown away the tracker.

The other chilling thought he had was how they knew he had come in on this bike. He came to the park on foot, so the FBI had to basically check cameras and trace him back to this garage, then play a hunch. He wondered how many other vehicles they put trackers on that would lead them nowhere.

He stared at the bike as he tried to figure this out. He wondered if he should keep the tracker in place, allowing the FBI to believe he was none the wiser. He would have to be careful. He could ride back to Vermont and dump the bike. But he would have to conjure up a plan to lose a physical tail. That in itself would create problems.

His main priority was to get back to Vermont.

Reznick figured that the best move was to do nothing. He decided to leave the tracker in place. He carefully put the sections back together again, screwing the seats in tight. He put away the repair kit. He pulled on the helmet and tied the strap tight.

Reznick straddled the bike, put the keys in the ignition, and fired up the bike. It roared to life. He flipped down the visor and edged his way down and out of the parking garage, paying the toll. The security barrier flipped up, and he turned onto the streets of Lower Manhattan.

He rode across town, through the Financial District. He noticed a black Suburban behind him. He quickly pulled onto FDR Drive as he headed north along the eastern fringes of Manhattan, beside the East River. Mile after mile through snarling, heavy morning traffic. He took a quick glance in his mirror. The black Suburban was still on his tail. He headed north, then on through Mott Haven and up into the Bronx.

He pulled up at a gas station and filled the tank for the long journey home. He bought a can of Coke, washed down a couple of Dexedrine.

Reznick got back on the road. He continued on, feeling more alert, wired. He wondered if he had maybe lost the Suburban. But as he headed along 95, he spotted the same black Suburban in the mirror. The same New York license plate.

No question, he was being tailed. It might be the NYPD. But more likely the FBI's Special Surveillance Group. He had met a few of them, investigative specialists, very smart and highly capable.

Reznick needed a strategy. A plan to get rid of the physical tail, get rid of the bike, and misdirect the electronic surveillance crew that was probably monitoring him from a mobile van. He needed to find a place between New York and Vermont. Ideally, he needed a person he could trust to help him out. The sort of person he could trust with his life.

He headed up through the suburbs and sped onto the highway north into beautiful Connecticut. He needed to find a place. He glanced in his mirror. He couldn't see the black Suburban. But that didn't mean another team hadn't taken over.

He headed off the highway at a truck stop. He was starving. He sat down to a hearty breakfast of scrambled eggs and toast, followed by homemade apple pie. He washed it down with a few cups of black coffee, discreetly taking a couple more Dexedrine to pep him up. Twenty minutes later, refreshed and loaded with enough amphetamines to keep him alert for days, Reznick got back on the bike and got back on the highway. He opened the throttle hard.

As the bike ate up the miles, gradually an idea began to form. It was a plan. A plan that might work. A plan that was going to need some outside help. He needed to create a false trail.

He rode up I-91 north until he got to Hartford. Then it struck him. He knew a guy. A good friend. A man he could trust who was close by.

His mind flashed back to memories of a wedding, a few years back, in Springfield, Massachusetts. Ex-Delta operator Ray "Mad Dog" Diaz was getting married. He had stayed at Ray's house before. He was even the best man at his wedding. Ray ran a garage on the outskirts of Springfield.

Reznick rode for another half hour until he reached Springfield. He headed along Bay Street. It seemed familiar. Then he remembered a diner. It was adjacent to an auto shop, so he headed there.

He spotted the diner sign and pulled up between a Chevy pickup and a Suzuki Jimmy. He switched off the Moto Guzzi's powerful engine and headed inside, helmet deliberately still on. A couple of diners sitting on stools at the counter, drinking coffee, checking their phones. No one so much as looked up when he entered. A jukebox played an old Guns N' Roses track.

Reznick took off his helmet. He headed over to a corner booth overlooking the rear parking area. Nice line of sight.

He picked up a menu and quickly scanned the options available.

A waitress walked up, pencil and pad. "What can I get you, honey?"

Reznick ordered a bacon sandwich, followed by blueberry pie and whipped cream. And coffee. Black.

"You got it," she said. The waitress returned with the mug of hot black coffee. "Enjoy."

Reznick pulled up a number for Ray Diaz. He hoped his friend would answer. He was pretty unpredictable on a bad day.

The number rang for a couple of minutes before it was finally answered. "Ray Diaz's Garage. How can I help?"

Reznick grinned when hearing his voice. "I was wondering when the hell you were going to pick up your phone."

"Who's this?"

"It's Jon . . . Ray, how the hell are you?"

"Are you kidding me? Reznick?"

"Yup, you got it."

"Good Lord. Jon Reznick?"

"How many Reznicks do you know, Ray?"

Diaz laughed. "How you doing, bro?"

"I've been better."

"What's the matter?"

"I've got a serious problem. And I'm calling in a favor."

"What do you need?"

"I need your help. Right now."

"Where are you?"

"Old-school diner on Bay Street, you know the one?"

"I was in there last week. Great place. Listen, what do you need? You need money? You need logistical help with something?"

Reznick quickly explained the events of the last few days. He also explained what he was looking for.

"That is off the scale, man."

"So, I want a car. A truck, something."

"I have cars. A lot of cars."

"In exchange, I have a vintage motorcycle. I know you like bikes."

"You can have the car for nothing."

"No. I want to exchange this bike for a vehicle. I don't want you out of pocket. This bike is worth quite a bit."

"You short on cash?"

"No. I need to lose a tail. It might bring you some heat."

"Never had a problem with heat."

"Have you got an old car or truck I can have?"

"Are you kidding me? My garage is full of cars. I have four cars and two bikes of my own."

"Great. Bring one of the cars."

"I see what you're going to do, man. Yeah, I get it. What else do you want me to do?"

"Wear jeans, black sneakers."

"You want me to bring some weapons?"

Reznick laughed. "Negative."

"You sure? I've got a lot of cool stuff I bought online."

"You're fine. Relax. Just bring some wheels."

"See you in thirty minutes, man."

"One final thing . . . When you arrive, see if you get a visual on a Suburban, black, New York plates, in the vicinity of the diner, within a mile."

"You got it. See you soon, bro."

The line went dead.

Reznick finished his lunch and was on his third coffee when Ray Diaz arrived. His old pal sat down opposite Reznick. "Man, nice to see you."

He shook hands with Reznick, the viselike grip unchanged. "Good to see you, bro."

"I appreciate you helping out."

"You kidding me? I love this sort of stuff. Sparks me back to life."

"So, off the bat, you see any sign of a Suburban around here?"

"Damn right you have, bro. You got a tail alright."

Reznick nodded. "I thought so. You get a visual?"

"Two hundred yards farther down Bay Street, on a side street in a parking lot opposite Berte Field, it's parked up. They have line of sight to the diner entrance. But not to the rear parking lot."

"Interesting."

The waitress fixed Ray a black coffee and brought some blueberry pie.

"Who are the guys in the car?" Ray asked.

"Feds, I think. Maybe their surveillance team."

"Jesus H. Christ, Jon. So, exactly who were the guys you deleted?"

"Two Chinese diplomats and one of their goons."

"Are you shitting me?"

Reznick shook his head. "If you think that's too heavy, I'll deal with it myself. Not a problem."

"I'm in. Fuck it. Can't let you have all the fun."

Reznick smiled. He leaned in close as he handed Ray the keys to the bike underneath the table, along with his black leather jacket. "So, they can't see us now, but they can clearly see the main entrance and side parking lot of the diner, right?"

"Correct."

Reznick pushed the helmet in Ray's direction. "Under the back seat of the bike is a GPS tracking device. Hardwired. Very professional."

"Where do you want me to take them?"

"First, get changed. Head east out of the parking lot so I can see that they're heading in that direction."

"Then what?"

"Ride east on 90 to Worcester."

"Perfect, just over an hour away."

"And then head back home. Take a detour if you want."

"You're seriously out of your mind, Reznick. Out of your fucking mind! Do you know that?"

Reznick felt happy and relieved to be in the presence of one of his closest buddies from his Delta days. "I have my moments."

"I miss the old days, man."

"Not me."

"Is killing three Chinese goons your idea of trying to enjoy the quiet life?"

"Fair point." Reznick winked at his old comrade. They had fought side-by-side in Iraq. Stinking back streets, dead bodies rotting in the sun. Terrified children screaming for help. A never-ending nightmare. At times when Reznick was alone at night, his mind was alive to the same horrifying images etched into his psyche. It wasn't the sort of story people really wanted to hear. Besides, like his father, he kept his thoughts on what he'd witnessed in war to himself, for him alone to deal with.

Diaz cleared his throat. "Take care of yourself, man."

"You too."

Diaz headed to the bathroom with the jacket and helmet. A few minutes later, he emerged, helmet on, black leather jacket zipped up tight to his throat. He strode past Reznick and walked out of the diner. He straddled the bike, put the key in the ignition, and kick-started her up. He revved it hard for a few moments. Then he edged away slowly. He stopped at the diner exit, carefully taking a right turn as Reznick had instructed him.

Reznick watched Diaz head down Bay Street, away from the diner. A minute later, a black Suburban was quickly on his tail. Reznick left a fifty-dollar bill on the table as he headed to the bathroom and freshened himself up. He waited fifteen minutes before he left the diner.

He opened the old Mazda Ray Diaz had left him, keys in the ignition. He adjusted the mirrors and took a few moments to get comfortable.

Reznick started up the car, reversing out of the parking lot before turning left along Bay Street. He glanced in his rearview mirror. No sign of the Suburban. He drove on, negotiating a few streets in downtown Springfield. Then he crossed over Memorial Bridge and out through West Springfield, headed northwest of town as he focused on getting back to Vermont.

Eighteen

Caroline Sullivan was exhausted. She hadn't slept since Reznick left her isolated Vermont home. She grew agitated, fearful something had happened to Reznick, expecting him back the previous night. But still nothing.

She checked her watch. It was just after three p.m. on the second day. The hours had dragged since Reznick had left. She had tried to stay busy. Cooking for Trevelle and Kevin and working on the new chapter of her book. She hadn't answered numerous calls from her editor. She assumed he had turned up at her house in Madison but found no one home.

Sullivan wondered if her editor would be worried for her and call the police. He knew that she had suffered mental health episodes in the past. If he contacted the police, saying he was worried about her and asking if they could do a welfare check on her home, it might lead them to the house in Vermont.

She needed to clear her head.

She had the address of a Sam Ripley if Reznick hadn't come back after forty-eight hours. That still gave him twelve hours to return. But realistically it was nine hours until midnight. Was she really going to wait and wait in the hope that he would return in the middle of the night?

Sullivan saw that time was of the essence. She needed to focus. She couldn't have the cops or Feds turning up in Vermont for her sake, being arrested along with Trevelle and Kevin. It would mean all her efforts would have been in vain. Her reputation would be trashed. And for what?

The more she thought about it, the more she realized she had a hard call to make. Either she sat and waited until Reznick's deadline expired after midnight, or she could cut and run with Trevelle and Kevin.

Trevelle walked into the kitchen, mug of coffee in hand. "Hi, Caroline."

"Hey, Trevelle, how're you feeling?"

"Not great. Reznick not back?"

"Afraid not."

Trevelle grimaced. "Fuck. I'm worried."

"Me too. I don't know what to do."

"Stay or go?"

"Exactly. I'm worried something happened to him."

"You look tired, Caroline. How're you holding up?"

"Stressed. But I'm fine, really."

"Listen, I'm worried about Kevin. Really worried."

"Is he in your room?"

Trevelle nodded. "The guy is tripping out. He's wrapped in a blanket. I don't know . . . he's talking to himself, muttering, repeating phrases."

"What phrases?"

"Stuff I don't understand. Mandarin, I guess. But it's like he's having a mental breakdown. I don't know. Mumbling and sobbing in his sleep. When he wakes up, he starts to shake. He's in a bad way. A real bad way."

Sullivan folded her arms and sighed. "Do you think he'll do anything crazy?"

"Like what?"

"I don't know. Running away in the middle of the night? Grabbing your phone and calling the cops?"

"He's not himself, I know that. I've never seen him like this before."

Sullivan walked over and hugged Trevelle. "I'm sorry about Amy. You must be struggling with all that too. You haven't really talked about it."

"I'll feel better when Jon is back."

Sullivan nodded.

"I know he's got our back," he said.

"He definitely does. Listen, I want to speak frankly in light of what you just told me."

"Sure. What's on your mind?"

Sullivan shrugged. "There are two main concerns. First, Kevin's state of mind. That worries me a lot. Is he a loose cannon? Is he going to do something stupid? Second, I don't know for sure that Jon will come back. And I feel scared."

"I know Jon. He will come back. He wouldn't leave us here."

"But what if the FBI has other ideas?"

"I trust Martha Meyerstein. So does Jon. She wouldn't compromise him."

Sullivan shook her head. "What does that say? Nothing is certain, except death and taxes."

"That's not a very subtle point you're making."

Sullivan realized how insensitive that sounded. "I'm sorry, I didn't mean—"

"It's fine. I know what you mean."

"I believe in Jon, too, Trevelle. I really do. That's why I'm doing this. He's doing a very courageous thing. But the FBI? I don't know if I would trust them."

Trevelle took a sip of his coffee. "So, what are we going to do about Kevin? Maybe you should see for yourself what I'm talking about."

Sullivan nodded. "I think I will."

Kevin Chang huddled on the bed, wrapped in blankets, eyes darting back and forth. He seemed genuinely manic. "What do you want?"

Sullivan took a couple of steps toward him. "Hi, Kevin. I just wanted to see how you are."

"What's taking him so long? Why has he disappeared without us? What about us?"

"Well . . ."

"I don't think he's coming back. Maybe he got arrested. So, what do we do then? Have you thought about that?"

"He'll be back."

"You don't know that."

"I don't know for sure . . . but I trust him."

"Caroline, I'm scared they're going to find me. Can I have a gun to protect myself?"

Sullivan thought that was a bad idea, seeing his mental state. "Let's not think like that. Let's be positive. I don't believe anyone will find you here."

"I don't want to go back to China! They're going to kill me! They killed Amy!"

Sullivan forced a smile. She realized she must have sounded like a patronizing, bleeding-heart liberal. "I'm sorry . . . this must be so tough for you. But we'll get through this, I promise. I won't leave you."

"Trevelle told me Jon is speaking to the FBI. Is that true? They already said they won't guarantee my safety."

Sullivan hesitated as she tried to strike an upbeat tone. "He's good friends with the Assistant Director. I told you about that."

"But can I really trust Jon? Can I trust you? What if the Chinese government finds me here? Have you thought about that?"

"No one will find you here."

Kevin scrunched up his eyes and began to sob like a frightened little boy. He let out a scream. "I can't face it again! I can't go back!"

Sullivan pulled up a chair and leaned forward to hold Kevin's cold hands. "We'll get through this."

"That's easy for you to say! You're not going to be deported! You're not going to be tortured and killed!"

"I understand that."

"No, you don't! How can you? Amy is dead! No one could protect Amy! I feel so stupid that I told her everything was going to be OK. She was scared. She thought they were following her. And I didn't believe her."

"I want you to hang on for a little longer. I know Jon Reznick will return. And hopefully it'll be with good news. He protected you in New York. He'll protect you for as long as it takes. He will not leave you. I promise you that."

"What about you?"

"I promise, as God is my witness, I will not leave you, Kevin. I want you to live free too. I'm putting myself on the line for you."

Kevin shook his head, still sobbing. "I can't do this."

"I'm going to make us something to eat and drink. Can I get you something, maybe an early dinner? A snack maybe?"

Kevin scrunched up his eyes. "I want to die. I want to die. What's the point?"

Sullivan got to her feet and left the room. She was shaken up by what she'd seen. She headed back down the path into the main house and into the kitchen.

"So," Trevelle said, "you see what I mean?"

"I don't think he's going to be able to hold on."

"He lost his sister, Amy. We're all on edge."

Sullivan reflected on what Trevelle was saying. More than anything, the fragile state of Kevin Chang worried her immensely. "He told me he wanted to die."

"He said that?"

Caroline nodded.

"Holy fuck. That's not good."

"I think he needs help. Medical help."

"Caroline, under no circumstances can we take him to a hospital."

"I know. But he's got too much time to think. I think he feels like he's a sitting duck. And it's just a matter of time."

Sullivan looked up at the clock on the wall.

"You need to have faith in Reznick," Trevelle said.

"I do. I'm just fearful of what lies ahead. For all of us."

Nineteen

Reznick drove through the small towns of the Berkshires in western Massachusetts. He was taking the long way home. But he was now driving a Buick SUV.

He had decided, once he'd left in Ray Diaz's vehicle, that a quick switch might be in order. Ray was hopefully laying down a false trail for the Feds.

Reznick had driven to the outskirts of Pittsfield when he saw a near-deserted open-air parking lot. He spotted an old Buick SUV. It was then that he decided to switch again. He had been concerned that if Diaz had been stopped not far from the city, they would soon put out an alert for any vehicle in his name.

Reznick was relieved to finally get out of the city driving on US-7, headed north in the direction of Bennington. He wasn't far from Vermont. But he didn't want to take a route straight as the crow flew. He took a long detour instead.

He headed west on NY-2 and cut through the Taconic Ridge State Forest. Mile after mile of winding road through the heavily wooded area of the Berkshires. Rolling hills and light traffic, just the occasional passing car or truck for company.

The sky began to darken, then the rain began to fall.

Reznick drove on through the downpour, wipers sluicing away the water from the windshield. He wondered if he should call Trevelle to say he was on his way. But he wanted to make sure the coast was clear before he put himself on anyone's radar.

He headed toward Williamstown on the northwest edge of Massachusetts. It was the home of the private liberal arts school Williams College. He knew the area quite well, having visited Lauren when she was at Bennington. They often traveled into Williamstown for a meal or a drink.

Reznick thought of Lauren. He thought of what had happened in his life over the last few days. She would be shocked to the core. He thought of her, working for the CIA on the other side of the world. He couldn't help but worry. It was in his nature as a father. But he also knew she was more than capable. And she wasn't a risk-taker like he was. In a way, he was glad that she was out of the FBI. He knew the fallout for her, career-wise, of his latest escapade would have been immense.

The rain fell heavier as he drove on into the night.

Reznick's one saving grace was that Lauren would be unaware of what had transpired. Hopefully. Maybe Meyerstein had texted her. He couldn't rule that out. Maybe called her in Jakarta. But as far as Reznick knew, Lauren was oblivious.

It was plain to see that he had been released by the Feds, maybe after Meyerstein's intervention, in the genuine hope of tracking him back to Kevin Chang. It would have snared all of them at once if their plan had worked.

As it stood, it wouldn't be long until the FBI realized he had given them the slip. And they would be pulling in all the intelligence agencies in the hunt for him. He needed to be even more careful. He drove on.

He thought back to when he had left the motorcycle at the parking garage in Battery Park. The Feds had to have attached the GPS tracker overnight. Doubts began to crowd his amphetamine-fueled mind. He wondered if the old bike could be traced, through the friend of Caroline's late father. It was a possibility. A long shot.

Maybe the Feds had already gone to Caroline's beachfront home in Madison. He couldn't discount the fact that they might have even tracked down Kevin to the isolated house outside Shaftsbury, Vermont. But maybe he was just spiraling through possibilities, both real and imagined.

Reznick drove on, his mood darkening as he crossed over the state line, a sense of foreboding washing over him. He wondered if he was headed into a trap. He drove a few more miles of rural back road before he came to the turnoff for Caroline's house. It was cloaked in darkness. He switched off the engine. It was like no one was home. He got out of the car and tried the front door, but it was locked. He peered into a side window. No sign of life. He rang the bell a few times. Then knocked hard. Still no answer.

Reznick got a sinking feeling in the pit of his stomach. He had gotten there too late. They were gone.

Twenty

It was early evening when James Bradley arrived at the Hyatt hotel in Reston, Virginia, backpack slung over his shoulder. He sat down in the lobby and surveyed the room. It looked like the usual crowd. Businessmen, a concierge explaining directions to a couple from the Midwest on a "romantic" break, and a smattering of singles, all mingling around the lobby bar. Piano music played quietly in the background.

A waitress approached, smiling. "Sir, can I get you a drink?"

"A Bloody Mary, thank you."

"Of course, sir."

Bradley admired the soaring lobby with its tasteful lighting. The waitress returned with his drink. He swiped his card and left a handsome tip.

"Very kind of you, sir."

The waitress headed over to serve another guest at an adjacent seat. He looked toward the elevators and caught sight of an Asian woman wearing a mask. She walked toward him and sat down in a seat opposite.

"What's that you're drinking?" she said.

Bradley's shoulders fell in relief. Those were the code words. "My favorite. Bloody Mary." He uttered the authorized reply.

The woman got to her feet. "Leave your drink and follow me."

Bradley did as he was told. He followed her across to the elevator. They rode the elevator to the sixth floor in silence. The elevator pinged and they got out. He followed the woman as she turned right and continued down a long corridor.

She stopped outside the door of the end room.

The woman knocked twice on the door. The door cracked open. Inside was the female Chinese handler he had met in the park in Leesburg.

"Come in," she said, opening the door wide.

Bradley headed inside as the masked woman turned around and headed back down the corridor.

The woman from the park locked the door behind him. She sat down on a plush sofa and pointed to a chair opposite. "Please, take a load off."

Bradley sat down. "Nice place," he said. "I'm assuming you swept the room for electronic surveillance?"

The woman shifted in her seat. "Obviously. And I'm deploying our jamming equipment. Advanced military capabilities."

Bradley knew full well the capabilities of China. He had written CIA reports about their technological advancements years earlier. Quantum computing, nanotechnology—they were pouring hundreds of billions into usurping America's technological capability. They were looking toward the twenty-second century and beyond. He unzipped his backpack, pulling out an envelope, and handed it to the woman.

The woman took a few moments to carefully examine the seal. She ripped it open and pulled out the photos and documents she might find helpful. Black-and-white FBI photos taken with a telephoto zoom in Lower Manhattan. The picture showed Assistant Director Martha Meyerstein and Jon Reznick engaged in an animated conversation, taken minutes before Reznick was apprehended in New York.

"The transcript you have," Bradley said, "is the verbatim exchange between Meyerstein and Reznick."

The woman studied the photos and flicked through the transcript. "How did you get this?"

"I have friends still in various agencies. Intelligence sharing is a lot more common these days. And it allows such intel to be gathered from unlikely sources."

"In this case?"

"I don't want to be too specific."

"I need to know. Broad-brush clue?"

"Department of Justice. A friend of mine is on a team responsible for the FBI in New York. A lot of interesting stuff comes across his desk."

The woman took a few minutes to read the conversation between Meyerstein and Reznick. "So, this Reznick, is he in custody, I'm assuming, after this conversation with the Feds?"

"This is where it gets crazy. My source indicated that Reznick was released earlier today in New York after being interrogated by the FBI."

"That doesn't make sense."

"Who do you think ordered it?"

"Ordered his release you mean?"

"Yes, he was released. On the orders of Meyerstein. Reznick is free. And they don't know where the hell he is. They hoped he would lead them back to Chang. But he's smarter than them, apparently."

The woman burst out laughing. Bradley continued, "No one thought he should be released. At least that was the talk among the FBI's New York office. But Meyerstein is obviously very, very persuasive. Now he's disappeared. Probably for good."

The handler shook her head. "So, her involvement is a clear conflict of interest, right?"

"It's outrageous. I'm embarrassed to even feed this back. It doesn't show American intelligence in the best light."

"Indeed. It does, however, show you in a very good light, James. You did very well."

"I assume there will be a financial quid pro quo. Besides, my sources at the Department of Justice and the FBI will have to be kept sweet."

"Not a problem. Your offshore account will be credited. You might want to check it when you leave."

"You mind me asking how much?"

"Two hundred thousand American dollars. Keep us informed. This is a hot topic for us. And just so you know, we want to know about Reznick. We'll deal with him when we find him."

Twenty-One

Reznick sat in the truck and checked his phone for any new messages. The Buick's headlights bathed Caroline's empty house as the rain poured down. He wondered where the hell they had gone. He had called Trevelle's number countless times, but there was no reply.

It was an ominous sign.

It wasn't like his hacker pal. Trevelle was inextricably glued to his screens at all hours of the day. He wondered if the Feds had tracked them down. Maybe they were watching him now, waiting to drag him out of the truck.

His phone suddenly rang.

"Sorry, Jon." The harassed voice of Trevelle.

"You OK?"

"I'm fine. We're fine. And safe."

Reznick sighed. "Where the hell are you? You had me worried."

"I'm sorry for not getting back to you sooner. I was just reconfiguring some of my antitracking privacy features, so I've been offline for a bit."

"So, it's all good now?"

"As good as could be expected under the circumstances."

"Trevelle, where the hell are you? Actually, don't tell me where you are."

"All you need to know is we're safe, Jon."

Reznick wondered if Trevelle was already in FBI custody, speaking under duress. "And Kevin's safe?"

"He's . . . Jon, he's very agitated."

"Is he safe?"

"Yes, he is. But he's freaking out. And we're all on edge."

"Put Caroline on."

A few moments later, she got on the line. "Jon, we're fine."

Reznick was glad to hear her soft voice. "Thank God. I think you bolted before the forty-eight hours was up."

"I'm sorry. But I needed to do something. Kevin was climbing the walls with paranoia. So, I decided to get us on the move. I gave him a sleeping pill. That quieted him down."

Reznick was impressed by her taking control of the fraught situation. "Smart. Listen, don't tell me where you are. But can you confirm you have arrived at the address I gave you?"

"Correct."

"That's all I need to know."

"How long will you be?"

Reznick checked the luminous dial of his watch. "A while . . . I'll get there as soon as I can."

"Any guesses?"

"Four hours. Thereabouts. Then we'll talk."

"OK, I think that will work."

"Hang in there, Caroline. You made the right call getting them on the move."

"I didn't know if you'd be mad."

"Mad? Hell no. You're thinking on your feet. In my line of work, you need to respond to changing events. You need to think critically. I'm impressed."

Caroline was quiet for a few moments.

"Are you still there?"

"See you soon, Jon."

Reznick ended the call. He needed to stay switched on for a few more hours. He knocked back a couple of Dexedrine pills, washed down with a sports drink. He checked the route on his phone. He turned around as the wipers whisked the rain away.

He pulled away and drove off into the night. He drove through Bennington and headed south on US-7. He headed east on I-90 and stopped for gas in Blandford, Massachusetts.

He paid in cash and rested for thirty minutes at a truck stop, ate, and drove on through the night. He headed past Springfield once again. The rain began to ease as he drove through eastern Massachusetts. The headlights picked out a road sign for Cape Cod.

Reznick drove on, the familiar New England colonial houses on either side of him.

It was the dead of night when Reznick finally arrived at the house, a few miles outside Mashpee on Cape Cod.

Reznick pulled up Sam Ripley's driveway and tapped on the front door. The door opened. Ripley stood there, mug of coffee in hand.

"Never a dull moment with you, Jon," he said.

"Tell me about it."

"Glad you finally made it. Come in."

It felt good to be in the warmth of Sam's cozy home. He followed Sam through to the kitchen. "I owe you one. I really do. Sorry for the unannounced intrusion. I hope you don't mind."

"It's fine, man. Caroline told me the story. Kevin's asleep up in my attic."

"Where's Trevelle?"

Sam cocked his head upward. "He's in my guest bedroom. He's exhausted. They all are."

A few moments later, Caroline walked in, stifling a yawn. Her eyes were bloodshot, as if she hadn't slept. "Nice to see you, Jon."

Sam stretched his arms. "Listen, I'll leave you guys to catch up. I have some paperwork I'm behind on. IRS bullshit."

"Lucky you," Reznick said.

"Make yourselves at home. One question, Jon. How long you planning to stay here? Obviously it's not an open-ended invitation."

"Not a problem. We'll be out of here within the next few hours, I promise. Just wanted to get Kevin in a better mental place. But we need to get ourselves organized before we go again."

"That's fine. I have friends coming around tomorrow morning. So, twenty-fours hours' time."

"We'll be long gone, trust me."

Ripley hugged him tight. "Help yourself to any supplies or food or whatever you need."

"Appreciate that, Sam. I owe you one."

"Forget it, bro. I'll be in my office if you need me."

"Got it."

Caroline made fresh mugs of coffee for her and Reznick. "You've gone above and beyond what I expected."

"So have you," Reznick replied.

"Worth fighting for."

"Worth killing for?"

Sullivan sipped some coffee and sighed. "My father, God rest his soul, you know what his favorite saying was?"

Reznick shook his head, surprised she was opening up to him.

"Liberty has never come from the government. Liberty has always come from the subjects of it. The history of liberty is the history of resistance."

"I like it. Who said that originally?"

"Woodrow Wilson."

Reznick stared at Sullivan. "You think me gunning down two Chinese diplomats and a private detective in New York was an act of resistance?"

152

"In a way, yes. That's what America was founded on. It's about liberty. Kevin Chang's liberty. So, yes, this was resistance against tyranny. You gunned them down so they couldn't crush a young man who wanted to live free. You were fighting for his freedom."

"I'm not sure the FBI will see it like that. Nor, for that matter, the NYPD."

"You did the right thing, Jon. And that's not easy sometimes. Easiest thing in the world is to turn away. Takes a lot of guts to do what you did."

Reznick pulled up a stool. "Killing is not something to be explained away lightly. It was in the moment. Kill or be killed."

"Listen, you must be hungry."

"I'm fine. So, what exactly happened at your place in Vermont?"

Sullivan rubbed her face. She looked drawn and tired, dark shadows around her eyes. "It was a bit unnerving." She explained how precarious she thought Kevin's mental state was. "I'm not an expert, but it's like he's suffering an acute psychotic reaction to the death of his sister and the killings in Chinatown."

"Sounds like he's at the breaking point."

"It's beyond that. I think he's broken. He's a broken man."

Reznick wondered if they should get him some help.

"He told me that in the past he has suffered from acute anxiety, has flashbacks, and was treated for post-traumatic disorder after the protests in Hong Kong. Flashbacks to detention. Beatings."

"I guess me gunning down those Chinese spooks in front of him wouldn't have helped."

"Not to mention the death of his sister. For Kevin's sake, the sooner this is over, the better. He desperately needs psychiatric help. A clinical psychologist. Real quick. He needs more protection than we can provide. How did your trip to New York go? I take it you spoke to the FBI."

Reznick put down his mug. "The whole thing went to shit."

"How so?"

"I had hoped that it would be just me and Martha. We've worked together in the past. I thought I'd try one final time to persuade her. Anyway, Meyerstein and me were walking, discussing it. In a park in Lower Manhattan. Back and forth. Very frustrating. But we were talking. I was keen to keep this channel of communication open."

"That makes sense."

"I thought so."

"So, what happened?"

Reznick sighed. "She set me up is what happened. I genuinely didn't see that coming."

"Maybe she'd had enough. Killing three people is not small potatoes. I guess she needs to do what she needs to do."

"Point taken. I thought maybe I was putting too much stock in our past friendship. But I thought we could still talk frankly. So, I was in FBI custody from that morning. And held overnight."

"What I can't understand is why on earth they would release you . . . it doesn't make sense. The FBI knows you killed those people. You said so yourself."

"I didn't talk. But they must've found the bike at the parking garage. And they discreetly wired up an advanced GPS tracker underneath the rear seat of the bike."

"But you managed to ditch them?"

Reznick nodded.

"How?"

"I got an ex-Delta friend to meet me at a diner in Springfield, and we switched rides. The FBI tail, physical and electronic, would have had a visual on the bike."

"But not you?"

"I can only surmise that they thought that finding Kevin Chang was of paramount importance. And they could get me in the bargain, leading them straight to him."

"That's wild."

"I'm guessing it was Meyerstein who persuaded them to release me as I didn't talk. But I had a tail most of the way back to your place."

"I'm curious. You said you did a switch."

"It's an old-school trick." Reznick explained how his friend arrived at the diner in Springfield, put on the helmet and the leather jacket, and drove off on the bike.

"So, the FBI tail would have assumed the guy driving the bike was you. But it wasn't."

"Right. Not the most elaborate plan."

"But it worked."

"Right. Unfortunately, your father's bike is in the possession of a friend of mine. Sorry."

"Forget it. What about your friend?"

"He can look after himself. He probably rode around for a few hours, did a switch of his own. Before you know it, I'm off their radar. For now."

"I'm glad you made it back. Actually, I've never been so relieved to see someone."

Reznick's stomach growled from lack of food. "It was a long ride."

"Sounds like someone's hungry. You want something to eat?"

"That would be great."

"Sam is pretty cool putting us up."

"Sam's a stand-up guy. He's a Black Hawk pilot."

"Seriously?"

"The best there is. Does a bit of freelancing for NATO these days."

"What do you want to eat?"

"Scrambled eggs, toast?"

"My favorite too. You got it."

Caroline picked up her phone and put on some classical piano music. It played low from a speaker on the counter. She cracked a few eggs, added cream, and began to whisk the eggs in a bowl before pouring it all into a frying pan. She cranked up the heat and stirred and stirred. Then she toasted some rye bread.

"What's that you're listening to?"

"Chopin."

Reznick beamed as the music washed over him. "Very relaxing."

"You should try it some time. Relaxing, I mean."

"I try."

"I take it you're not a meditation sort of guy."

"Not really."

"So, what's your idea of relaxation?"

"Down in the Lower Keys, drinking a cold beer, staring out at the sea. That does it for me."

"That sounds like my kind of speed." Caroline served up a portion of scrambled eggs and toast in double-quick time with a fresh cup of black coffee. "Enjoy."

Reznick ate the food, grateful to get some sustenance and home cooking inside him. "This is really good."

"I don't know. It's food, right?"

Reznick nodded as he ate his toast. He pointed to the speaker. "That's not a smart speaker, is it?"

"Relax, Trevelle already asked that. He freaked out. But no, it's not a smart speaker. It can't pick up what we're saying. It's just a simple, good old-fashioned Bluetooth speaker."

Reznick nodded. "You like music?"

"I played piano when I was younger."

"Were you any good?"

"I was hopeless. Beset by nerves."

"Hey, if you enjoy it, that's all that matters."

"That's what my dad used to say. I used to practice and practice. But I just couldn't get it."

Reznick looked over and saw a MacBook with a notepad beside it. He cocked his head. "You been interviewing the guys for your book while I was gone?"

"I managed to get some fascinating details. And it augments what I've learned in my research for my book on Chinese intelligence operations in America."

"What have you learned?"

"What do you want to know?"

"Give me what you've got."

"Well, one aspect that I'm investigating is that China has surreptitiously set up more than one hundred unofficial police stations in the world. The one in Lower Manhattan appears to be a travel agency that specializes in tours to Hong Kong. But the two guys running it, brothers Jimmy Kao and David Kao? Their links are deep within the Ministry of State Security. Counterintelligence, foreign intelligence, primarily focused on the United States. They've lived in the country for thirty years. But they have one loyalty."

"Beijing?"

"And the party. They ran a nightclub in Boston for a few years. Links to crime syndicates back in Hong Kong too. But they're running operations for Beijing to monitor, harass, and repatriate dissidents, rounding up American green card holders to send them back to China."

"Why?"

"They want to punish dissent. But they also want to send the message to people—friends, family—back in China that the party will find you, wherever you are in the world, and bring you back. It's incredibly frightening. But it's not just on the thug level."

"What else?"

"The spying is done by all sides, right?"

"Sure, it's a given."

"The problem is Chinese spying is also very adept at thieving intellectual property, thus harming American economic interests. And that's what worries America. They worry that China, targeting corporations in the US, stealing the technology, will in turn build China up economically and ultimately enhance Chinese national security through biotechnology, patents, and copyrights.

"And our intelligence community views this as a real and present threat to our interests, not only now but for the next twenty or thirty, maybe even fifty years and beyond. They are gaining the technological edge. The economic edge. And that's why they can't have brilliant minds fleeing to America. They allow their brightest students, artificial intelligence experts, robotics, all that, to study and learn in America. But they want them back. To develop China. To empower China to become the dominant power in the twenty-second and twenty-third centuries."

"Glad I won't be around to see that."

"And to compound matters, they're hacking our systems like never before. We've discovered the digital footprints to malware and myriad new technologies to subvert our systems, subvert our companies, and ultimately subvert American influence throughout the world."

"So, why is the FBI not going after the Chinese operatives? Why are they worrying about me neutralizing a few of their goons?"

Sullivan shook her head. "The FBI must have been asleep. The level of Chinese operations across North America is scandalous. We want cheaper goods, and the Chinese make them, employing millions of their own people. But in return, they get to start bringing in major economic benefits by trading with us, and that allows their expansion on all continents, not just North America. A byproduct of globalization."

"How dumb are we?"

"Don't get me started. You want to know something else?"

"What?"

"My research has shown that Chinese spies are buying citizenship in Vanuatu."

"Where's that?"

"Country in the South Pacific. The Chinese are investing heavily in scores of countries around the globe to buy influence. But it also means they can gain entry to the United States on visas with Vanuatu passports. If a Chinese businessman, for example, racks up one hundred and fifty thousand dollars' worth of investment there, he acquires citizenship. Also by buying property. Namibia is another country. But there are others. It allows access to a country."

"What a mess. We're wide open."

"Pretty much."

Reznick sighed. "Let's get back to how this started. Tell me about the death of Amy Chang."

"I've looked into this. I believe she was pushed, as Trevelle told you. No surveillance footage from the platform or in and around the subway. But NYPD sources have told me off the record that two separate eyewitnesses saw a masked Asian woman push through crowds and stand behind Amy. They didn't see the push. But one reported that the woman ran away. The rest of the people on the platform stayed and gave statements to cops. So, that would indicate deliberate, targeted intent."

"What a piece of shit to do that."

"Whatever it takes."

"Anything else on this?"

"Get this. I learned that Amy received a LinkedIn message from a daughter of David Kao, Kimmy Kao, and had been told there was a job opportunity. Amy turns up for an interview but instead gets a stark warning to pack her bags and return home within forty-eight hours or face consequences."

Reznick shook his head. "So, they reached out to her through LinkedIn?"

"Correct. It's a very common way to invite people for jobs, maybe give lectures, and that's when they get their tentacles into you. Trevelle and Kevin told me that she had reported sightings of suspicious activity outside her apartment the day after the meeting. Her phone rang. She answered. The person on the other end hung up. And then she was pushed."

Reznick looked at her. "Listen, if I can play devil's advocate for a minute. It's very, very persuasive what you're saying. But it won't be the first push on the subway. Especially recently, Asians have been particularly vulnerable. Some people thinking they're Chinese or whatever and with links to the Wuhan lab and all that Covid bullshit."

"I mentioned that to Trevelle and Kevin, that it could be a random event. But I think knowing what we know now, and the subsequent targeting of Kevin in New York too . . . I think that's too much of a coincidence. I'm open-minded. It's a possibility, I guess. But I think it would be foolish to rule out foul play. I believe she was murdered by Chinese government operatives."

"But impossible to prove in a court of law."

"Precisely. So, it's a moot point."

"Were there others?"

"Deaths?"

Reznick nodded.

"I believe so. What happened to Amy and Kevin—the threats to have them disappeared if they didn't return home—was not an isolated case. I have gathered documentary evidence of seven other cases in New York alone of Chinese dissidents and green card holders who opposed their government simply disappearing or dying in suspicious circumstances. One died after jumping from her apartment on the Upper West Side."

"Not unheard-of in New York."

"I know. But the victim's cousin was also killed by a hit-and-run driver on Broadway in Midtown a week earlier. The driver who was arrested worked as a junior cultural attaché at the Chinese consulate."

"How very convenient."

"No charges could be brought. Diplomatic immunity. There are five other cases of Chinese dissidents disappearing or dying in strange circumstances. One found floating in the East River. This is all documented by the NYPD and FBI, according to my sources."

"That's way more than a coincidence."

"It's a pattern. In one city. And I'll be stating that in my book. Which reminds me, I'm falling further behind with my deadline. So, what now?"

"What do you mean?"

"I mean, what now? Where are you going to take Kevin? You can't stay here indefinitely."

"I don't know. I was wondering if Sam could fly us up to a little town in Upstate New York, close to the Canadian border. Maybe hide out there for a few months."

"You would go that far?"

"It's not a game. You're either all in or you go home. I've decided I want to help the kid. Besides, I have a network of ex-Delta guys I know. Like the one that did the bike switch. That might be another route for me to take. But to answer your question, I don't know. I think it's an hour-by-hour thing."

"What about Meyerstein?"

"What about her?"

"Are you holding out for her to have a change of heart?"

Reznick shook his head. "I've burned that particular bridge. I think my actions have caused irreparable damage."

"To your professional relationship with her?"

"I think so. I think I've got to assume there's no mending that. It's just the way it is."

"Do you have a personal relationship with her?"

"I'd rather not go there."

Sullivan was quiet for a few moments.

"What about you?"

"Me?"

"I mean, is there anyone in your life? Are you married?"

"Divorced five years."

"I'm sorry."

"I'm not. He was an asshole."

"What happened, if you don't mind me asking?"

Sullivan sighed. "The usual bullshit. He ran off with a new girl in the office. Fresh out of college. She's a lawyer. And she's also a twenty-something blonde. My ex-husband is a corporate lawyer in Manhattan. Takeovers, mergers."

"That must have been tough for you."

"Things happen, right?"

"You've just got to roll with it. No other way."

"So, are you married . . . sorry, that's none of my business."

"It's OK. No, I'm not married."

"Divorced?"

Reznick knew he had to be careful. His wife's life as a CIA agent operating in Switzerland for more than two decades was classified. He was sworn to secrecy. He decided to stick to the official version. "She . . . she died on 9/11."

Sullivan covered her mouth. "God, I'm so sorry. That's terrible."

"It was a long time ago."

"Trevelle mentioned you have a daughter."

"I do. She's out in Indonesia. CIA."

Sullivan looked surprised. "Are you kidding me?"

"She was previously mentored by Martha Meyerstein."

"Come on, seriously?"

"It's true."

Reznick was beginning to warm to this rather unconventional journalist.

Caroline looked at her watch. "I better be going soon. I need to get back to that goddamn book of mine. I hope you understand."

"Of course. I really, really appreciate everything you've done, Caroline."

"I'd really appreciate a full off-the-record interview with you when this is over, one way or the other."

"Count on it." Reznick grinned. "There's a possibility you might be interviewing me in some goddamn penitentiary doing some serious time."

"I hope that's not the case. But it would be great if you could keep in touch."

"You bet."

"You know where to find me. Madison."

"On the beach, sounds nice."

The sound of heavy footsteps coming down the stairs. "Jon! Jon!"

Trevelle burst into the kitchen. "It's Kevin! He's not waking up!"

Reznick rushed up the two flights of stairs and burst into the attic bedroom. The kid was lying face down, an empty pill bottle on the floor. Reznick flipped him over. Caroline and Ripley arrived. Reznick checked his pulse. Nothing. He slapped Kevin's face hard a few times, trying to rouse him. But nothing. "We need to get him to a hospital. The fucker's overdosed!"

Twenty-Two

Meyerstein avoided the calls she knew would come from her higher-ups. She had given the final go-ahead to release Reznick. She wanted to kill two birds with one stone. Reznick would lead the Feds to Kevin Chang. That was the plan. It was a high-risk strategy. But she knew that. She had anticipated that at some point Reznick might find the tracking device. However, his decision to keep the tracker in place, signaling to the FBI that he hadn't found it, was a clever ploy. A double bluff. And then Reznick's adroit switch of the bike to an ex-Delta friend had allowed Reznick to make his escape. Simple but brilliant.

The more she thought about what had happened, the more she wondered if she hadn't subconsciously engineered Reznick's getaway. Was that it? Was that really it? She knew she was going to be forced out of the FBI anyway. Did she, also knowing Reznick's formidable special ops military capabilities, actually intend for him to evade capture? She had worked with him for years and knew his high-functioning skill set. She had to have known what would happen by allowing Reznick to leave New York. Maybe, just maybe, that was her final way of letting him go for good. To be free. Did she really want the infuriating, brilliant soldier, a warrior, a man she still cared about, to be thrown in prison for the rest of his days? But it was all too late for supposition. The writing was on the wall.

She should have listened to the other special agents in the New York field office. Everyone, apart from a reluctant Don Laslow, thought it was crazy and that it was too high a risk. But her voice carried the day, despite the serious concerns. She had brushed away legitimate complaints with a smidgen of high-handedness.

Now the FBI was back at square one. The fallout, when it came, was going to be brutal. She wasn't so stupid as to believe her seniority would allow her to walk away unscathed. The ramifications would be serious. Someone was going to take the fall. They had already earmarked her for an early exit from the FBI. But now? She was going to be the fall guy. No one else. And on reflection, she deserved nothing more.

Her phone rang and her heart skipped a beat. "Assistant Director Meyerstein."

"Martha, it's Bill." The brusque voice of FBI Director Bill O'Donoghue.

Meyerstein felt a tightening of the knot of tension in her stomach. "Evening, Bill."

"What a mess we've got on our hands."

"I know."

"Listen, I'm going to be blunt. This is going to be it. I'm sorry."

Meyerstein closed her eyes, knowing what lay in store.

"I just got off the phone with the Department of Justice. You know how these things work. I know what you were trying to do, Martha. It might have been a sound idea on another day with another person. But not with someone like Reznick. I think you're too close to him. It has clouded your judgment."

Meyerstein ordinarily might have objected to taking the sole blame. But this was her mess and she knew it.

"It was a crazy strategy. A roll of the dice. But the gamble failed. And the team in New York along with everyone at the Hoover building can't believe this went ahead."

Meyerstein wondered if she should take the time to explain that Laslow had given lukewarm support for the move. She quickly decided what was done was done. No use bringing that up. "I take full personal responsibility."

"Damn right you do. The buck stops with you on this."

Meyerstein felt her throat tighten at the verbal onslaught. Her mood was low, and he wasn't helping. "I thought it was the right thing to do. We needed to get Chang back, no matter what."

"Doesn't matter now. The Attorney General is headed up to New York as we speak."

Meyerstein didn't know how much she could take. She felt as if she was being buried alive.

"Beijing is kicking up a shitstorm over this. And he's in the cross fire. You see what I'm saying?"

Meyerstein cleared her throat. "Yes, I do."

"The Chinese government is going to engage in a full, protracted diplomatic war because of this. They have threatened mass expulsions of American diplomats, nongovernment organizations, and any US charities operating in China. The State Department and the CIA are frantic."

"What about the role of the Chinese diplomats at the New York consulate? What about their role in all this?"

"Enough! We have no witnesses; that's the fucking problem. Reznick was a witness. He was the culprit. And you let him go. He killed three Chinese nationals. You know what's next?"

"What?"

"This shitstorm is going global. The Secretary General of the United Nations is talking about a Security Council resolution in the next month criticizing the actions of the United States, blaming its agents. Russia will be voting with China, not surprisingly. And I'm hearing France is lining up behind them too."

"I don't know what to say . . . It's awful."

"They're going to throw the book at you. Then they're talking about reorganizing the FBI. Anything to placate the Chinese government. And yes, you might be looking at jail time. And as it stands, there's nothing I can do."

"Do you want me to resign right now? I will offer my resignation this minute if required."

O'Donoghue sighed. "That's not happening. Not right now."

Meyerstein suddenly saw the ploy. "They want me to stay in place and then fire me, right? I'm the patsy. The figurehead."

"I think that's the plan. Besides, the Chinese government seem to know a hell of a lot about you. And they have intimated they want you to stay in place too. They want you to be held responsible and not enjoy an early retirement. They don't want you to be rewarded for failure."

"Who the hell is running the FBI?"

"This suits all sides."

"I see."

"I think they also want to humiliate you in the press; that's what I'm hearing."

"Who's officially running this investigation now?"

"You are."

"Why?"

"I've already explained why. They want you to be in place when they apportion the blame."

"Why has this not been handed back to the Special Agent in Charge of the Criminal Investigative Division in New York?"

"The Chinese government wants to hold you to account. The president's national security team wants you in the frame. That might be the trade-off with them. We keep you in place for a little while, and they desist from holding a Security Council vote."

"I can't believe it got so crazy."

"It's politics. And it's a dirty game. Listen, it means you're still heading this investigation. The one crumb of comfort is that we believe you do have a connection to Reznick, albeit at times misguided and highly dangerous. But if you are able in some way to mitigate this disaster, even at the eleventh hour, it might be something. We don't want to close the door on finding Chang or Reznick. That still remains a priority."

"Are you giving me enough rope to hang myself with?"

"You do what you think is best."

There was a sharp knock at the door, and a young rookie FBI agent popped her head in. "Ma'am, we got something!"

"Bill, stay on the line." Meyerstein switched the call to speaker so O'Donoghue could hear the conversation. "Spit it out!"

"Kevin Chang and Jon Reznick have been ID'd by a surveillance camera at a hospital on Cape Cod."

"Are you sure?"

"Less than an hour ago. A source within the hospital tipped us off too."

"Francine, tell Boston to get their guys there. You getting this, Bill?"

"Copy that. Get the chopper ready to get you up there. I want every available agent up there! I want Reznick and Chang alive! This ends now!"

Twenty-Three

Reznick paced the corridor outside Kevin Chang's private hospital room. He glanced across at Caroline Sullivan, who sat, her head in her hands. "He's in the best place possible," he said. "Let's have some faith."

"I'm responsible. I gave him the sleeping pills."

"You gave him a couple to get him to sleep. But he stole the rest from your purse and swallowed them all. He did this. You didn't."

"Why couldn't I have anticipated this?"

"You're not a psychic, Caroline. This is on Kevin." Reznick sat down beside her and held her hand. "I swear to God, this is not your fault. Kevin overdosed. He did this. The poor kid was out of his mind with fear, worry, depression, grief over losing his sister, having a gun pointed at his head, and watching me taking those people out. He was the victim of those circumstances. You did your best. So, come on. Enough! Snap out of it!"

Sullivan shook with tears. "This is my fault!"

"There is a good chance the cops will be here. You might want to head back to Madison. Get out while you can. I've got a bad feeling about what will happen if you hang around."

Sullivan shook her head. "I'm not going to abandon him."

"How are you abandoning him? You've gone above and beyond. You've put your neck on the line again and again. The cops will be looking for me, not you. But you'll be in their crosshairs if you stick around much longer."

"I want to stay. With Kevin. With you. Until this is done."

Reznick squeezed her hand. "This isn't the time to give up your life. I pulled the trigger. This is on me. I went on the run with Kevin Chang. I will face the consequences. And trust me, the FBI won't release me again."

"So, that's it, then? What will happen to you?"

"What do you think? There will have to be a trial. It'll get messy."

Caroline glanced at the closed door. "I'm not going to run away."

"Who says you're running away? I got this. The medical staff will make sure he's fine."

"We've come this far. I want to stay. For now."

Reznick shook his head and sighed.

"Kevin is alive. They've pumped his stomach. But they've got to check on his condition over the next seventy-two hours. I just want to ensure that he's really going to be OK. I couldn't live with myself if something happened to him."

Reznick's gaze was drawn farther down the corridor.

A masked doctor wearing a white coat walked toward them, talking into her phone. "I'm going to need the results by tonight," she said. She ended the call and put the phone into a pocket of her white jacket.

She stopped a few yards away and took out a pager, clipped to her pocket. She checked it for any messages before she walked past, giving a small nod.

Reznick watched her head down the corridor and disappear through a set of doors. "I don't like it," he whispered to Sullivan.

"What don't you like?"

"The doctor who just strolled past. I don't know. Sixth sense—I don't know."

"It's just a doctor, Jon. We're in a hospital."

Reznick sensed there was something off. A gut reaction that something wasn't right. He could feel it in his bones.

"You think that doctor was one of them?"

"I don't know. Maybe."

"Shit, Jon, that's taking paranoia to a new level."

"They want to neutralize Kevin. We already know that."

"What are you saying?"

"I'm saying we have broken cover. Maybe the Chinese operatives have face-recognition scanning surveillance cameras. Who the hell knows."

Sullivan nodded. "Maybe we could move him?"

"Where?"

"A different floor."

"That would work. I like it."

A few moments later, a male doctor and a couple of nurses in blue scrubs headed down the corridor.

Reznick watched closely. Sullivan, as if reading his mind, rose to her feet. She smiled coquettishly, tucking some loose hair behind her ear. "Excuse me, doctor," she said, hand on hip, "I'm sorry to bother you. Our friend, Kevin, is in the room opposite. We were wondering if there are any other private rooms on a different floor we could move him to?"

The doctor looked surprised at the request. "The patient is resting," he said. "It's best if he rests."

"I understand. But I think his life might be in danger. I believe people are trying to cause him harm."

The doctor stared at her. "I beg your pardon?"

"His life is in danger. We would like to move him for security considerations."

"Are you serious?"

"You need to trust me. We brought him in. He's scared of certain people who are out to get him. And that's why he overdosed."

"This is very irregular. I'm not sure . . ."

Reznick got up and smiled at the doctor. "My name is Jon Reznick, Doctor"—he checked the ID hanging around the doctor's neck—"Benjamin . . . We brought him in. And if you could just move him to a private room of your choice on a different level, right now, it would be better for all concerned."

The doctor looked at the nurses, who nodded. "Are you a friend of the patient?"

"I'm a friend of a friend. This is urgent. It needs to happen now."

"Have the police been informed?"

"The police and FBI. I assume they will be here at any moment. But this is a time-critical situation. We're not asking to move him out of the hospital. Just to a different room. Under your medical supervision, of course."

The doctor nodded. "I'm not sure."

"Listen, Doc, either you move him or I'll do it. Your choice. Get security to move him. But he needs to move. Doing nothing is not an option."

"Are you police?"

"I've worked in the past with the FBI. That's all I can say."

The doctor directed the nurses, "Get Mr. Chang up to one of the empty rooms on level six. I'll accompany him too."

Reznick shook the doctor's hand. "Good decision. I really appreciate that, thank you."

Sullivan got up. "I'll accompany Kevin too, if that's OK."

The doctor nodded. "Appreciate that, thank you."

Reznick watched as the nurses went into Kevin's room and quietly maneuvered the gurney out of the door. They wheeled it past Reznick and down the corridor to an elevator, accompanied by Caroline and the doctor. And they were gone.

Reznick felt a sense of relief wash over him. His instincts told him something was amiss with the masked doctor. He wondered whether he should head up to the floor where Kevin was.

A few minutes later, his phone rang. "Yeah, Reznick."

"Jon, it's Caroline. He is safely in a private room. The door is locked. I'm with him, along with one of the nurses."

"Great. I'm just going to hang around here for a little while. I want to make sure that no threat arises."

"Are you expecting any?"

"My gut says yes. But I don't know."

"Look after yourself."

"You too. And maybe shut the blinds."

"Already done."

"Good work."

Reznick ended the call. He stared down the empty corridor. Not a soul in sight. He wondered if the threat was real or imagined.

His mind flashed images of the masked doctor through his head. A sense of foreboding washed over him. The threat level was critical.

Twenty-Four

The minutes dragged as Reznick sat in the chair outside the room the hospital had originally allocated for Kevin Chang. He considered heading up to where Kevin was now. But just as he was about to decide to move, three people came into view. The masked doctor flanked by two cops.

Reznick's senses heightened as he considered the trio. The cops looked Chinese and were chewing gum. The whole thing felt off.

The masked doctor approached him, standing over him, hands clasped. The cops fixed on him. "Sir," she said, "I'm going to have to ask for some identification."

Reznick rubbed his hands together and got to his feet. "Not a problem, Doctor," he said. He reached into his jacket and pulled out his Beretta, pointing the gun straight at the doctor. "Now let's see some ID from you, whoever you are."

The doctor's dark eyes stared at him from behind the mask. She raised her hands in the air. "Don't shoot! I'm a doctor!"

"You said that already. Where's your ID? Show me your hospital ID. Where's the lanyard around your neck? Let me see it."

"It's in my office, sir."

The cop on Reznick's left reached for his gun.

Reznick shot him once in the head. Blood splattered the corridor walls.

The doctor screamed. The second cop's eye began to twitch. He raised his left hand slowly in the air. "I'm going to show you my ID. It's in my back pocket."

"Nice and slow."

The cop reached into his back pocket and flashed a cop badge. "Barnstable Police Department. See? That was my partner."

Reznick glanced at the ID. "That's an out-of-date ID, pal, for a Caucasian cop. You get that on eBay, knockdown price?"

The cop glared at Reznick long and hard. "You're making a terrible mistake . . . I was just transferred."

"Bullshit."

The cop nodded slowly. He slowly raised both hands. "It's just a misunderstanding . . . You need to trust us."

Reznick knew the cop's unfazed, almost Zen-like nonreaction to his killing a fellow cop showed the hallmarks of a trained killer. He should know. He knew the signs. He knew how to disassociate. To compartmentalize. He knew all about that. "Just so we're clear," Reznick said, "this is how it's going to—"

The cop crouched and pulled out his gun.

Reznick quickly fired two deafening shots into the man's forehead. The man collapsed, lifeless, blood spilling across the linoleum floor.

The masked doctor screamed again as she stared at the fake cop, blood seeping out of his open mouth. Two dead fake cops. She dropped to her knees very theatrically, hands on head. "What the hell have you done? You just killed two cops! Help! Help! Someone!"

Reznick took a step forward. The sound of alarms. Footsteps and screaming in the distance.

The masked doctor's hand reached into a pocket of her white coat. A flash of metal. A handgun appeared.

Time seemed to slow.

Reznick fired only one bullet into her forehead. A clean head-shot. She collapsed face-first, smashing her bloody head on the floor, sprawled between the two other Chinese operatives. He stared down at the scene. Three more dead. He knew he had taken out a Chinese hit team. Two men, one woman.

He sensed people were behind him.

A man's voice shouted, "Freeze! FBI! Drop the gun! Drop it!"

Reznick opened his fingers, letting the gun drop to the floor.

"Nice and easy, Reznick. Hands on your head. And get on your knees!"

Reznick complied. He kneeled motionless, hands on the back of his head. He stared at the three bloodied bodies of the Chinese assassination team prone on the ground. His instincts had been correct. They had tracked down Chang, after all.

A team of highly armed FBI SWAT guys swarmed all around him. "On your feet, motherfucker!"

Reznick was hauled to his feet before he could get up. He felt the barrel of a long gun pressed tight against the back of his neck.

"Not one move!"

He was quickly handcuffed and frog-marched out of the hospital to a waiting truck.

Twenty-Five

It was dark when James Bradley walked into the near-empty restaurant in Rockaway Beach, Queens. A Mexican restaurant, sombreros on the wall, black-and-white photos of Mexican revolutionary leader Zapata with a sword and rifle. A handful of diners.

Bradley felt bone weary. It had been a grueling five-hour journey up from Great Falls, Virginia. He had earlier checked into a nearby boutique hotel three blocks away. He surveyed the restaurant until he fixed on a smartly dressed guy nursing a Scotch on the rocks in a booth at the far side of the restaurant. He walked past the tables and sat down opposite the man. "Sorry I'm a bit late," he said.

Thomas Kelly, the FBI's head of counterintelligence in New York, set down his glass, eyes cold, unforgiving. "Long time no see, James," he said.

"Yeah, likewise." Bradley ordered a Scotch on the rocks for himself and another for Kelly, along with a menu. He leaned in close when the waitress was out of earshot. "I think I might have a proposition for you."

"We'll talk about that in a little while . . . First, you look good."

Bradley forced a smile. He always hated the awkward encounters with Kelly, a man prone to mood swings veering into violent rages, especially when drinking. But he fitted the profile a corporate client of his in Asia wanted to head up their operation in the Far East.

"So, how's retirement treating you, James?"

"It's working out OK . . . but I'm still busy. You know how it is."

Kelly nodded. "I just want to check. No devices?"

"Absolutely not."

"I'm not going to frisk you. I'm trusting you."

"I know how it works."

"I hope so."

The waitress returned with their drinks and handed Bradley a menu. Bradley clinked glasses with Kelly in a toast. "To friendship."

"To friendship."

"Nice to meet up, Thomas. Sorry it's been so long."

Kelly looked at his watch. "I don't have long. Let's get down to business. My plans for the future. The last time we spoke, I mentioned that I was looking further down the line at fresh challenges in the next year or two. And you said you might be able to help me."

Bradley nodded. "I've been working on deals for several private companies, global entities, and I've been very, very discreet in reaching out. I hope you understand."

"As it should be."

"Right. So, I have a proposition for you that I think you might find interesting. I think this would be a perfect fit for your skill set and experience."

Kelly grinned. "I'm listening."

"A Singapore businessman spoke to me."

"Singapore, huh?"

"Right. So, his company is looking to leverage your knowledge of counterintelligence operations against some of the big players on the geopolitical stage: China, Russia, Iran. But your position would be to protect his corporation from such foreign states, which are based mostly in Singapore. There is one caveat."

"What's that?"

"It would mean you being based abroad. In Singapore."

"Singapore?"

"Think about it, Thomas. High quality of life, no crime to speak of, and they want to keep it like that, as you would be working alongside the cops and the state."

Kelly sipped his drink, narrowing his eyes, as if trying to figure out his move.

"The businessman is worth eight billion dollars. And it's considered a start-up. So, spectacular chances of growth over the next five to ten years in the global security consulting sphere in the Far East. I mentioned that you have been very forthcoming over the last few years when I've reached out. Investigations you're working on. Knowledge is power, data is everything, that kind of thing. But we all know this comes at a price."

"Damn right it does."

"You mind me asking you a personal question, Thomas?"

Kelly shrugged.

"What are you making?"

"Salary? Not enough. Not by a long shot."

Bradley nodded. "I'd estimate a hundred and fifty thousand a year, plus bonuses and expenses, right? Give or take."

"Close."

"My Singapore guy is offering you a nonexecutive directorship, a guaranteed million bucks a year, with a handsome five-year contract."

"Interesting."

"Plus . . . they will also pay your tax obligations. You will have a rent-free, three-bedroom duplex overlooking the harbor. Full deluxe family medical coverage. Corner office. The works."

"Sounds like a blast. What's the catch?"

"The catch is you have to live in Singapore, and you will attend meetings once a month. And over the course of one month, you will be working ten hours, maximum. The absolute maximum. So, three hours a week, or thereabouts."

"Very interesting indeed."

"So, it would be retirement with major, major perks."

"And in return?"

"In return, during meetings, you will be advising his company on the direction and implementation of counterintelligence policies and strategies to ensure his business operates and aligns with American and Western geopolitical aims. They are pro-Western and pro-capitalist. But they foresee themselves coming within the growing sphere of influence of the Chinese government. In particular, they want to protect their company against intellectual property theft."

"Do they allow you to drink in Singapore?"

"There are strict conditions. You won't be served alcohol after 10:30 p.m."

"I can live with that."

"The job has wide powers. So, you would have free rein over the vetting of all employees and directors, including the chairman, protecting the company's interests and those of the shareholders, alerting the company to nefarious interests or activities of employees or their families."

Kelly sipped some more of his Scotch. "I'm still listening."

Bradley had been softening up Kelly for the last year. He estimated he had passed from his Chinese handler no less than two hundred thousand dollars in cash, a fair chunk of that to Kelly. A slow burn with a high price.

The cultivation of Kelly began in earnest when Bradley learned that Kelly had a mistress. He had secured the photos from a private detective, hired by Kelly's wife, for a five-figure sum. Bradley had leverage. The mistress was Kelly's weakness. As well as booze. And so began the cultivation of a burgeoning relationship between Thomas Kelly and James Bradley. Maybe it was more a tacit understanding.

Kelly's scruples slowly eroded.

A drip, drip, drip of information followed. Highly classified intel that crossed his desk. The FBI was one of seventeen federal agencies that collected and occasionally shared intelligence.

It was clear that Kelly didn't know anything about James Bradley's growing links with Chinese foreign intelligence agents in America. If he had, the intel would have dried up. But Kelly thought Bradley's clients were bona fide US corporations who needed hard intel on geopolitical and intellectual property issues.

When the cash started changing hands in the last few months, Kelly began to let his guard down. He grew more and more forthcoming. His previous belligerence and aggression became assuaged by the money.

Kelly opened up to Bradley. Snippets of information flowed Bradley's way. Booze loosened Kelly's tongue even more. It concerned the surveillance of prominent diplomats and politicians based in and around New York. The close surveillance of Chinese businessmen in and around the United Nations. The comings and goings of Chinese diplomats and their families. It was all very useful for Bradley. And he in turn fed it back to his Chinese handler. And the money flowed back to Bradley as a sweetener, with a generous slice for Kelly.

Kelly picked up the menu, sidestepping the issue. "I'm starving. Do you want to eat?"

Bradley quickly perused the menu. "Me too. Beef chili enchiladas, my usual."

Kelly ordered the same, along with two more Scotches. It always kept Kelly sweet. "Hell of a day."

"Is that right?" Bradley wondered how much intel Kelly would be divulging. He knew that free Scotch and the promise of a serious cash injection into Kelly's bank account always loosened his tongue. "I thought you'd be winding down at this stage of your career. Before you retire, I mean."

"So did I."

"I thought you said you were six months from retirement."

"I am."

"No second thoughts?"

"Not a chance."

"Tough day?"

Kelly shook his head. "You don't want to know. Seriously, you would blow your brains out if you knew the shit I have to deal with."

"I heard you guys have been dealing with some killings in Chinatown."

"Who did you hear that from?"

"People I speak to. Friends of mine."

"Well, let me tell you, the shit has well and truly hit the fan. The last few days I have barely fucking slept."

"You want to talk about it?"

"Just a situation . . . it's complicated."

Bradley sat quietly, not saying anything, allowing Kelly to be the one to break the silence. He sipped his Scotch as he took stock of his surroundings.

"Thing is, it's a major shitstorm that came out of nowhere. And the optics aren't good. We look like idiots. Asleep on the job. You know what I'm saying?"

"We talking about Chinatown?"

"Correct."

"What the hell happened?"

"It's a monumental fuckup. And the FBI is in the crosshairs as we are indirectly responsible. A special forces guy gunned down two Chinese diplomats in Manhattan."

"Are you kidding me?"

Kelly shook his head. "And listen to this. It comes at the same time we're investigating unofficial Chinese police stations in and around the city intimidating Chinese dissidents in the city. None too subtle either."

Bradley feigned surprise. "In New York?"

"Yeah, in fucking New York. Military tough guy was responsible. Went on the run with some Hong Kong dissident kid after killing the two diplomats and a private dick. Then the fucking kid overdosed up in Massachusetts. That just happened literally a few hours ago."

Bradley listened intently, absorbing everything, making mental notes.

"And to compound matters, the special forces guy gunned down three Chinese up on Cape Cod. Six dead!"

"I knew you had your hands full, Thomas, but that's nuts."

Thomas shrugged. "I'm getting it from all sides. *Why didn't you see this coming?* I'm up to my eyes in bullshit from Islamists just off the boat driving around town in cabs and vans, and now we've got the Chinese government going crazy. Threatening all sorts of diplomatic repercussions."

"The pressure must be intense."

"To make matters worse, I have the Assistant Director all the way up from DC asking me a million and one questions."

"About what?"

"The Chinatown stuff. What do you think?"

"So, she's looking over your shoulder."

"Worse than that. She's taking over the whole thing."

Bradley leaned closer and got a whiff of the booze on Kelly's warm breath. "She's running the field office?"

"I know. That's part of the problem. The chain of command as we understand it within the Bureau has become compromised. She's in and out of my office at all hours of the day and night."

"You don't need this shit, Thomas."

"No one needs this shit. She's breaking my balls over my need to spend so long overseas. I just got back from Albania ten days ago. And before that I was in Bosnia and Ukraine and before that Saudi Arabia. We have multiple threats. And we need to keep abreast of it."

"I get it, trust me."

"Know the thing that gets me? I've learned, well, actually I've known for a while, that the Assistant Director, Meyerstein—"

"I've heard of her."

"Everyone's heard of her. She's a major league pain in the ass. But you're not going to believe this."

"Believe what?"

Kelly picked up his glass and stared at the booze, swishing his Scotch and ice. "The Assistant Director is romantically linked with the special forces crazy who killed the Chinese diplomats."

Bradley's senses became heightened in a nanosecond. "How is that possible? That can't be right."

"Think again. She's fucking him while he's killing these Chinese guys. See what I'm saying?"

Bradley feigned surprise. "That's unbelievable."

"You better believe it. I was the one who began the investigation two years ago into Chinese police stations across the country. My team got the ball rolling. We have informants in Chinatown, out in Queens, Brooklyn, and they told us things. We opened a new file. And that's how it began. Now I've got this fucking nutcase woman trawling through our files, questioning how we do things."

"You need a vacation."

"I need to be retired. I want out of New York. It's killing me. I need less stress."

Kelly nodded. He smiled as the waitress put down their plates of food. *"Muchas gracias,"* he said.

The waitress blushed. "You want any more Scotches?"

Kelly pointed to Bradley's glass. "Two more. Set 'em up."

"Right away, sir."

Bradley started his meal. He took a couple of large mouthfuls; it was blazing hot. He felt sweat sticking to his back. "Damn, a lot of fire in that, huh?"

Kelly laughed. "Nice little place, out of the way. Manhattan isn't a good place to meet."

"So, you were saying this crazy stuff about the special forces guy."

"Chinese are going apeshit."

Bradley tried to ask his question in the most tactful manner. "And you've still got this special forces guy in Manhattan?"

"That's right. But we've got a tight rein on him. Hyper-tight security in and around his room."

"The Javits building?"

"Of course."

"What about the Assistant Director?"

"Meyerstein? She'll still be where she always seems to be. In the fucking office. Actually, in my office. Do you know she's using my fucking office? You believe that?"

"She's not hot desking it?"

Kelly shrugged. "Hot desking? Bullshit. It's driving me crazy."

Bradley made a mental note of that vital, time-sensitive intel that Kelly had divulged. "That's a lot of crazy stuff coming at you."

"James, I'm telling you straight, after the week I've had . . ."

"Well, my client would love you to join his team in Asia. No stress, huge salary, great perks, expense account, first-class travel. What do you say?"

"Tell him I'm very interested. Very, very interested."

"Leave it to me, Thomas."

Thirty minutes later, Bradley finished his meal, which he paid for, and caught a cab back into the city. He switched on his specially modified Samsung Galaxy phone, and it rang immediately.

"James?"

"Speaking?"

"We've been trying to contact you."

"I've been meeting with an *old friend of mine*." The code words for Kelly.

"Does he want to work in Singapore?"

"He's very interested."

"That would be wonderful. But in the meantime, we would need intel on the whereabouts of Reznick."

"I might be able to help you."

"Where is he?"

"I've just been told Reznick is back in FBI custody. Manhattan. Javits Federal Building, Lower Manhattan. Twenty-third floor."

"And you know this for sure?"

"Quite sure. Assume a ring of security around his interrogation room. So, limited chance of getting access to him."

"And what about the Assistant Director?"

"What about her?"

"Where is she?"

"Same place. She's working around the clock on this case, based in the office of the head of counterintelligence, Thomas Kelly."

The line went quiet for a few moments. "I think he will fit in well in Singapore."

"Guarantee it. Do you want anything else?"

"Not at the moment. But stay available. And keep your phone charged. For now, thank you. Good work. Very good work."

Twenty-Six

Reznick was handcuffed and back in the interrogation room in New York, a couple of special agents watching him closely. Three more stood stationed outside of the room. He paced like a caged animal for what seemed like hours, glaring into the two-way mirror running across one wall.

Reznick stopped and held his handcuffed wrists out. "Do you mind taking them off? I'm not running away. Besides, the door is locked."

The younger of the two shrugged. "Not a problem."

Reznick was uncuffed, and he stretched his wrists and arms. "I appreciate that. Thanks."

He felt tight around the shoulders and the back of his neck. He did a few stretching exercises. Then he lay spread-eagled on the ground and did a couple hundred push-ups. He needed to keep sharp. He was bored. And he had time to kill.

The older of the two Feds shook his head. "Reznick, sit the fuck down."

Reznick got to his feet and ran himself through a few more stretching exercises.

"Did you hear what I said?"

Reznick nodded. "I heard you."

"So, what are you waiting for?"

Reznick sat back down, arms crossed. "Happy now?"

The special agents averted their eyes, clearly pissed off at his attitude.

Reznick had had his fill of the FBI. He liked them as individuals. And they did some seriously good stuff in the intelligence field. But from his time with Caroline, he learned it was increasingly clear that government overreach by agencies like the NSA and the FBI encompassed way more than investigation of crimes and tracking criminals. Now the alphabet agencies encroached on an individual's life. Unnecessary surveillance and infringement of First Amendment rights were part of their mandate.

The door was unlocked from the outside, and Reznick shifted in his seat.

Meyerstein walked in, a pile of papers and files in her hand.

"So, here we are," she announced.

Reznick eyed the two Feds.

"Look at me, Jon." Meyerstein pulled up a chair opposite. "Quite a couple of days you're having."

Reznick sat in silence.

"Quite a couple of days."

"You mind getting to the point?"

"You have no idea the damage you've done."

"That's where you're wrong."

"You comprehend the magnitude of your actions?"

"What the hell do you mean by comprehend? Do you believe I don't understand the threat and know what I've done? I knew full well."

"We will be dealing with the ramifications of your actions for years." Meyerstein leafed through the papers on the table between them.

"Where is Kevin?"

"He is in a secure location."

"How secure?"

"Secure unit at a hospital in the tristate area. Round-the-clock protection. Happy now?"

"So, he's still alive?"

"Barely."

"But he is alive."

"He is lapsing in and out of consciousness."

"I'm glad he's alive."

Meyerstein shook her head. "How did it come to this, Jon?"

"You really want to know what I think?"

"Yes, I do."

"It came to this because the American government didn't realize the ongoing threat from operatives of the People's Republic of China. If you had, you would have shut down the scores of unofficial so-called Chinese police stations they have dotted around the country. Including in New York."

"You don't know what you're talking about."

"Don't I? I heard that there are over one hundred locations around the world. Harassing innocent Chinese dissidents just wanting to make a new life in the West. People like Kevin. Frightening them to death, literally. He tried to escape the clutches of the regime. But those bastards still got their claws into him."

"Jon, this is not why I'm here."

"People like Amy Chang. She was pushed to her death."

Meyerstein flushed, clearly exasperated with his insolence.

"You ask how the hell it came to this? It came to this because someone was asleep at the wheel. I spoke to someone that knows about this sort of thing. *Transnational repression* is the phrase. And we are allowing this to grow without anyone getting rid of this cancer metastasizing in our midst."

"This is deflection, pure and simple. You have lost your mind, running around killing people. The Vienna Convention is in place to protect their rights."

"I don't give a shit about the Vienna Convention. This is America."

"Jon, America is built on laws. And international agreements."

"It is built on freedom, individual rights. Rights and freedoms that people gave their lives for. And we don't give them up easy. We protect our own."

Meyerstein looked at her watch. "In thirty minutes, I will be meeting with Don Laslow. The Department of Justice is calling for blood. Your blood, to be exact. You're going to be held accountable."

"What do you want from me?"

"A bit of humility."

"You want me to get on my knees and say I'm sorry?"

Martha rolled her eyes.

"I'm not going to go down on bended knee to you, the FBI, or anyone. I will defend myself in court. I'm not afraid. And I'll tell you something for nothing: when the judge and jury hear what happened, what really happened, they might wonder what the hell the FBI was doing all this time to protect people like Kevin Chang."

"You are talking about a world of espionage you know nothing about."

"Did the FBI know these unofficial covert police stations were operating under its very nose? You see where I'm going with this. Oh, and before I forget, do you want me to talk about my dealings with the FBI? Does Congress know you were employing a former black-ops specialist on classified missions here on American soil?"

Meyerstein took notes on a legal pad.

"Write it down, that's it. I was protecting the life of Kevin Chang, nothing more and nothing less. If I hadn't got involved, Kevin would have been disappeared by Chinese operatives and never seen again. Maybe there would have been an extraordinary rendition straight back to a torture cell in Beijing. How does that sit with you? Make no mistake, Martha. That's how this would have ended."

"Are you finished?"

"I haven't even started yet. You said to me I had no idea what I'm dealing with. I know exactly what the fuck I'm dealing with. I was dealing with Chinese killers masquerading as diplomats."

"What about Lauren? Do you think she will agree with your views on summary execution as she pursues her career?"

"You leave her out of this!"

Martha bowed her head. "I thought there would be more contrition, Jon. But instead, you're doubling down."

"Didn't the FBI release me and then try to track me back to Kevin Chang with a little device on the motorcycle? Did you get legal authorization for that? I'm sure the court will be interested. I sure as hell would be."

"I wanted to help you, Jon. It didn't have to be like this. There's no going back to the way it was."

"I get that."

"Can I ask you something? Now that Kevin Chang is safe, how about you let us know where you took him and kept him all this time."

Reznick sighed and shook his head. "You want me to become an informant, is that it?"

"Even at this moment, you are still not willing to cooperate?"

"I cooperated by reaching out to you and the Feds, Martha. I just wanted assurances about Kevin's safety, that's all."

"I understand. I do think it's important as we go forward to show us some contrition. That could start by saying where you were with Kevin. If you give us some intel on this, it would be looked upon very favorably further down the line. I'm asking you to think of your personal and professional interests by telling us where you kept him. This is very important."

Reznick slowly shook his head.

"Final word? I can't help you after this interview."

Reznick said nothing.

"I'm trying to help you, Jon. Tell me who was helping you."

"I guess we're done here."

Twenty-Seven

Meyerstein gathered up her papers. "I wanted to help you. I thought you would listen to me. I'm sorry it has to end like this."

"It is what it is."

Meyerstein got up and left. She headed back to her temporary office and locked her door. She sat down and placed her notes down in front of her. She took a sip of her coffee and noticed a slight tremor in her right hand. She had felt increased heart palpitations in the last few days. She wondered if it was simply symptoms of increased anxiety.

She closed her eyes and began a few breathing exercises. She had begun listening to guided meditation to improve breathing and ultimately help with relaxation and sleep. She noticed her triggers. Increasingly and invariably they were work-related. She was tempted to get her AirPods Pro on and take a few minutes for herself. But she knew that she needed to try and stay focused, at least for the rest of the day.

A sharp knock at the door disturbed her brief moment of solitude.

Don Laslow shut the door quietly behind him. "Wanted to see how you were . . . I'm told you had a tough time with Reznick."

"Nothing I can't handle."

"You OK?"

"No, as a matter of fact, I'm not."

"I'm sorry. This has been awful. I just wanted to say I've had a few days like this. It's not nice."

"Don, I messed up."

"It happens to everyone. We make wrong calls. It's tough."

"It's not just the events. It's the emotional impact. It's all gone to shit. And I'm to blame."

"Martha, please, we all make wrong calls."

"Do we? I don't. Never."

"We got Chang. Reznick is with us. So, it's better than nothing."

Meyerstein cleared her throat. "In four hours, the Attorney General is paying me a personal visit. Here."

"Here?"

Meyerstein nodded.

Laslow pulled up a chair opposite. "Martha, listen to me. I get it, this thing is a mess. But it's all because of Reznick."

"Is it really?"

"He's the one who killed six people. Three in New York, three in a goddamn hospital on Cape Cod. Who the hell could have foreseen that?"

"The shooting on Cape Cod was avoidable. What was I thinking? He was in custody. We had him. But I thought I was playing it real smart."

"Martha, listen. The only reason Reznick took Chang to the hospital was that he overdosed. So, there's no way Reznick went looking for the Chinese agents. It was the other way around. I didn't agree with your move to try and track Reznick—I had misgivings, everyone did—but I understood your logic. The tracker on the bike would have gone undetected ninety-nine times out of one hundred, no question."

Meyerstein rubbed her eyes. "Yeah, but it didn't in this case. I've done this for decades. I know Jon Reznick. At least I thought I did. How could I have been suckered into thinking that was a smart move?"

"You managed to get him into custody after agreeing to meet him face-to-face. That couldn't have been easy for you, knowing you were leading him into a trap."

"Don, I fucked up. I shouldn't have let him go the second time."

"Then we've got the small matter of Article 35."

"What?"

"This will be Reznick's defense, just wait and see. Under Article 35 of New York Penal Law, use of physical force in defense of a person is a proper defense. Reznick's lawyers could argue that straight off the bat. And that's why it was worth trying what you did."

"I understand that. I think I've tolerated Reznick's crossing of boundaries for too long. I guess this is the natural conclusion. The train has come off the tracks."

"The FBI as an organization has to take some of the blame."

"Don, you sound like Reznick."

"I'm going to tell you something. These goddamn covert Chinese police stations were operating under our noses for years before we got up to speed. That's on us. I am responsible for that. That was my fuckup. And we allowed cells of Chinese agents to operate with impunity. We need to look at counterintelligence, if you ask me. We need to look at how we operate. We need to overhaul our operations. Our job is to see threats before they arise. This is New York, after all. But our focus has to be on counterintelligence across New York."

"And that would be Thomas Kelly?"

"Correct. It wasn't Thomas who brought us the intel on the establishment of Chinese police stations across the city. Know how we really found out?"

"How?"

"A low-level informant, a restaurateur loosely involved with a triad-run human-trafficking crew first mentioned it to one of my team. That's how we got onto this. So, this didn't come from Counterintel, Kelly, or any of his team."

"Where is Kelly?"

"At this moment? Meeting a source, apparently."

"Hasn't he got other agents to do that kind of legwork?"

"Thomas enjoys working at street level. He likes to keep his ear close to the ground. That's the way he is."

"Is that the best use of his expertise?"

"I've asked myself that before. I've asked him that. But Thomas does his own thing. He's a law unto himself."

"What does that mean?"

"It means he doesn't like being told what to do. He's not the best team player. Maybe it's poor oversight on my part."

"Does he share intel when he gets it?"

"He does. Eventually. But he likes to store it for a while until he's good and ready."

"Interesting."

"It's the way he operated in DC before he was transferred here."

A loud knock at the door disturbed the conversation as a young agent stuck her head in. "Ma'am, there's a diplomat in reception asking to speak to you."

Meyerstein shrugged. "A diplomat? I'm due to see the Attorney General in a few hours. It'll have to wait. Tell them I'm in a meeting."

"Ma'am, the person showed a diplomatic ID from the Chinese consulate. A military attaché. She specifically says she wants to talk to you as a matter of urgency. She has some information you might find helpful."

"Never a goddamn break. Thanks, Gina. That'll be all."

Meyerstein gathered up her papers and coffee. "I'm sorry for cutting this conversation short. Thanks for listening."

Laslow smiled. "Any time. You want me to sit in with you?"

"Thanks, Don, but I'll handle this."

Meyerstein finished her coffee, dropping the Styrofoam cup in the trash can under her desk.

She picked up the phone and called reception. "It's Assistant Director Meyerstein. Send the diplomat up."

A few minutes later, a knock at the door. "Yes, come in."

The Chinese diplomat was a young woman. She wore an N95 mask, had her hair tied in a tight bun, and carried an expensive brown leather briefcase. The woman wore a black crepe blazer with matching trousers. "My name is Lucy Heung, military attaché for the People's Republic of China consulate here in New York."

"Please take off your mask. No requirements for that now."

"I'm taking personal precautions because of my health."

Meyerstein sighed. "Very well, if you insist."

"I insist."

"Take a seat."

Heung sat down demurely, hands on her lap, briefcase at her feet. "Thank you for seeing me at such short notice."

"I believe in open communication at all times."

"I appreciate your honesty." The woman reached into her briefcase and pulled out an envelope.

Meyerstein noticed the woman was wearing plastic medical gloves. "What on earth are you wearing medical gloves for?"

"I have a skin condition. It has flared up with all my stress. Just a precaution my doctor has advised me to take. My brother, who is a doctor, thinks it might be an allergy to detergent chemicals."

Meyerstein thought it odd. Highly odd.

The military attaché handed over an envelope.

Meyerstein looked at it. Handwritten in neat black ink were the words: *Private & Confidential, FBI Assistant Director Martha Meyerstein, New York.* "And what's this?"

"Open it."

"I'm asking what's inside."

"This is a formal complaint from the consulate here in New York. And we would like to know how the deaths of six Chinese citizens, all of whom either have diplomatic status or have links with our consulate in New York, could have happened. It's all in the letter."

Meyerstein stared at the woman's eyes above the mask. She noticed the woman never blinked. Not once. "I'll read it over later, thank you. We are, as you can imagine, snowed under on this investigation. I want to reassure you that we are intent on leaving no stone unturned."

Cold brown eyes fixed on Meyerstein. "I want to be clear. We hold the Federal Bureau of Investigation directly responsible. And we want to know about your relationship with Jon Reznick. It is all outlined in the letter."

Meyerstein sat dumbstruck. She wondered how much more they knew about her and Reznick.

"Such a relationship is most irregular. Would you like to say anything?"

"The FBI will investigate this case thoroughly and judiciously, like all the cases we undertake."

Meyerstein felt uneasy. She had dealt with Chinese military attachés any number of times. No big deal. But the mask and the gloves made her distinctly suspicious. What the hell was that all about? She knew from visits to China and other parts of the Far East that mask-wearing was widespread in big cities. Something to do with cultural norms developed since the SARS epidemic swept across Asia in early 2003. But masks also were worn to protect against suffocating car exhaust fumes and industrial pollutants in the atmosphere.

"Anyway, we just wanted to show you the courtesy and go through the official channels. I trust this is in order."

"I will read the letter carefully and get back to you within the next few days as to our response."

"We would like to meet up to discuss this in the very near future."

"That can be arranged."

The military attaché picked up her briefcase, stood up, and stepped forward, offering Meyerstein a handshake with the medical glove.

Meyerstein kept her hands folded, reticent.

"I thought a handshake was customary in the West, no?"

Meyerstein nodded. "Of course." She reached out and shook the woman's hand, the touch of the plastic against her skin.

"My name is Lucy. I work at the consulate."

"You said that already."

The woman handed Meyerstein her card. "Any time, day or night, please call me on my cell. Email too."

Meyerstein scanned the details.

"Don't hesitate to speak to me or reach out."

"Will do."

"I'll see myself out."

Lucy turned and quietly opened the door. She closed it softly behind her.

Meyerstein took a few deep breaths as she tried to compose herself. It was a very, very surreal exchange. What the hell had just happened?

Twenty-Eight

The hours dragged on in the locked interrogation room.

Reznick gave a perfunctory nod to Don Laslow. He was just the latest Fed to interview him. "Are you going to charge me, or am I free to go?"

"You're not free to go. So, get that out of your head, Reznick."

"Thanks for the clarification."

"It didn't have to go down like this, Jon. I just wanted to say, man to man, I understand your thinking behind your actions. I'm not condoning it. But I wish this had gone down a different path. I can't see any way out for you."

Reznick sat in silence.

"Your daughter, Lauren, she was always so proud of you when she worked here with us. She was great."

"Appreciate that."

"She's a smart girl. I was sorry to see her go."

Reznick tried to determine whether Laslow was being sincere or playing an angle. He said, "Thank you."

"Listen, here's where I'm at. I'm going to reach out to some people I know close to the White House."

"Don't put yourself on the line for me, Don."

"We all have lessons to learn from what happened. And that goes for the Bureau, how we operate. And in particular, this field office."

"All I wanted was for Kevin Chang not to be handed over to the Chinese government. Can you understand that?"

"Yes, I can. Let's not retread old ground. I can make my recommendations, and I will be making my recommendations. I can't reveal what they are. But I will be making my own special submission before any Senate or House intelligence hearing if necessary."

Reznick appreciated Laslow's candor.

"Can I get you anything? Food? Coffee?"

"No, thanks."

A sharp knock at the door. The door cracked open; a young special agent announced, "Don, we got a problem."

"What kind of problem?"

"You need to come quick."

Laslow and the agent disappeared from the room.

Reznick tapped his fingers and again tried to look through the mirror, to see if this was a game or not.

Laslow returned, flushed, four special agents with him. "Get up!"

"What?"

"We need to move. Now!"

Reznick was quickly handcuffed and frog-marched out of the room and down to the basement. He climbed into the back of a waiting SUV, sandwiched between two burly agents. "What the hell is going on?"

Laslow slid into the front seat. "Drive!"

"I said what the hell is going on?"

Laslow pointed right, and a few minutes later, they were speeding across the Brooklyn Bridge. "Never you mind."

"Don, talk to me. What the hell happened?"

"You'll know soon enough."

The SUV hurtled over potholes and bumps in the road. They sped through downtown Brooklyn, up through Williamsburg, and accelerated fast along the Brooklyn-Queens Expressway. "Don, what the fuck is happening?"

"Be quiet, Jon!"

Soon they were in dense traffic. The SUV slowed to a crawl, snarled New York traffic bunched up tight, bumper to bumper.

Laslow craned his neck to see what was causing the problem up ahead. "What the hell is it now?"

The driver shrugged. "The GPS isn't indicating any real-time incident."

Laslow banged his palm down hard on the dashboard. "Fuck!"

Reznick could see something bad had happened. He wondered if there had been news on Chang. A few minutes later, the traffic was beginning to move again.

"Let's hurry up, Enrique, for fuck's sake," Laslow said.

The driver edged the SUV forward. "OK, it's moving. Finally. Not long now."

Reznick figured it was to do with Chinese operatives still at large. Did they want to move him because of a threat? The SUV sped across the Kosciuszko Bridge from Greenpoint and into Maspeth, Queens.

It looked like a solid, blue-collar neighborhood so typical of older industrial areas of New York. They headed along the Long Island Expressway, the Van Wyck Expressway, then onto Union Turnpike for a few more miles. Where the hell were they taking him?

Laslow pointed to a twelve-story office building in Kew Gardens. "That's it," he said as they turned a corner and into a parking garage.

The SUV pulled up sharply and plunged down a ramp.

Reznick was hustled out of the car and into the building. "Easy, guys."

Laslow led the way.

Reznick and the special agents followed close behind. He was escorted to the elevators and headed straight to the eleventh floor. The doors opened, and they were shown into the reception area of an office suite.

Laslow tapped in a four-digit code next to a security door. He clicked it open, and they headed inside.

Reznick looked around at the monitors on the wall, a few special agents at their desks. It looked like he was in an FBI satellite office. He followed Laslow down a series of corridors before he was shown into an interrogation room.

A young agent quickly uncuffed Reznick. "Take a seat."

Reznick complied, sitting down at a desk, glad to be out of the handcuffs.

Laslow headed out of the room for a few minutes before returning with a couple of strong black coffees. He looked at the other Feds. "That'll be all, guys. I'll take it from here."

The agents left and locked the door behind them.

Reznick's gaze wandered around the bleak room. Not much different from the one he had just left, except there was no mirror, just bare walls and gray paint flaking in corners.

"So, do you mind telling me what the hell is going on? That was a sudden change of plan."

Laslow was pale. He looked shaken.

"We had a situation back in Manhattan."

"So, what happened?"

"It's Martha."

"What about her?"

"She has been rushed to the hospital."

"What?"

"She began to vomit, her temperature skyrocketed, and then she started having a seizure in her office."

"Jesus Christ, that's terrible."

Laslow nodded.

"Is that why I was moved? Hang on, did she come into contact with anybody?"

Laslow nodded. "Very perceptive."

"We got any details?"

"I'm not entirely sure."

"Where is she, Don? Where has she been taken?"

"I can't reveal that."

"What do you mean you can't reveal that?"

"It's a private matter. It's national security. All I can say is she is in a hospital at this moment."

"Is she going to be OK?"

"We don't know. I mean . . . the doctors don't know. Listen, I know you and Martha go back years."

"I just want to know that she's OK."

"She's not OK. She's fighting for her life."

He wondered if Martha had been targeted. Poisoned in some way. But by who?

"She is receiving the best possible medical care. We can rest assured of that."

"I know."

"I'll try and let you know if there are any updates. That's the best I can do."

"I'd appreciate that."

Laslow took a gulp of his hot coffee. "I forgot to say that I was told an attorney has been appointed to represent you. She's on her way over here at this moment."

Reznick's senses were heightened as he stared back at Laslow. "I don't have an attorney."

"You do now. I hope you have deep pockets."

Reznick wondered if Laslow was fucking with him. "I swear to God, that's not my attorney. You might want to make sure it's not someone that's been sent to neutralize me."

"Don't worry. Your lawyer will be getting thoroughly checked, vetted, et cetera, before she is allowed in here. She will be put through all our detection machines."

Reznick ran his hands through his hair. He thought back to the moment he had arrived at Forsyth Street with Trevelle. He wondered if he had, inadvertently, stumbled into an active operation by Chinese operatives in the city. A small glimpse into a high-risk Chinese intelligence operation. But had Reznick's response ratcheted tensions up to new heights?

He wondered if an operative had managed to slip into the FBI field office in New York and poison Meyerstein. In some ways, it was a move that risked inflaming US-China relations, already at a low. Why would they do that? Diplomacy was all about exerting influence, soft power. Making connections. Establishing links and networks. But this was hard power, pure and simple. Raw power. It was almost like the Chinese government didn't care what the response from America would be.

None of it was good.

It would only lead one way. The path to confrontation. Maybe all-out confrontation. Maybe war. Maybe that was what they wanted. Were they trying to prod and poke and provoke America into lashing out?

Reznick had listened to what Caroline had told him. The growing power of China, its influence on the world, the multibillion-dollar infrastructure projects in dozens of countries around the world. Buying up land. Buying up countries. It was getting more powerful. Economically. Politically. The Belt and Road Initiative included 150 countries around the world. Roads, loans, Chinese labor for building hospitals and harbors. Geopolitically, the country was flexing its muscles in the South China Sea. Taiwan was in its crosshairs. Always had been.

He remembered the incident of the high-altitude Chinese spy balloon that had to be shot down after it was tracked over Canadian and then American airspace. The more aggressive Chinese foreign policy was being rolled out. Year after year, they were pushing back.

Laslow cleared his throat, snapping Reznick out of his ruminations. He checked his phone. "Right, she's here."

"The lawyer?"

"Yeah. Come with me."

Laslow escorted Reznick out of the interrogation room, back down the corridor to an office. They stood beside the door. "Your lawyer is in there."

"So, are you guys going to charge me?"

"We need to formally interview you again at length. And I think we've got to wait to see how this plays out. I can't say any more."

Reznick nodded. "What's the attorney's name?"

"Abelman. Hot shot, by all accounts. How did you get her name?"

"I told you, I didn't."

"You must have a secret admirer."

Reznick shook his head. "Yeah, right." He knocked on the door and walked in.

A smartly dressed fifty-something woman was sitting behind a desk, papers in front of her. She got up and shook his hand. "Naomi Abelman, senior partner at Schwartz, Houlihan, and Perreri here in New York. Jon Reznick, right?"

Reznick shut the door behind him and shook her hand. "Correct."

"Pull up a seat, Jon, and we'll get started."

Reznick sat down. "First off, I'd like to know who hired you, if that's not too much to ask."

"I was contacted by a long-term client of mine. I can't disclose their identity."

"Listen, if we're going to have a lawyer-client relationship based on mutual trust, I need to know. Otherwise, I'll have to pass."

Abelman clicked her pen open and shut, making a decision. "I was instructed by my client, who is also a personal friend, to help you. Her name is Caroline Sullivan."

"So, she's paying for this? I can pay for it, thank you very much."

"Caroline insisted. If this goes to trial, you're talking perhaps hundreds of thousands of dollars, maybe millions. It depends."

"And she's going to pay for that?"

"Yes, she is."

"And she's given you the lowdown on what happened?"

"She did."

Reznick considered what the lawyer was saying. He needed representation from a legal expert. He needed someone to defend him and his interests. He was prepared for the consequences further down the line, whatever the outcome of his trial. But he needed the best in his corner. Someone who would fight hard. "What do you think my chances are?"

"Of?"

"Of . . . being cleared."

"First, I need to know that I can represent you. You are perfectly at liberty to explore other options. There are many other fine, eminent criminal attorneys in New York. I can recommend a couple if you wish. Second, I need you to sign a legal document confirming that I represent you. So, what's it going to be?"

"Naomi, let me ask you something."

"Shoot."

"When you embark on a legal case, how hard do you fight for your client? I mean *really* fight for them."

"If you are my client, I will do whatever it takes to represent you. I fight dirty. I fight smart. This is not a game for me. I go all in. My attention to detail is well known. I could pick apart prosecution cases on technicalities. And work back from there. I am relentless. I like winning. I hate losing. Trust me, you don't want to face me in court."

Reznick smiled.

"Anything else?"

"Where do I sign?"

Abelman grinned. "Wise choice." She picked up a contract from her briefcase and pointed to the bottom of the second page of the document. She handed him her pen. "Sign it, date it, and we're good to go."

Reznick signed and dated the contract.

Abelman checked it over and rejoiced, hands clasped. "Now the hard work really begins. I'll get a full interview with you after I speak to the FBI off the record about what they've got. Caroline filled me in. She told me all about you. What you did."

"What about Kevin Chang? I'm assuming he's going to get first-class representation."

"Kevin will be represented by a leading criminal attorney in Boston who I recommended."

"Good. Is there any update on his condition?"

Abelman began to take some notes. "He is, I believe, slipping in and out of consciousness. His condition with regard to liver damage is sketchy. He's going to take a while to get over this—that's assuming he pulls through. But my concern is you. I'd like to start by asking you a few basic questions so I know where I stand."

"Fine."

"My first question to you is, did you kill three people in Chinatown, three others at a hospital on Cape Cod, all the while protecting a green card holder?"

"One hundred percent correct."

Abelman scribbled down his response on a legal pad. "This is not the time to get into the minutia of what transpired and why. We'll get to that. I'll try and schedule a full interview sometime tomorrow that aligns with the FBI. I need to speak to them first to get a sense of the precise charges you may be facing."

Reznick nodded. "I'm guessing the Chinese government, China's embassy in DC, and the consulate in New York will be working overtime to put pressure on the State Department and the FBI."

"They wouldn't be doing their job if they didn't. Don't worry about them."

"I'm not."

"Criminal cases related to national security would ordinarily be supervised by the Assistant Attorney General of the Department of Justice's National Security Division. I'll be speaking to him tonight."

"Already?"

"You need to get out on the front foot. We need them on the back foot. I'm guessing the Foreign Intelligence Surveillance Court might be exploring surveillance warrants. A whole host of sensitive stuff, all national security related. Under state secrets privilege, the federal government can resist court-ordered disclosure of information during litigation. And this refers to government contractors. That is an avenue they will be exploring."

"I don't want to compromise American national security or my links with the FBI, Meyerstein, and various intelligence agencies. That would be damaging."

"Maybe it would. And that might possibly be an avenue that I'll be exploring. They don't want this disclosed, but neither do you, for perfectly understandable reasons. Jon, we're going to take the fight to them. You saved an innocent man. A man being terrorized by an authoritarian dictatorship. I checked the State Department website. And they state unequivocally the Chinese government is responsible for genocide and crimes against humanity, predominantly the persecution of Muslim Uighurs but also other religious minority groups in and around Xinjiang."

"You're not messing around."

"I will not only represent you. I will fight for you, and I fight to win."

Twenty-Nine

It was just past midnight.

Bradley idled in his hotel room on Rockaway Beach after his earlier meeting with Thomas Kelly. His mind had been fizzing since the face-to-face. It wasn't just the Scotch. The move to Singapore, which he was helping engineer, would also set up Bradley financially for the future. He would hand over an intelligence expert who could be leveraged. And Bradley would get his usual fee, ten percent of Kelly's gross salary. A win-win all around.

He yawned as he picked up the remote and clicked on Fox News.

Bradley stared at the TV. A live breaking story from Lower Manhattan. His attention was piqued when he saw the headline: *Government Building Evacuated.*

Bradley sat up. He recognized the building right away.

The reporter held the microphone tight to her face, occasionally glancing behind herself. "I'm standing in downtown Manhattan, outside the Jacob K. Javits Federal Building. I'm hearing from police sources inside the NYPD that the entire building has been evacuated. Hundreds of workers streamed out this afternoon. And I'm hearing that the incident is believed to be centered on the twenty-third floor, where the FBI has its New York field office. I have contacted the FBI, but no one is available to comment officially. However, a source in the FBI did say it was believed to be a chemical leak incident, which led to at least one member of the FBI being rushed to the hospital. No further details are available at this time."

Bradley muted the volume. He wondered if Thomas Kelly had been affected. But if he wasn't, maybe he knew more. He called Kelly's private phone number.

"Kelly speaking," he growled in greeting.

"Thomas, it's James Bradley. I just heard there was some incident downtown. Are you guys OK?"

"Not a good time. We've got a serious situation developing."

"Fox is saying your building was evacuated. I was worried you might have been hurt or affected."

"I was affected."

"My God, James, are you OK?"

"I'm OK. But it was someone else who was directly impacted. Chemical leak. We've had to move out to our satellite office."

"In New York?"

"Yeah, in Queens."

Bradley made a mental note. "All of you have moved there?"

"Just a few senior people, and the special ops guy who we needed to get to a secure place."

Bradley felt exhilarated that Kelly had thrown him a tidbit of intel. "Thomas, you stay safe. I just wanted to know you were OK." He ended the call. He opened a cold bottle of Schlitz from the minibar. He took a couple of gulps as he contemplated his next move.

He needed to play this right. His tone needed to be neutral. He had shown them he was indispensable, but this was an opportunity beyond even that.

He needed to be sure of his facts first. He checked his phone. He saw an FBI office in Kew Gardens, close to Jamaica, Queens. That had to be it.

Bradley called his handler. The phone rang five times before she answered.

"What is your date of birth?"

Bradley gave the verification details.

"Good evening, James. How can we help?"

"Have you been watching the news?"

"Not since breakfast."

"It's all over the networks. FBI and the entire federal building in Lower Manhattan have been evacuated. An FBI person taken to the hospital."

"We know that already."

Bradley felt his heart sink. "I have some intel I thought I'd like to share. I want to know that this is something you would not only welcome but also reward the person who shared it with you."

"Is it about Kevin Chang's whereabouts?"

"Sadly not. It is with regard to Jon Reznick."

"We would be incredibly and forever grateful if you could share whatever you have on where he is located."

"I thought you would. Kelly told me that he, along with several senior Feds, have been transferred to the Kew Gardens satellite office in Queens. And that's not all."

"What?"

"He said the special ops guy is being kept there."

"Reznick?"

"The one and only. That's where he is."

"Right now?"

"Right now. This moment."

"You know this for sure?"

"The building has been evacuated. It's all over Fox. Kelly just told me that he is at the Queens satellite office, along with the special ops guy. That's how he was referring to Reznick during our conversation about the killings in Chinatown."

"I've just brought up the location on a map. You are sure?"

"I spoke to Kelly five minutes ago. He knows a lot of people."

"We are grateful as always for your insights."

"How grateful?"

"We would like to show you."

"I'm listening."

"How would you like to earn a bonus of five hundred thousand American dollars?" the voice asked.

Bradley sat up. "It does."

"Good. You see, we believe you are a man to be trusted. You've shown us that."

"Five hundred thousand dollars. Did I hear correctly?"

"You heard correctly."

Bradley's stomach tightened. He knew the huge windfall would wipe out all his debt. He would get back on his feet again. He thought of his three college-age kids. He would be able to help them out too. This was a once-in-a-lifetime opportunity. "Tell me, what sort of information would you need to make that level of transfer?"

"It wouldn't be for information."

"It wouldn't?"

"No. Let me explain. We may call upon you to perform a task that we think you would be uniquely suited for."

"A task . . ."

"If you perform that task to completion, and to our satisfaction, you will be compensated."

"When will I hear from you again?"

"Soon."

"I'll await further instructions."

Thirty

Reznick was being watched in his grim new interrogation room by two special agents. "Relax, guys," he said. "I don't bite."

The pair of young, fresh-faced Feds just stared back at him, nonplussed.

Reznick paced the room to keep himself occupied. "So, when am I going to be charged?"

A Fed with an earpiece in nodded as if he was receiving instructions. He looked over at Reznick. "Hands out in front, tough guy."

Reznick began to do some stretching exercises, his calves feeling tight from sitting for so long with his lawyer. "Come on, guys. I'm not going anywhere."

"We're not asking; we're telling."

Reznick walked up to the Fed with the earpiece and stretched out his arms in front of him. "No need for this."

The Fed clicked steel handcuffs tight on Reznick's wrists.

"You want to ease up on that? It's biting my fucking skin."

The guy got a key and loosened the handcuffs ever so slightly.

"Take a load off," the other one said. "Someone wants to see you."

"My lucky day, huh?"

Reznick sat down, handcuffed wrists resting on his lap. He wondered why they weren't charging him and moving him to jail. But he also wondered what the hell had happened in Manhattan to provoke such a quick evacuation.

The sound of the heavy door being unlocked.

A tall, gray-haired man wearing a navy suit, FBI ID lanyard hanging from his neck, walked in. He cocked his head at the two special agents. "I'll take it from here, fellas."

The door was locked from the outside again. The man pulled up a seat.

Reznick saw the guy's details from his ID badge on his chest.

"Hi, Jon. My name is Thomas Kelly, head of counterintelligence for the FBI across New York."

Reznick smelled the drink wafting off his breath.

"How are you?"

"I've been better."

Kelly nodded. "Quite a few days you've had."

"So, are you going to charge me, or do I have to sit around here for another day or two?"

"I can't answer that at this time. I believe you've spoken to your lawyer."

Reznick nodded.

"Your lawyer would be better equipped to tell you all about that."

"She's not here. I'm asking you."

"Well, I don't know is the answer."

"Why not?"

Kelly folded his arms as if bored. "Here's the thing, Jon. This isn't just a simple case of who killed who."

"The complication of the Chinese operatives running amok, the diplomatic fallout, State Department calling the shots?"

Kelly applauded quietly. "You're a smart guy, Jon. Here's the thing, we're trying to piece together how you got hooked up with this Kevin Chang. And from what I've read in a preliminary report, it was simply a phone call from Trevelle Williams, some sort of hacker pal of yours."

"Listen, I want to help. But I will not incriminate anyone. I know how this works."

"How what works?"

"Don't play games, Thomas. How the FBI operates. I understand how you guys work."

"I hear your concerns, and I get it. We're imperfect. We're a bureaucracy. And sometimes we do the end-justifies-the-means thing. We get stuff wrong. There are a lot of lessons to be learned from this whole episode."

Reznick sighed. "What exactly do you want to know?"

"OK, so you're not telling me how you hooked up with Trevelle Williams before all this went down."

"Don't try and fuck with me. I'm not in the mood."

"No one is trying to fuck with you. You're probably wondering why you were whisked here."

"Security risk?"

"And then some. Now I know you and Martha go way back."

"Professional relationship, you know that."

Kelly stared at him, eyes heavy with drink. "Martha is in the hospital. It was a serious security breach. A lady walked into our FBI offices in Manhattan. A Chinese woman."

"Shit."

"We believe the woman might work for the Ministry of State Security. Low-level operatives in the main intelligence directorate. We have reason to believe that such operatives are spreading out across the country, looking to neutralize any Chinese dissidents. It is a growing threat. But what happened in Manhattan, and in particular what happened to Meyerstein, is something completely different. This is not their usual playbook. They are becoming much, much more assertive in the global area."

"They've caught you off guard?"

"Most certainly. The Chinese . . . they're usually very risk averse. But this is pushing the boundaries."

"Why?"

"Who knows. Maybe they're looking for a response. Maybe they're getting more confident on the global stage. But this is state aggression, pure and simple. A way of humiliating us in the eyes of the world."

"Why are you telling me this?"

"It's just me and you shooting the breeze, Jon. Two guys being honest and upfront."

"Thomas, that's all very interesting. Very plausible. And you're probably right."

"I am right."

"But it's a transparent ruse to get me to open up, yes? You have to do better than that."

Kelly grimaced at him, eyes hooded. "I don't dislike you, Jon. You know, what you did, taking out those three Chinese operatives on Forsyth Street, you most certainly saved the life of Kevin Chang. I believe he will be a valuable information source for us in the coming years."

Reznick could see that Kelly was seriously inebriated. "I'm sure he will. He's a nice kid. Smart kid. But I just wanted to keep him alive. I didn't want him to be extradited to China. He is terrified of the Chinese state. That's the only reason I went all in on this."

"I'm glad you did. He's alive. There is a long, long road ahead for him. But rest assured, he is in a safe and secure place. A secure facility."

Kelly's eyes seemed to become more hooded. "Your lawyer got a pretty impressive Boston lawyer for Kevin."

"What about Meyerstein? What's the latest on her?"

Kelly shook his head. "I got an update twenty minutes ago. We believe they got to her. Preliminary tests are still being carried out. Very serious attack on an American intelligence facility. Blatant. Who knows where the hell this will lead."

"What exactly happened?"

Kelly cleared his throat. "Don't know if I should be telling you this." He let the words hang in the air.

Reznick just sat in silence and waited to see if Kelly was going to be more forthcoming.

"You ever heard of thallium?"

"The poison chemical?"

"Yeah, nasty stuff."

"What was the method of delivery?"

"I guess this will all come out over the coming days and weeks . . . So, it was a very, very shrewd operation. The Chinese operative posed as a defense attaché. ID and all that were checked. It appeared fine. But she was wearing one of those N95 masks and had put on forensic gloves. We believe the door handle to Meyerstein's temporary office got smeared with a thallium compound gel. Also an envelope Meyerstein handled."

Reznick closed his eyes.

"Foreign intelligence agencies work according to agreed rules. It's an international, rules-based order. What this means—"

"The rules have been ripped up."

"Precisely. They're telling us, 'We do what we want, when we want.' They're trying to find out how far they can go. What will our response be? Will there be a response? They know the freedoms Americans have. The only problem is that when their operatives are over here, it gives them carte blanche to move around at will. In

China, our operatives are under surveillance from the moment they step out of the door until they go to bed at night."

Reznick leaned back in his seat. "Why are you telling me all this? This is a lot of intel you're sharing. Why?"

"Let me explain. Your actions have created an international diplomatic crisis. I believe the National Security Council is meeting to discuss the ramifications in the early hours."

"As they should."

Kelly shrugged. "However, in these matters, you have to tread carefully. This is in an escalatory pattern. Where do we go from here?"

"What do you think it will entail?"

"It won't be a military response from us, that's for sure."

"Asymmetric warfare?"

Kelly smiled. "You know about this stuff, don't you."

"Just a bit."

"So, we could be talking about remotely disabling a power plant. Cutting underwater internet cables. Gas pipelines. You know what I'm saying?"

"As a warning not to fuck with us?"

"Let's call it a reminder. The only problem is that they have the capabilities too. So, it's a fluid situation. And it might be Kevin Chang who would become the fulcrum in the middle of this."

"Hand over Chang and we'll call it quits?"

Kelly rubbed his eyes. "Then again, maybe it'll be hand over Reznick and we'll call it quits."

Reznick sighed. He saw through what Kelly was doing. Psychological mind games. "None too subtle, Thomas. A word to the wise: don't fuck with me."

"I need you to be aware of the ramifications. That's why if you can help me piece together the missing parts of the jigsaw, like who else helped you and Chang, it would help you. Really, it would."

Reznick bowed his head. He wondered if anyone had given Kelly authorization to try this ruse with him. Maybe Kelly, boozed up, not thinking straight, was on a one-man mission to show his intelligence chops.

"Give us more, Jon. That's all I'm saying. We need something to work with. We need to fill in the blanks. Because, whether you like it or not, there has to be a fall guy. And I figure it'll come down to either Chang or you."

Reznick sat in silence. He knew this would be a typical FBI interrogation ploy. Inject the fear of God into an interviewee. And let them stew. But he doubted that an intoxicated senior FBI agent would be the conduit.

"I've got to be honest, Jon, Chang means nothing to me. Bright kid? Who cares. We've got plenty of bright kids in this country. Fleeing persecution? Get in line. You see what I'm saying."

Reznick sensed Kelly wasn't bluffing. He felt a raw, seething hatred emanate from him. The guy exuded malevolence. But Reznick wasn't unnerved by Kelly or anyone.

"I have no qualms dealing with bad guys, Jon. I deal with them every day. It gets me up in the morning. And that's why a guy like you must realize that America sacrifices its citizens occasionally for the greater good. Nothing personal. We're talking national interest. Spheres of influence. They would much rather give up Chang than you. But I've seen it happen, Jon. Our people, good people, are sacrificed. American spies in Beijing? They're cut loose if it threatens to bring down a foreign intelligence network. The kind your wife was part of. Can you imagine if that stuff got out in the media, huh?"

Reznick could see the full extent of Kelly's ploy now. He could see that Kelly would be more than happy to reveal the true story behind his wife's disappearance on 9/11. Her new identity abroad in Switzerland. Before Reznick and his daughter tracked her down. But Reznick stayed composed. Kelly was needling him.

"I know she's on American soil. But if this came out, can you imagine? It might compromise her life to bring out that whole elaborate cover story. That ain't good."

Reznick sat in silence. But one thing was for sure: Reznick would never compromise her security or her life to save his own skin. Never. How the hell had Kelly gotten the story?

Kelly slurred, "I know a lot of people's secrets. That's what counterintelligence teaches you. Everyone has a secret. We trade secrets."

Reznick shifted in his seat.

"Here's the thing. I want answers. I want names. And you're going to give them to me. To protect Elisabeth, you need to tell me where Kevin Chang was kept during your little road trip."

Reznick's mind flashed back to the beautiful, sleepy beach town of Madison, Connecticut. He had found refuge there thanks to Caroline Sullivan. She had put her neck on the line for total strangers. She never wavered.

Reznick opened his mouth and sighed.

"Not a big talker, huh? I get it. I respect that. This is not the hill to die on. For Chang? Who gives a shit about him? Me? I'd give up Chang in the blink of an eye if we could. But events have a way of snowballing when the story comes out. Do you care for Chang more than Elisabeth, living in her sleepy New England town?"

Reznick was shocked that he knew Elisabeth was in New England. "You finished?"

"You help me and I'll help you. It's a side deal. And it's the best you'll get."

"You're full of shit."

"You think so?"

"I know so. You stink of booze."

Kelly tilted his head, shrugged. "The stunt you pulled with the motorcycle, that was interesting. The switcheroo. Nice. So, you had accomplices. One to hide you, and one to throw any surveillance tail off the scent. So, I'm guessing, minimum, two people you need to tell us about."

"Go fuck yourself."

Kelly chuckled. "Like I said, it would be in your interests to come clean."

Suddenly the piercing sound of a fire alarm rang out.

Kelly scrunched up his face. "Never a goddamn break." He got to his feet and pointed down at Reznick. "Wait here, tough guy. I'm going to see if this is real or not."

"So, I'm supposed to sit here during a fire?"

"I'll be back in a minute. Don't fucking move."

Thirty-One

The high-pitched, piercing sound of the fire alarm seemed to grow louder.

Reznick sat handcuffed and alone in the interrogation room, alarm bells of a different kind ringing in his head. He sensed this was no drill. Not a malfunctioning detection system.

His senses became heightened. A switch had been activated inside his head. First, the sudden dash from the FBI's downtown Manhattan office to Queens. Now, fire alarms sounding throughout the Queens office.

A diversionary tactic. The purpose? To sow confusion, chaos. But also get people moving around the building as they exited.

Reznick got to his feet and headed toward the door. He needed to get out of there.

The door banged open, Kelly with gun in hand. "Reznick! We need to get the hell out of here."

Reznick saw pure fear in Kelly's eyes. "Get me out of these handcuffs!"

Kelly grabbed Reznick's arm and yelled, "Active shooters in the building!"

"Get me out of the cuffs!"

"I can't do that."

"Kelly, either you get me out of these cuffs, or I will take matters into my own hands. Do you understand?"

Kelly pointed the gun at him, the smell of liquor still on his breath. "You make a run for it, and I will kill you. Do you understand?"

"Copy that. Now get me out of these fucking cuffs!"

Kelly took a key from his pocket and unlocked the handcuffs, throwing them onto the floor.

"Who's got eyes on the shooters?"

"Special Agent Ramesh checked the surveillance footage."

"So, where are they?"

"They're here. They've entered the building. But we're unsure where exactly they are. No idea if they're spread out. They've taken out the agents posted in the lobby."

"I need a weapon! Where're your weapons? Secure storage, right?"

Kelly stared in shock.

"Where is it, Kelly? You need to trust me."

The sound of gunshots, screaming, and shattering windows.

Reznick instinctively threw himself to the floor as he craned his neck, looking around the corner. Further down the office suite, he saw a couple of Feds with handguns drawn, crouched behind filing cabinets. He wondered if the shooters were just out of sight. "How do you get onto this floor?"

"FBI security key card. The shooters at the outer reception on this floor have them."

Reznick signaled Kelly to get closer. "Give me the key to the secure room."

"That ain't going to happen, buddy."

Reznick squared up to Kelly. "I will help you. But you need to give me the tools to deal with this."

Kelly shook his head. "I can't do that."

"You need to help me help you. Where is the secure room?"

"You're not getting the key. That's out of the question."

The sound of shouting and threats. A gunshot rang out. A Fed down the hallway collapsed, blood spilling out of his neck.

"Give me the key! Now!"

Kelly looked paralyzed by fear.

Reznick grabbed Kelly by the throat. "Are you for real? Give me the key!"

Kelly reached into his back pocket and handed him a set of keys. "This opens all secure FBI gun stores in this building. Three doors down on the right."

Reznick peeked around the door.

The screams of a woman from the far side of the floor, thirty yards away. "Help me! I'm a civilian!"

Reznick could only watch as she was gunned down.

"Where is Jon Reznick?" someone shouted.

Reznick still couldn't see the shooters. They were just out of sight. He needed to move.

"Where is Jon Reznick?"

The woman was screaming for help on the ground.

Reznick fast-crawled out the door and down the corridor, mentally blocking out the woman's screams. More shots rang out.

"Get down!" Kelly shouted from behind. "Everyone get down!"

Reznick crouched low outside the secure gun room. He took out the biggest key on the chain and put it into the lock. He slowly turned the handle, and the door opened. He got in and quietly shut the door behind him. Heart pounding.

He studied the locked rifle racks. He tried the key for the door. But it didn't work. He tried a second key. But still the rack wouldn't open. He tried a third, smaller key. It opened the full gun rack.

He quickly grabbed a Heckler & Koch submachine gun. He unlocked a separate ammunition cabinet. Thousands of rounds of ammo, 9 × 19mm Parabellum. He locked and loaded. He flicked off the safety. He grabbed a 9mm Glock and clipped in a full magazine. He pushed the handgun into the waistband of his jeans.

Reznick held the submachine gun tight. The cold metal familiar on his skin. He cracked open the door and looked outside. He spotted two masked shooters. Both with semiautomatic rifles. He had a mental picture of what he was going to do.

The men approached the screaming, terrified woman. "Where is Jon Reznick? You want to die? Tell us where Jon Reznick is!"

Reznick broke cover and raked the shooters with rapid shots, a deafening burst of noise from the submachine gun. The sound dulled his hearing. The pungent smell of nitroglycerin from the fired ammo quickly rose into the air. He scanned the area as he moved forward. Hyperalert. "Keep down!" he shouted. "Two shooters down, east side of the office! Stay on the ground!" He quickly approached the two shooters, who were dead, blood pooling around their heads.

The woman who had been shot lay on the ground, bleeding out fast, sobbing and crying. "Help me," she said.

Reznick grabbed her by the wrist and moved her toward a crouching special agent. "You got first aid?"

The special agent nodded. "Yeah."

"Grab some bandages and stem the blood loss!"

The guy opened a drawer, pulling out a first aid kit.

Reznick scoured the rest of the floor. A few agents peered up at him from behind desks and filing cabinets. "Get on your feet! Now! There are more of them! We're going after them! They've breached your outer security. We need to find them. We need to fight them. Then we kill them. Now!"

Thirty-Two

Reznick stalked carefully through the offices as he headed for the exit to the floor, submachine gun at the ready, eyes fixed where the weapon pointed. He whispered to Kelly, who had fallen in just behind him. "How many shooters did we have in the lobby?"

"Four shooters in the lobby."

"Two down. So, where are the other two?"

"I don't know."

Reznick grabbed Kelly by the arm. "We need to clear the building. The woman over there needs urgent medical treatment. We need to move her. Fast."

"This is a live situation. We have cops and other Feds en route."

"ETA of the cops and Feds?"

Kelly shrugged.

"What is the ETA of the police and paramedics? Status update?"

"Four minutes and the first units will be here!" Kelly said. "Four minutes!"

"Are you kidding me? We don't wait for help. We need to get the fuck out of here. Get that woman out of here before she bleeds out."

"So, what do you suggest?"

Reznick pointed to the door leading to a fire exit. "North stairwell, fire exit route."

"The two other shooters might have that covered."

"You with me or what?"

Kelly seemed trapped in a maelstrom of indecision.

Reznick brushed past him as he went back over to check on the bleeding woman. The agent had bandaged up the injured woman's shoulder. Reznick crouched down beside her. "We're getting you out of here now. I will take you out."

The woman's eyes were rolling around in her head as if she was ready to lose consciousness.

Reznick grabbed her arm and leg and flung her over his left shoulder. "You still with me?"

The woman moaned.

Reznick headed back through the office toward Kelly, the woman spread-eagled over his shoulder and back. "Cover me! I'm heading down the north stairwell."

Kelly motioned for the rest of the agents to evacuate.

Reznick cracked open the first door, the weight of the woman bearing down on him. Finger on the trigger, he craned his neck forward. He knew from training drills that slicing the pie when clearing a room was dangerous. It was all about getting your angles correct. Knowing when to move. The dangers were inherent. And real.

The woman was breathing hard, moaning. The sounds of fire alarms and smoke detectors blared, drowning out most other sounds.

Down the stairwell, Reznick caught a fleeting glimpse. A figure holding a handgun.

A shot rang out, narrowly missing him, ricocheting around the concrete stairwell.

Reznick pointed the submachine gun around the corner, raking gunfire in the person's direction. The gunman collapsed in a hail of bullets.

The woman screamed.

Reznick adjusted her weight as he headed down the stairwell. He passed the dead gunman lying in a pool of blood, face down. "Shooter down in the stairwell! One to go. Let's move."

Kelly, red-faced and sweating profusely, rushed down past him and took the lead, as if now energized. He headed down a flight of stairs. He signaled for Reznick to proceed.

Reznick headed quickly down the stairs. The rest of the FBI special agents and staff followed, guns drawn. "Let's pick up the pace, people!"

Kelly headed down another two flights of stairs. "We're clear so far."

Reznick signaled the burliest Fed toward him. "You! Carry this woman!"

Kelly pointed at the guy. "That's an order, Tony."

Special Agent Anthony Russo hauled the bleeding woman over his broad shoulders and back. His navy suit and white shirt quickly became soaked in her blood.

Reznick moved toward Kelly. "I'm going to go down first. If there's a shooter, I'll take him. If he takes me, get a couple of agents by your side, armed and ready."

Kelly stared at him.

"Do you understand?"

"Got it! Let's go."

Reznick headed down the stairwell, submachine gun sights scanning for anything. It was important to slow down. *Slow is smooth; smooth is fast.* People streamed out of side doors into the stairwell from offices below. "Shooter on the loose!" he shouted. "Get back inside! Lock all doors until the all clear!"

The men and woman went back through the double doors into their offices.

"Lock the entrance. Deactivate electronic ID for the entrance. And call the cops!"

Reznick looked down. Several floors below, a shadow. Imperceptible. Moving.

Reznick showed the palm of his hand to stop the descent of the FBI team. He glanced at Kelly and indicated there was movement down below. He peered over the edge.

A voice below shouted, "Anyone up there?"

Reznick crouched down low, weapon in hand.

A radio from below crackled into life. "This is the communication dispatch office, do you copy? Identify your code."

Reznick put his finger to his mouth. He headed slowly down the stairs. A flight down, he turned. Two Asian firefighters, one with an ax in hand and the other with a 9mm gun in his hand. "Freeze!" he said.

The firefighter with the ax dropped the weapon. "Easy, buddy. We're here to rescue you."

Reznick sensed they were disguised. A classic ploy. He pointed the submachine gun at the other man. "Drop the gun and hands in the air, pal! Now!"

The man glared as he did what he was told. "We're here to help. New York Fire Department. What the hell are you doing, buddy?"

"I'm not your buddy, so shut the fuck up. On your knees. Now! Both of you."

The pair of them slowly complied.

"You're not FDNY. Your hands are office worker hands. Desk work. And I don't know any firefighter that carries a gun when responding to a 9-1-1 call in a building."

The guy who had the ax bowed his head.

Reznick kept the submachine gun trained on them. The sound of the injured woman moaning echoed from a couple of floors above. He figured they must be the second pair of the four-man team. A second entry point.

The guy who had dropped the gun hadn't taken his eyes off Reznick.

"Don't get any ideas, pal," Reznick said.

"You're making a big, big mistake."

The woman cried out in pain. "I need medical attention!"

The man continued to stare at Reznick. "I'm a firefighter paramedic. I can help you, lady. But this man needs to put his weapon down."

Reznick still had the submachine gun trained on the man.

Suddenly, the guy reached behind him.

Reznick pulled the trigger, expecting to hear a hail of bullets. But nothing. Silence. A misfire. Fuck! He crouched down and pulled out his 9mm handgun.

The Asian guy fumbled as Reznick took aim.

Reznick saw the man pull a pistol from a side pocket. He blasted the guy twice in the head. Blood splatter and gunfire and smoke filled the air. The smoke began to clear. He trained the handgun on the second man.

The guy pulled a knife out of his jacket and lunged at Reznick.

Reznick gave a double tap to the head and one to the chest and the guy yelled and screamed as the bullets hit him. He reached over and grabbed the guy by the neck. He was unbelievably still alive, blood pouring from his mouth. Then he rammed the gun into his mouth. He pulled the trigger once. He blew off the back of the man's head.

Thirty-Three

The minutes that followed felt like a slow-motion nightmare. Images of the bloodied bodies were etched into his brain.

Reznick felt nothing. He was back in the kill zone. He stood over the bodies of the two dead fake firefighters. Piercing alarms cut through the air. A couple more Chinese operatives neutralized. The fire and smoke alarms were a smart way of getting everyone down the stairwells, into their line of fire.

Reznick stared at the blood on the floor and the red-splattered walls.

He signaled for the agents to head down with the critically injured woman. He would cover them.

Kelly stepped down toward Reznick. He slumped down on one of the stairs, head in his hands. The sound of fire alarms still blaring.

"You OK?" Reznick asked.

"No, I'm not OK. This is fucked up. As fucked up as it gets."

"What did you want me to do? Get shot to death?"

Kelly shook his head. "Where the fuck is the NYPD?"

The sound of distant sirens.

"I think they heard you," Reznick said.

"What a shitshow. I would never have believed—"

"Believed what?"

"I don't know. This is not how intelligence agencies behave. This is not rational. This is insanity. Are they starting the war on our soil?"

"We need to wake the fuck up. They are a psychopathic authoritarian regime, Kelly."

"What kind of game are they playing? What the hell did they hope to gain?"

"Fear. They want to plant the seeds of fear in us. In our government."

"There are examples of the Iranian regime killing dissidents on American soil. But the Chinese acting like this? It's madness. Total fucking madness."

"Maybe the mask has slipped. Maybe they're showing their real face. Their true side to the rest of the world."

"To what end? They're the second most powerful country in the world."

"Maybe so. But why do you think no one is risking their life to get into China? Why do people like Kevin Chang and his sister risk their lives to get onto American soil? I'll tell you why. We're free. And they're not."

Kelly looked up at Reznick and sighed.

"They'll never beat us. What they've done is show what they're capable of. What Kevin Chang came here for. To escape persecution. To live his life."

Kelly nodded.

A sound like firecrackers and stun grenades down below.

A SWAT team burst up the stairs. The lead guy pointed at Reznick. "Freeze! Drop your weapon!"

The SWAT team smuggled a handcuffed Reznick and Kelly out of a basement garage into a waiting SUV. They were driven to

One Police Plaza in Lower Manhattan. Reznick was hustled out of the vehicle and escorted via a freight elevator to the eighth floor.

Kelly identified himself and he was frisked, then taken away for questioning.

Reznick was taken to a separate interrogation room by two besuited detectives. He was shown to a chair behind a desk. He sat and waited, the handcuffs chafing his wrists.

Two cops stayed in the room. The younger of the two stared at him and shook his head.

"What?" Reznick said.

"You're having quite a day, man."

Reznick sat in silence.

His colleague looked at Reznick. "You want a cup of coffee? Sandwich?"

"Black coffee."

"Sandwich? What do you like?"

"Any chance of a sandwich from Katz's?"

"Sure, we can get that sent over."

"Corned beef and pastrami. And a large Coke."

The young cop grinned. "Out of sight, man."

Thirty-Four

Kelly sat glumly by Meyerstein's hospital bed. As soon as she had regained consciousness and the doctors saw positive signs, she had demanded to get back on the case. Too weak to stand and leave, though, she had Kelly come to her, bringing a tablet where she could see the closed-circuit feed of Reznick wolfing down a sandwich as if he didn't have a care in the world.

Kelly shook his head. "You wouldn't believe that guy, Martha," he said. "I mean, they could have wiped us all out."

Meyerstein felt shattered. She watched him finish his sandwich, washing it down with a large Coke. She felt conflicted about the carnage that had unfolded over the past few days. But as she looked at Reznick, she couldn't help feeling more than a touch in awe of this man. A man she had known. A man she had trusted. A man who didn't walk away. He never gave an inch. It was selfless. It was crazy.

Kelly started to nod off at the side of the bed. Meyerstein couldn't blame him, given what he'd been through, but there was something else bothering her. Through the antiseptic scent of the room, she caught the smell of liquor on his breath. She couldn't be bothered to find out why he was under the influence while supposedly on duty. "How are you feeling now?"

"Shaken up, that's all."

"You look like shit."

Kelly nodded. "I feel like shit. Is he for real?"

Meyerstein sighed. "Yeah, he's for real. As real as it gets."

"I owe him my life. We all do."

Meyerstein felt her throat tighten. "Where were you earlier? I was trying to contact you. Your phone was turned off."

"I was meeting a source."

"An FBI source?"

Kelly shrugged. "Not an official source. A source I speak to."

"An informant?"

"It's an unofficial thing."

"You know as well as I do, Thomas, that with FBI informants, special care has to be taken."

"What are you getting at?"

Meyerstein sensed an uneasiness in Kelly as she broached the subject. "So, you had a few drinks with this source, informant, call them whatever you want."

"Correct."

"And then you returned to Kew Gardens. So, you had been drinking on duty?"

"Meyerstein, you don't have authority over me."

"Not directly, Thomas. You're right."

"Your relationship with Reznick crossed numerous boundaries and laws, so I'm told. So, if you don't mind, cut the bullshit. This whole thing got out of hand because your close relationship with Reznick clouded your judgment when we had him in custody. We had him. But you overruled the FBI's senior special agents, including Don Laslow. And me."

Meyerstein felt herself flush with anger listening to Kelly. The problem was, he was right.

"If this ever got out, your reputation would be in the shithouse, Meyerstein. We'd never recover. So, you need to think long and hard about casting aspersions on my working methods. What I do on my time is my business."

Meyerstein shook her head. "Point taken. But this is a failure of the intelligence in New York. How did we not see this coming?"

"It's a failure of the FBI as a whole. We were fully cognizant of the threat."

"They were operating in plain sight. De facto Chinese police stations on American soil? New York? Gimme a break."

"Who the hell do you think you are? I've heard all about you, Meyerstein."

Meyerstein faced Kelly. "And what have you heard?"

"You want me to spell it out?"

"Spit it out."

"Your relationship with Reznick is unethical and illegal, and on countless investigations you have overseen with Reznick in the mix, crimes have been committed. Murders have been committed. Want me to go on?"

"See that guy on the monitor?"

Kelly nodded.

"He's not perfect. I'm not perfect. But he will fight for what he believes in. He will fight for his country. And you know what? He doesn't give a shit about what we say or do. He operates on a different code. A code of honor."

Kelly laughed. "A code of honor? You've got to be kidding me. He's a raving lunatic. A psychopath."

Meyerstein slapped Kelly on the face. She was weak, he was exhausted, but she put enough behind it to knock him back. "How dare you! That man saved your life and the lives of everyone in Kew Gardens. And he also saved the life of Kevin Chang. Thanks to

Reznick's intervention, I believe America will never give up Kevin Chang. Don't ever forget about that."

Kelly's eyes blazed with fury and indignation. He stood up, turned, and left, leaving his tablet behind.

Meyerstein had only her thoughts and regrets for company. She stared through the tablet one final time at Reznick. She wondered what he was thinking. She felt tears spill down her face. Her heart was broken. Broken by everything that had transpired. How she had been compromised. But at the end of the day, she couldn't hate Jon Reznick. Not for one minute.

Thirty-Five

The following morning, Reznick sat wedged between two Feds as he was driven through Lower Manhattan and out to LaGuardia. He was escorted onto a waiting Cessna. He had no idea where they were taking him from there. He wondered if they would take him down to Washington to be interviewed at FBI headquarters.

The Cessna took off and flew low out of the city, over Citi Field, where he had seen Springsteen years earlier with Lauren. Then the urban sprawl of Queens disappeared below the clouds.

Reznick was flanked by a special agent in a seat across the aisle. The Fed dozed during the eighty-minute flight down to Reagan National Airport in Washington, DC.

A Suburban picked Reznick up and sped the four short miles to FBI headquarters, the Hoover building. He was taken to a window-less room on the fifth floor, the same floor where the FBI Strategic Information and Operations Center (SIOC), the command center, was situated.

He remembered the first time he had been shown around here by Meyerstein. He was interested in the technical capabilities and entranced by the round-the-clock surveillance, keeping an eye on events around the world, and in real time.

Reznick wondered what was taking them so long to charge him and haul him to court. He paced the room for several hours under the watchful eye of a special agent assigned to be with him. He was escorted to a bathroom break before he was given a light lunch: a ham sandwich, a Coke, and a black coffee. He sat back down in a wooden chair behind a table and looked across at the FBI special agent.

"So," Reznick said, "are you guys going to charge me, or what the hell is going on?"

The Fed checked his watch. "Your lawyer arrived an hour ago."

"My lawyer? Why didn't you tell me?"

"She can explain all that. But there is someone who wants to speak to you first. He'll be along soon."

Reznick was sick of all the games. He wished they would just get it over with.

Twenty minutes later, there was a knock at the door.

The young FBI minder opened the door. A tall, imposing man walked in. He wore a navy suit, white shirt, black tie, and shiny black oxfords. An FBI ID hung from a lanyard around his neck.

The guy sat down opposite Reznick. "Hello, Jon. Sorry for the delay in speaking to you."

Reznick shifted in his seat. "It happens."

A wry smile. "Can I get you anything before we start?"

"I'm good. I've eaten."

"Firstly, I don't believe we've met. My name is Peter Bouvelle, deputy director of the FBI. I oversee every domestic and international FBI operation, investigative and intelligence. I've worked with Martha Meyerstein for a long, long time. Has she ever mentioned me?"

Reznick shook his head. "Can't say she has."

"Fair enough. I know you and Martha have worked together on several classified operations. It has been a bone of contention here in the Hoover building."

"Why is that?"

"It's unconventional. It's problematic. But that's not why I'm here."

"Why are you here?"

"I'm here . . . First, I'd like to remind you that you still have top secret security clearance. Do you understand the ramifications of that? Your obligations, under law."

"Peter, you've read my file, I'd imagine."

"I have."

"I worked Delta Force for too many years to mention, was a CIA operator in black ops, and after that had a loose relationship with the FBI."

Bouvelle nodded.

"I know full well my obligations."

"Just so we're on the same page. I want to reiterate that intentionally disclosing classified information without authorization is a federal crime under the Espionage Act. This act from 1917 is United States federal law."

"I get it."

Bouvelle laughed.

"What's so funny?"

"I've never met you, but Martha told me all about you. What you're like. I've been wanting to meet you."

"Listen, Peter, I just gunned down a crew of Chinese agents or operatives. I'm not in the mood for pleasantries. Why aren't you throwing me on the mercy of the courts? What the hell is going on?"

"Jon, my job is complex. It encompasses myriad aspects of intelligence operations at home and abroad. The threats we face, real threats to our way of life, our freedoms. And make no mistake, this country is under threat."

"I'm listening."

"The threats change over time. This is just the latest phase. This isn't the Cold War. What we're facing now in the twenty-first century is, potentially, far more dangerous. A multipolar world is emerging. Russia, China, India on the rise. Brazil. And South Africa with its vast mineral wealth."

"The BRICS, right?"

Bouvelle smiled. "You're very informed."

"I have my moments."

"America's position as the head of the free world is under threat, economically and militarily. This is a challenge. A monumental challenge we have to face up to."

Reznick wondered why he was getting a lecture on geopolitics. He was interested in what was going to happen to him. He expected to be languishing in a jail cell before a trial. But he sensed that Bouvelle was taking a bureaucratic, long way around to explain what was going to happen to him and why.

"That's why I've looked at your situation . . . and how it impacts and fits into what I've just said. The stakes couldn't be higher. If we don't defend ourselves and our allies, we will lose our influence in the world."

Reznick sat in silence.

"We have to fight to defend our liberties, near and far. Sometimes thousands of miles from home. Sometimes in our own backyards. We need to be vigilant. And sometimes we need to assert ourselves. We have to fight. We have to kill to stay free."

"You ever served or fought overseas?"

Bouvelle went quiet for a few moments. "I'm sorry. I don't see what relevance that has."

"It's a simple question. Have you ever fought for your country?"

"I've served my country. That's what I do, every day when I come to work."

"You serve your country. That's fine. But have you ever fought for your country?"

"No, I haven't."

"Well, I have. I'm the sort of person, the sort of man, they send overseas to fight these wars. You ever had friends die in a stinking alley, thousands of miles from home? You ever see tough men bleeding out, crying for their mothers in some ditch in Iraq? Have you?"

Bouvelle bowed his head. "No, I haven't. What's your point?"

"My point is until you have made such a sacrifice, seen such things, the horror of it all, you might think twice about sending Americans to fight in far-off shitholes. Afghanistan . . . twenty years. Twenty fucking years. I've been there. And it was wretched. And we ran away. Vietnam? My father served there. He lost countless friends. Comrades. Cut down in their prime. And for what? Huh? For global, bullshit games."

"I get your point."

"I don't know if you do."

Bouvelle shifted in his seat. "Maybe you're right. I was just trying to paint a picture of my thinking, the FBI's thinking, regarding what to do with you."

"I'm sorry, I overstepped. I'm strung out just now. I'm sleep-deprived, you name it."

"I hear you. Maybe we should tread more carefully."

"You mind if I ask you a question?"

"Sure."

"Where's Martha Meyerstein in all this?"

Bouvelle sighed. "The Assistant Director is dealing with other business. Her recovery is continuing. So, she's not available."

"Can I speak to her?"

Bouvelle shook his head. "You'll have to deal with me. Is that alright?"

"Can I speak with my lawyer?"

"You will."

"When?"

"Very soon. I think we have gotten a lot of lessons we could learn from what has happened here. The issue of de facto Chinese police stations operating on American soil is a source of embarrassment to us. Acute embarrassment."

"Why didn't you guys put a stop to it?"

"Like I said, we've got a lot of lessons to learn. I believe when we initially became aware of what was happening, we were slow to get a handle on it. Then we took the decision, the wrong decision, to allow them to continue operating so we could try and understand how they operated. Was it via the embassies or consulates, or was it from Beijing? Who was giving and taking the orders? Was it ad hoc?"

"What was the answer?"

"The answer was it was all those things. And we left it too late. Way, way too late."

"You figure the Chinese operatives were probing and suddenly realized, hey, we can operate with impunity?"

"Maybe. Listen, I get it. It's a failure on our part. On sharing intelligence with police forces, including the NYPD. But that runs two ways. They haven't been as forthcoming about some of their intelligence operations and informants operating in Chinatown and in parts of Queens."

Reznick stared at Bouvelle. "Where do we go from here? What's going to happen to me? That's what I'm interested in."

"What you did . . . was very reckless. But it took guts. Maybe you could have handled it differently. But I don't believe, in your shoes, there were any good options."

Reznick sensed Bouvelle was laying the FBI's cards on the table.

"That's not to say that you shouldn't face justice. No one is above the law."

Reznick sat quietly as he wondered where this was headed.

"The meeting I just concluded with your lawyer was confidential, of course; the discussion was overseen by the Attorney General himself. He is upstairs with the Director now, briefing him."

Reznick stared at him.

"I just want you to know that your point about not serving, fighting—maybe I should have. To get a better understanding. The ramifications."

"I was out of line. Whether you fought overseas or not is neither here nor there. We all serve the best we can. And I shouldn't have disparaged you. I was out of line."

Bouvelle waved it off. "My father served. He was in Vietnam too. He stopped me from joining the Marines. He saw it all. He didn't want that for me."

"Your father was a smart man."

Bouvelle cleared his throat. "Tomorrow morning, I'm attending a meeting of the National Security Council. Maybe I shouldn't be telling you this. But your lawyer will be giving you an update."

Reznick sighed.

"I will be explaining, alongside the Director and the Attorney General, our actions. The rationale. We have already notified the State Department. And they are now fine with it. So, we are, in light of what we know now, on the same page."

"Can I ask you something?"

"Sure."

"Kevin Chang?"

"I thought you'd ask me about him."

"How is he?"

"He is receiving the best medical treatment. He is alive. And he is going to do just fine."

"What's going to happen to him?"

"I don't know for sure."

"That's disappointing."

"Why?"

"Everything I did was in vain."

Bouvelle shook his head. "Quite the opposite, Jon. While I don't know exactly the path Chang will be given, I do know he will categorically not be extradited to China, now or in the future. Categorically not. Furthermore, he will become, in time, a full-fledged American citizen, if he so wishes."

Reznick rolled his eyes. "That was all I wanted."

"Aren't you looking for guarantees?"

"You told me that. That's the guarantee I was looking for."

"You have my word. This is the red line you talked about with Martha. We should have accepted that, given you that guarantee. But like I said, lessons have been learned. Hard lessons." Bouvelle extended his hand across the table. "No hard feelings, man."

Reznick shook his hand with an iron grip.

Bouvelle got to his feet and stared down at him. "Nice meeting you. I'll show your lawyer in."

A few minutes later, Naomi Abelman breezed into the room, briefcase in hand.

She wore a heavy black overcoat, a pink scarf around her neck. She hung up the items on a chair at the far side of the room. She walked over to the table. She looked at the Fed still watching over Reznick. "I need some privacy to talk things over with my client, if you don't mind."

"Of course, ma'am. I'll be outside if you need anything."

"Thank you."

The Fed shut the door on his way out, locking it behind him.

Abelman put her briefcase on the table. "Sorry for keeping you waiting so long. My meeting went long."

"How did it go?"

"As well as could be expected. I met Deputy Director Bouvelle and the Attorney General and a representative from the State Department upstairs."

Reznick finished his cold coffee.

"So, how you holding up?"

Reznick smiled.

"They looking after you OK?"

"No complaints."

Abelman sat down and took out a sheaf of papers. She took a few moments to compose herself. "You're probably wondering what you're facing."

"I know what I'm facing."

Abelman leaned forward. "Do you?"

"I have a good idea. A long time inside, right?"

"What did I tell you?"

Reznick shrugged.

"Didn't I tell you I would fight for you?"

"Yes, you did."

"I fight for my clients. And you are no exception."

"Give it to me straight."

"So, under normal circumstances, you would be facing thirty, forty, who the hell knows what sort of jail time."

Reznick sat quietly as he wondered where she was going with this.

"I'll lay out what just happened upstairs. The Attorney General is directly involved in the final decision as it involves national security. Strategic interests. Not to mention confidential human sources. And that area is what I focused on."

"What is that, exactly?"

"I focused on your previous classified relationship with the FBI, in particular with Assistant Director Martha Meyerstein. True?"

Reznick nodded.

"Bouvelle, the Director, and the senior executives of the FBI in general don't have the authority to make any promise or commitment that would prevent the government from prosecuting you. By that I mean a promise that holds water. Bottom line? The government could jail you for life and throw away the key, ordinarily. It's a slam dunk. But your case, your actions, and you as a person, your history, your career trajectory, are rather unique, wouldn't you say?"

"I guess, maybe."

Abelman laid out legal documents on Department of Justice letterhead. "Here's the heart of the matter. It's only the Attorney General that can agree to a deal with immunity."

"Immunity?"

"Immunity from prosecution. This document has just been signed by not only the Attorney General but also the Secretary of State, the Director of the FBI, and myself. All it needs is your signature."

Reznick took a few minutes to read the two-page letter, absorbing the magnitude of what this meant. He felt as if he must not be reading it correctly. "I don't understand. I'm free to go?"

"Absolutely right. They have reviewed the chain of events that led up to this, Jon. And they can see multiple failings within the FBI intelligence networks, NYPD intelligence sharing, and Homeland Security. A complete mess. So, a major element of responsibility for this was down to the government."

"It had gone undetected?"

"Yes and no. It had been detected by some. They had passed it on. Others hadn't. What transpired under the nose of the FBI? The Chinese government had activated a complex spying operation in New York, their sleeper agents, assassins—call them what you will. But with your actions, they have been neutralized, and the remaining diplomats that were involved have fled back to Beijing. Every one of them."

Reznick leaned back in his chair and rubbed his face, trying to wake himself up. The full extent of what he was being offered hit him like a freight train.

"So, here's the thing. We have this document. It just needs a signature."

"And that's it?"

"This is a take-it-or-leave-it, one-time deal."

Reznick stared at the document and shook his head. "I'll take it."

Abelman pointed to the space for his signature and handed him a pen. "Sign it and you're free. It's legally binding. But on the proviso that it remains strictly confidential, as this matter concerns national security. Do you understand your obligations?"

Reznick signed and put the date on the bottom of the page. "Most certainly."

"You are free to go. You are not at liberty to talk to anyone about this. Not a soul."

"I don't know what to say."

"How about, 'Naomi, you're great, and how fantastic that I don't have to pay your ridiculous fee'?"

Reznick laughed.

"What are you going to do now?"

Reznick shook his head. "Me? Have a beer. Close my eyes. And thank God for lawyers."

Thirty-Six

Reznick had been truly blindsided. He hadn't seen this coming. But in a way, it made sense.

He contemplated the reasons why America would have made such a deal. The diplomatic pressure from China would be immense. But the risks to America if Reznick was put on trial, exposing the full extent of his links to the FBI, CIA, and American intelligence agencies for the better part of twenty years was a bridge too far. Far better to whitewash the killings.

Who was responsible? the media would ask.

Reznick walked with relief, escorted by Bouvelle, back down to the parking garage underneath the Hoover building. He sat in the back of an unmarked Lincoln with the FBI Deputy Director and was driven back to Reagan National Airport.

When the car pulled up at the drop-off, Reznick turned to Bouvelle. "So, that's it, then. You guys going to be talking to the Chinese officials about this?"

"Pretty much. Word to the wise: stay out of trouble. You're a lucky man."

"Listen, for what it's worth, I just want to say thank you."

"For what?"

"For having the wherewithal to do this deal. It couldn't have been easy, I understand that."

"If you ever mention this to anyone other than your lawyer, and I mean anyone, we'll be meeting again. And we'll be turning up at your door and putting you on trial. No ifs, no buts. Are we clear?"

"Crystal. You mind me asking you something?"

Bouvelle looked at his watch. "Make it quick. I've got a meeting with the National Security Council in an hour."

"How did that Chinese crew know I was in the FBI's satellite office?"

Bouvelle averted his gaze to the entrance of the airport terminal. "It's a long story."

"I'm interested in how they knew."

"Suffice it to say, we're having an internal review of operational decision-making in New York. I'm overseeing a review of this case over the next few weeks."

Reznick spoke softly. "You might be looking for a mole in the New York field office."

"How did you come to that conclusion?"

"Connect the dots. Maybe the Chinese operatives have hacked the FBI systems. Maybe they have someone who needs a cash infusion into their bank account. It wouldn't be the first time."

Bouvelle assessed Reznick. "I'm going to keep an open mind."

"What's that saying? Follow the money?"

Bouvelle cleared his throat. "I hear you." He handed Reznick his trusty 9mm Beretta.

Reznick put his gun in his backpack and shook Bouvelle's hand. "Take care of yourself. Till next time."

"Just make sure there isn't a next time."

It was a short, ninety-minute flight from DC back to LaGuardia.

Reznick had contemplated catching a connecting flight back up to Maine. He figured he needed to get home and try and drop off the grid for a while. Maybe a long while. But despite the alluring prospect of getting back to his beloved home beside Penobscot Bay, he couldn't settle. He felt as if he needed time to process what had transpired.

Reznick caught a bus from the airport which dropped him off at the 61st Street-Woodside station. He caught a train to Times Square. He stepped off the train and looked around. The hustle and bustle, people moving, some running. The pungent aromas of marijuana and urine hung in the air. He knew for sure he was back in New York. Then it occurred to him.

He was back where it had all started. The place where Amy Chang had been pushed in front of a train.

A homeless, disheveled white guy with wild-crazy bloodshot eyes and infected sores on his arm was swigging from a bottle of White Lightnin' as he shuffled up to Reznick. "You got forty-three cents, buddy? I need to get some soup. Who doesn't like soup, right?"

"Forty-three cents, huh?"

"That's right. Don't tell me you can't spare forty-three cents. 'Cos that's bullshit."

"I think you might need more than that, buddy."

The guy huffed at Reznick, eyes hooded and sad.

Reznick reached into his pocket and pulled out a twenty-dollar bill, handing it to the guy. "Get some food. Soup. Actual soup. You need to eat."

The guy clutched the bill for what seemed like an eternity. He scrunched up his face and began to sing some long-forgotten country ballad.

"You take care."

The guy nodded. "I ain't got no one, pal. Not a goddamn soul. No one knows me. But thank you all the same."

Reznick patted him on the back and walked away. He headed toward the hellscape that was the Port Authority Bus Terminal. A dystopian, never-ending vista of grim urban life, people milling around who looked as if they would rather be dead. Maybe he was one of those people.

He stood in line for the Greyhound bus north to Portland. A long wait. But then the driver signaled them on.

Reznick was just relieved to get on board. He sat in the back and watched the passengers get on. Eventually, after a ten-minute delay for a harassed woman who had temporarily lost her elderly mother, the bus pulled away. Through the congested streets of Midtown, the bus crawled through the city. It headed due north.

Reznick felt his eyes get heavy. He wanted to sleep for a hundred years. He wasn't the supremely fit twentysomething man of his Delta days anymore. Not by a long stretch. But he was still in great shape for a man in his forties. A few more aches and pains along the way. A reminder of how the time had passed.

He felt himself drift away into a sea of darkness. Suddenly, he was floating. Millions of stars twinkling in a black sky.

It was dark when Reznick awoke. He sat upright and looked outside, failing to stifle a yawn. He checked his phone to see their location. He saw that the bus was on I-90, just outside Worcester. He had been sleeping for more than four hours. He couldn't remember when he had last slept that long.

As he took a few moments to get his bearings, his phone vibrated in his hand. It was a FaceTime video call. He answered and put on his AirPods for privacy. The face of Meyerstein appeared on his phone, smiling at him from a hospital bed.

"Hey, Jon."

Reznick stared at her face on the screen. He wondered what she wanted. He had assumed they would never see each other again. He thought that time had come and gone. "Martha . . . are you OK?"

"I'm fine. I was about to ask you the same thing."

Reznick rubbed his eyes. "Don't worry about me."

"I hope I'm not disturbing you."

"It's fine. Getting a bit of shut-eye."

"I just wanted to say I'm glad you're OK."

Reznick stared out into the darkness, at the headlights of the passing cars and trucks on the interstate in Massachusetts. "I appreciate that."

Meyerstein closed her eyes for a few moments as if what she was about to say was difficult to talk about. "I've been thinking about my future. Thinking about it a lot. The FBI wants me out of the way now. Maybe I've overstayed my welcome."

"Are you serious? They want you out?"

Meyerstein smiled at him through the screen. "It's just the way things turn out. But it's more than the FBI forcing my hand. Easing me out of the door. However, I've been reflecting on my feelings . . . You see, for me, it's way more than the FBI and my job."

"What is it?"

"I don't know . . . the pressure. The sickening feeling I get when I consider what lies ahead. The dread . . ."

Reznick cleared his throat. "Martha, I just want you to know that I wish none of this had happened. I wish I could turn back the clock."

"But you can't. It happened. And it keeps on happening. It's like you're stuck in a doom loop. *We're* stuck in a loop. The same never-ending cycle of killings. The recriminations. The lack of accountability. The feeling that I don't know what you'll do next. Jon, cards on the table, I'm scared."

"I didn't mean to scare you. I would never hurt you."

"Not intentionally, I know. But there comes a time when your world is too much to take. I feel like this might be an opportunity to find myself again."

"What can I do to make this right?"

Martha dabbed her eyes. "I can't go on. Not like this. I resigned with immediate effect. My resignation was accepted by the Director."

Reznick felt hollowed out, knowing he had played a part in her career coming to an abrupt end. He had never wanted that.

"I've dedicated decades of my life to the job. I've decided now is the time to call it quits, while I still can. While I still have all my faculties."

"It seems really sudden. Is there nothing I can do to change your mind?"

"This is about me, Jon. Besides, when one door closes, another opens."

"That sounds promising."

"I've been offered a new position in DC very close to my home in Bethesda."

Reznick took a few moments to process the enormity of the decision. It would be strange not to think of Martha Meyerstein behind her desk in her office on the seventh floor of the Hoover building.

"Where are you going, if you don't mind me asking?"

"I've been very lucky. I will be splitting my time between teaching at Georgetown and the National Intelligence University."

"I think I might enroll. Sounds interesting."

"It is. I'll be reviewing some of the curriculum, modules, and the subjects. But it'll be a labor of love. I've learned a lot. And I think my experience will be of great benefit to future generations of intelligence specialists. In total, I'll be teaching about eight hours per month."

"I'm pleased for you. Gives you plenty of spare time."

"Absolutely. And in addition, the rest of the time, I'll be employed at a private firm in Bethesda, a consulting firm that offers corporate and government advice on intelligence matters and geo-political issues. The office is close to where I live. Means I work two days a month, and I'll be bringing in a lot more money. A heck of a lot more money. Without the hassle."

"Always a good thing . . . So, the end of an era for you."

"Turning the page."

"You sound relieved."

"You have no idea. Anyway, I just wanted you to know that I'll miss all the excitement and the unpredictability you bring to my life. I've given these things a great deal of consideration. And I need to change my life in a fundamental way."

Reznick sensed where she was going with the conversation.

"It means . . . it means I won't be seeing you again."

Reznick looked at her impassive features. He took a few moments to absorb the news.

"I need a different life. And it means a life without you, Jon."

"I see."

Meyerstein smiled through a veil of tears. "This is difficult."

"Martha, hey, listen, I hope there's no hard feelings."

"Quite the opposite. I just have fond memories. We change. We move on."

Reznick sighed. "I'm a pain in the ass, always have been for you. And I want to say sorry for all the hurt I've caused with my actions."

"I'll miss you, Jon."

Reznick felt his throat tighten. "I'll miss you too."

"I'm glad you're OK. But my nerves can't take it any longer. And I wish you nothing but the best."

The screen went blank as her face disappeared.

Thirty-Seven

The hours that followed on the bus passed like a strange dream.

Reznick headed north on the interminable journey, interrupted by a thirty-minute stop for a bathroom break and food at a diner. But at least he had serious time to reflect on what Martha had said. She had made it clear it was over between them. Her decision felt final.

She was, in many ways, like him. A maverick, independent-minded. Fiercely hard-working. And she had gone to the ends of the earth over the years to help Reznick as they worked together on numerous classified intelligence investigations. He was going to miss her. He would miss the woman he had grown to admire and respect before growing closer as their personal relationship began to develop. But when all was said and done, there was something missing.

The more he thought about it and the more he thought about her, about them, the more he realized that he hadn't ever really allowed her into his world. Not in a meaningful way. He had tried. And they had grown intimate, but he could never really subsume himself, his special ops mindset, his personality, his propensity for solitude, introspection, and ultimately, violence. Killing was his business. Maybe he was damaged. More than he realized. Maybe he couldn't truly give himself over to another person. Not entirely. Even if that person was Martha. Maybe she saw through him. Was that it? Maybe she had known all along that he couldn't let go of who he was and what he had become. She probably knew she couldn't change him. Not one iota, even if she wanted to.

Reznick understood full well that someone as brilliant, talented, and loyal as Meyerstein could never fully align herself with a man who was, at heart, a machine. No matter her wise counsel to rein in his vengeful tendences, whether hunting down a Mafia boss responsible for killing his friend Bill Eastland and his wife, or finding and neutralizing his archnemesis, Adam Ford, a psychotic ex–special forces medic who had blown up the yacht Meyerstein was on. Time and time again, he had gone against the legal niceties of the FBI. She had come under enormous pressure from within the Bureau to ditch the relationship with Reznick. But she hadn't.

Until now.

He closed his eyes for a few minutes as sleep began to take him again. He wondered if Meyerstein's resignation might also have been connected to Reznick discovering Elisabeth. He had first noticed, on his return from Switzerland, that he hadn't heard from Martha. She usually called at least once a week to see how he was. But nothing.

Despite Reznick having zero contact with Elisabeth, Reznick sensed Meyerstein couldn't be part of his life now that his legal wife was back in the picture. Except she wasn't. He couldn't meet up with her. Besides, he had no feelings for his wife anymore apart from a feeling of betrayal. He wanted her to be safe. Which she was. That was his sole concern. But he could understand why Martha would want nothing to do with him.

Reznick felt himself drift off. He slept for hours. He dreamed of floating on dark waters again, inky-blue sky overhead. Shooting stars through the air. Then blackness.

He awoke at first light as the bus pulled into Portland, Maine.

Reznick picked up his bag, blinking against the harsh sun. He got off the bus and headed to a nearby diner. He sat down to a full breakfast, drank a few cups of black coffee. He began to feel better.

He went to the restroom and freshened up, splashing cold water on his face, cleaning his teeth. He stared at his reflection in the mirror. He rubbed the heavy stubble on his skin. He looked rough, black shadows under his eyes.

Reznick left the restroom and headed to a nearby gas station, where he caught a ride from a truck driver who was headed to his hometown.

He made small talk with the guy, who was picking up frozen fish and lobster to be flown down to Florida that evening. He was dropped off at the Rockland Ferry Terminal. He looked around at the old coastal town. It never seemed to change. It wasn't as rough around the edges as it was when he grew up. But it was home. A home he loved.

He breathed in the salty air. He felt a little better. A little more centered.

Reznick walked the mile back to his house on the edge of town, backpack slung over his shoulder. Down the same dirt road his late father had walked a thousand times before him. In the distance, he saw his property and the sea just beyond.

All he wanted to do was close his eyes and forget.

Reznick's phone vibrated in his back pocket. He stopped and checked the screen. A message flashed *Urgent: Intruder Alert.*

His house stood like a sentinel guarding the rocky headland.

Reznick opened an app and stared at his phone. A spectral figure sat alone in his living room. The figure crossed his legs, comfortable enough to suggest that he had been there a while. It was clearly a man.

Reznick had a visitor. An uninvited visitor.

The man's presence had been detected by an infrared motion detector concealed within a carbon monoxide detector.

Reznick kept his distance as he plotted his next move. Was it the Feds? Maybe the cops? But why no vehicle outside? Would they really have broken in? How long had they been there? Minutes? Hours?

He wondered if the FBI had reneged on the deal.

Reznick needed to approach from out of any line of sight. Away from the living room with views to the front of the house. He took a sandy path, little used. He headed down, partially shrouded by undulating sand dunes and a scattering of trees, to the beach. Slowly his senses grew sharper. He headed down a steep slope to the sandy cove below his home.

The sound of the waters of Penobscot Bay crashing onto the rocks below masked any sounds he made.

Then he began to climb.

He ascended the steep dunes and traversed farther along and then up the rocky headland to the wild, long grasses fringing the back of his house. He lay on his front, spreading himself low as he crawled toward the rear of his home.

He carefully made his way out along the edge of a rocky clifftop ridge.

Reznick stopped and stared across at the house his father had built decades earlier. The wooden house by the sea, overlooking Penobscot Bay. He stayed still for a few minutes. The sound of gulls overhead. His mind raced. He took out his gun, carefully flicking off the safety.

He checked his phone one final time.

The figure was looking around the living room as if slightly bored.

Reznick put his phone away. He approached the house, skirting the rear deck. Down a concrete path to the side of the garage.

He quietly unlocked the side door. He edged closer to the farthest door. The door that led to his utility room, adjacent to his kitchen.

He turned the key, unlocking the door to the house.

Reznick pressed his ear to the door. Listening for any sound. Vibrations from footsteps. But nothing. Just the sound of his heart beating.

He turned the handle softly and cracked open the door to the small room inside.

Reznick stepped forward. Past the washing machine and dryer and toward the kitchen. He stopped and waited. He held his breath.

The kitchen door was open. He craned his neck as he listened. Not a sound. But he could see down the dark hall and into the corner of his living room.

The silhouetted figure sat alone, his back to Reznick.

He edged through the kitchen and into the hallway. One step. Two steps. Eyes on the motionless figure. The figure spun around, gun in hand.

Reznick fired two shots that hit just below his right clavicle. The man screamed and slumped slowly onto the floor, dropping the gun.

Reznick quickly kicked the gun away and held his Beretta at the man's throat. "That's not a very nice welcome home, pal."

"What are you waiting for? Just kill me!"

Reznick reached over and switched on a lamp. The light bathed the room in a soft glow. Dark-red blood pooled on the hardwood floor. The man's eyes were terrified. A fifty-something white man. "Who are you?"

The man shook his head.

"Name?"

The man closed his eyes for a moment, scrunched up in pain.

"Who sent you?"

"Go to hell."

Reznick reached over and rifled in the man's back pocket and pulled out a wallet. He flipped through his credit cards and scanned his driver's license. "James Bradley. You mind telling me why you decided to visit me here at my home? You been paid to kill me? Is that it?"

Bradley clenched his teeth.

"You were waiting for me, James, weren't you? Why would you do that? Who are you working for?"

"Why don't you kill me?"

"All in good time. First, who sent you?"

"Kill me. Please, kill me. I'm begging you."

"You wanted to kill me, didn't you, James? You are in my home, uninvited. So, who the fuck are you working for?"

"It's too late. I have nothing to live for now! I can't face it now! I know what lies ahead. I know what fate awaits me."

"The same fate awaits us all."

"Reznick, just put a bullet in my head."

"Why should I do that?"

"I have nothing! I'm dead already." Bradley looked up at Reznick, tears in his eyes. "I want you to kill me! I order you to kill me! Give me a good death."

"A good death? You piece of shit. But that can be arranged. You working for the Chinese government, is that it? That would make sense."

"What do you know about the Chinese?"

"I know a bit. I know they've got money to throw around."

"Reznick . . . you're a man of honor. That's what they say. Do the honorable thing and just fucking kill me. Don't let me die like a dog. Put me out of my misery. Think of my kids having to look at me in a courtroom."

Reznick stood up, gun still trained on him.

"What are you waiting for?"

Reznick took off his jacket and ripped off his T-shirt. He kneeled and pressed down on the bloody wounds, trying to stem the blood flow.

Bradley screamed in pain.

"Be quiet! We need to stop the blood. Otherwise, you'll bleed out."

"Let me bleed out. I need to die. I can't stand the humiliation that awaits."

"Stop talking, you stupid fuck!"

"I can see it now. The national humiliation. The personal humiliation. The shame. I know what I've done. I'm prepared to face the consequences. Just do it!"

Reznick looked down into Bradley's watery eyes. He was pitiful. "Who are you, James? Who are you really working for?"

"I used to work for the Agency in my younger days. Just like you used to."

"CIA?"

Bradley gasped as a fresh wave of pain rolled over him. "Why so surprised? I wouldn't be the first Langley operative to spy for a foreign government."

"Give me your motive. How did you end up here?"

"Money. What do you think? I'm broke. I need money."

"You'll face worse than financial ruin, Bradley. You will be put on trial. And you know what they'll do to you once you're safely inside your cell? You have any idea of what prison is like?"

"Don't. I don't want to face that. I'm begging you, in the name of God, please, kill me. Kill a traitor. I know you can."

Reznick felt a burning rage within him. Just ready to explode. To destroy. To kill. He wanted to kill Bradley.

"Shoot me, you cold bastard! Shoot me in the head! Now!"

Reznick pressed Bradley's left hand to his injured shoulder. "Hold the T-shirt to the wounds tight! Stem the blood flow!" He took out his phone and pulled up Meyerstein's number. It rang five times.

"Who are you calling?" Bradley demanded to know. "Are you calling the cops? Please don't call them."

The voice of Meyerstein said, "Yeah, who's this?"

"Martha, it's Jon. Don't hang up."

"I thought we were done."

"We are . . . but there's still some unfinished business."

"What kind of unfinished business?"

Reznick stared down at Bradley, who was blinking away the tears, blood soaking through his T-shirt. "You need to get your guys up to my place."

"What happened?"

Reznick stared down at Bradley, who was beginning to shake with shock and trauma. "I'll need paramedics. FBI team, right here, right now. This is a national security classified situation."

"What happened?"

"I'll send you a picture. He's still alive. He's losing a lot of blood. Two shots to the right shoulder. His name is James Bradley. Ex-CIA. In my house."

Reznick ended the call. He took a photo of Bradley and sent the picture to Meyerstein.

Bradley stared up at him. "Who was that?"

"None of your business."

"Why didn't you kill me when you could? You're trained to kill. Why didn't you kill me?"

"On another day, I would have. I guess you caught me on a good day, James."

Epilogue

Three months later, on a warm summer night, Reznick was standing in the sandy cove below his home. He gazed over the black waters of Penobscot Bay, thinking of nothing in particular.

His phone rang.

Reznick wondered if it was Lauren, who hadn't called for a couple of weeks. He took his phone out of the pocket of his jeans. "Yeah, Jon speaking."

"I hope it's OK to call you." A familiar woman's voice. But it wasn't Lauren.

Reznick took a few moments to recognize the voice. "Caroline, is that you?"

"Glad you remembered."

"Well, I'll be damned." Reznick hadn't heard from Caroline Sullivan since they had sat together in the Cape Cod hospital.

"How are you doing?"

"I'm OK, thanks."

"Listen, Jon, are you near a TV?"

"Not at the moment. I'm close, but I'm outside."

"Turn on CNN."

"Give me a minute." Reznick clambered up the beach and back into his home. He switched on the TV in his kitchen and changed it to CNN. The ticker said, *Ex-CIA operative in court charged with spying for the Chinese.*

He watched a rerun of a handcuffed man in his fifties shuffling into a courtroom, accompanied by a phalanx of FBI special agents.

"You got it?" Sullivan said.

"I got it."

"James Bradley. Ex-CIA, heavily in debt until the Chinese made him an offer he couldn't refuse. He was spying for them. I heard the FBI might have one or two special agents who were on his payroll too. Crossed the wrong people, apparently. They had to delay his trial while he recovered from two bullet wounds. The penetration of American intelligence is devastating."

Reznick realized it was the guy he had shot in his home in Rockland. "Son of a bitch."

"Yeah, just what I was thinking. He was feeding classified information on the Kevin Chang investigation back to the Chinese as they were hunting for him."

"You got an inside track on what happened?"

"The story is unfolding. My sources have told me very worrying details about security lapses, holes in our intelligence."

"So, how did this Bradley character operate?"

"He got intel from a source or sources from within the FBI. Maybe the Department of Justice as well."

"Seriously?"

"Unbelievable, I know. And that's how they tracked you down to the hospital and made that attempt on your life at Kew Gardens out in Queens. Bradley got the intel from an unnamed senior FBI agent. Very, very senior. In New York."

"You know that for a fact?"

"I know that for a fact. I've spoken to numerous sources that are saying the same thing."

"You got any names?"

"I do have names. One in particular. But of course I can't reveal it."

"You've got quite a story to work on, then."

"That's why I haven't been in touch. I literally have enough material for a follow-up book."

"That's a good thing, right?"

Sullivan laughed. "Very much so."

"Let me ask you something, Caroline. You didn't get any knocks at your door from the Feds?"

"I didn't, thank goodness. I have heard from a source that we were spotted together entering the hospital and sitting together in the hospital. And they worked back from there. But in light of what happened, nothing came of it. So, my lawyer says I'm fine."

"That's a relief. Caroline, listen, I owe you one."

"For what?"

"Helping me out. Saving my neck. And Kevin's."

"I was pleased to help. Quid pro quo and all that, right?"

Reznick laughed. "There's something else I need to talk to you about."

"What's that?"

"Let me pay you back the costs of the lawyer."

"It's on the house. But I'll tell you what. How about you buy me a drink, and that'll make us even?"

"Next time I'm in Madison, we'll meet up. Definitely. Drinks on me."

"Why not meet up now?"

"Now?"

"Unless you've got other plans."

"At this moment?"

"Jon, do I have to spell it out to you? I'm in town. Now. Your town."

"Rockland?"

"Gorgeous place."

"Where exactly are you?"

"Trackside Station bar."

"Know it well. How about I see you there in ten minutes?"

"I'll be waiting."

Reznick ended the call, put on a fresh shirt, and headed out. A few minutes later, he was going down Union Street. He walked into the bar.

Caroline was sitting on a stool, sipping a beer. She turned around and flashed him a grin. "Hey, Jon. Long time no see."

Reznick was dumbstruck. He couldn't believe she had come all this way. Here she was in person. He pulled up a stool and ordered a beer and a fresh beer for Caroline. "This is a pleasant surprise."

"What can I tell you?"

"So, how's the book coming along?"

"It took over my life. Actually, it's taken on a life of its own. It's a monster."

"I can imagine."

"But I'm almost finished. I'll have to write at least another chapter focused on this Bradley guy."

Reznick handed her one of the beers and raised his bottle as if to salute her efforts. "Good work. Very good work."

"Thank you."

Reznick took a gulp of the cold beer. It felt good. He cocked his head. "You want to take a table over by the corner? Bit more private."

"Sure thing."

They took their drinks and sat down at a table well out of earshot.

"So, I'm interested in what you were saying about Bradley getting help from a Fed."

"I have the name. And I know there's a high-level investigation into the New York field office. That's all I know."

"My daughter used to work out of there. Seemed like a really smart crowd of people. What have you heard?"

"I've heard they're trawling through a bank account opened by this FBI special agent, someone very senior in the New York field office. And the bank is based in the Cayman Islands, which is a bit unusual."

"What a piece of work."

"More to come, as they say."

Reznick sipped his beer. "I just wanted to say thanks again for your help."

"You put your neck on the line, not me. But OK, I'll take the appreciation."

"Seriously, though, the lawyer bill, please send it to me."

"Not happening."

"Do you mind me asking you something, Caroline?"

"It depends on what you want to know."

"Why did you go out on a limb? I mean, you didn't have to do that. You went all in."

"I think that's the question I wanted to ask you. And more."

"But seriously, why did you do it?"

"It felt like the right thing to do."

Reznick took a sip of his beer and stared at Caroline. She was beautiful. She had a dry sense of humor and was ridiculously easygoing. He liked her. A lot.

"It wasn't simply about me being altruistic and helping out. I got a story; I admit that. The growing influence of China on America and its institutions. And what happened to you, Kevin, and Trevelle encapsulated exactly that."

"What about Chang? What's the latest? How is he? Where is he?"

"Chang is fine and well, still traumatized by his sister's death. He's getting some intense counseling from a psychologist."

"And Trevelle? I haven't heard from him."

"He disappeared after Kevin's overdose. He went into hiding. Dropped off the grid."

"But he's OK?"

"He lost Amy. But yeah, he's fine." She stared at his jacket. "I see you're carrying."

"At all times. What about you?"

"It's in my purse."

"What've you got?"

"Me? Sig P365."

Reznick whistled. "Very nice."

Sullivan finished her beer as she gazed at him. "I heard Assistant Director Meyerstein retired."

"You hear a lot of things, don't you?"

"Nature of the job. I talk to people. People talk to me."

Reznick sighed. "Meyerstein . . . yes, I believe that's correct."

"A little bird was telling me that you and she worked side by side for a few years."

"I wouldn't say side by side. But there was a collaboration of sorts. I think this case and my actions and the ramifications were the final straw."

"You still seeing her?"

Reznick smiled. "You're very direct."

"So are you, Jon."

"You seem to know a lot about me."

"This and that. You haven't answered my question."

"No, I'm not seeing Martha. That part of my life is over. She's moved on."

"What about you?"

"What about me?"

"Have you moved on?"

"I have. I'm sitting here with you, aren't I?"

Caroline tilted her head, eyes clear, alluring. "You were brought up in Rockland?"

"Me? Born and bred. This is home. My father built the house I live in with his own two hands."

"What about your mother?"

"She died a long time ago. When I was a kid."

"So, it's just you?"

"Pretty much. My daughter . . . she's in goddamn Indonesia. When you called, I thought it was her."

"I also heard you were married before."

Reznick leaned back in his seat and swigged his beer. "You ask a lot of questions."

"I'm a journalist. That's what we do."

"She's not around anymore, if that's what you're asking."

"That is exactly what I'm asking."

"Why do you want to know that?"

"Curious, I guess."

"You just up for the evening?"

Caroline shook her head. "No, I was thinking about sticking around for a week or two. I don't know."

"A week or two? Why?"

"I like it up here. And I wanted to meet you again. To interview you at length."

"Where are you staying?"

"A cute little boutique hotel on Main Street." Caroline called over a waitress. "What do you want, Jon?"

"Scotch on the rocks. And a beer."

Caroline smiled up at the waitress. "Two Scotches on the rocks. And two cold beers."

The waitress winked at Reznick. "Coming up."

"You know her?" Caroline said.

"Her? Sure, she plays pool at the Myrtle Street Tavern."

"I play pool."

"Is that right?"

"Pretty hot shot, they say."

"I think the Myrtle is open late tonight. I'll take you over there."

"Sounds like a plan. I think I'm going to hang around for a while, Jon. If that's OK with you."

"No objections here."

Caroline's gaze wandered around the bar.

"What are you thinking?"

"I was thinking . . . I think I like it here."

Acknowledgements

I would like to thank my editor, Kasim Mohammed, and everyone at Amazon Publishing for their enthusiasm, hard work, and belief in the Jon Reznick thriller series. I would also like to thank my loyal readers. Thanks also to Faith Black Ross for her terrific work on this book, and Randall Klein, who looked over an early draft. Special thanks to my agent, Mitch Hoffman, of the Aaron M. Priest Literary Agency in New York.

Last but by no means least, thanks to my family and friends for their encouragement and support. None more so than my wife, Susan.

About the Author

J. B. Turner is a former journalist and the author of the Jon Reznick series of political thrillers (*Hard Road, Hard Kill, Hard Wired, Hard Way, Hard Fall, Hard Hit, Hard Shot, Hard Target, Hard Vengeance, Hard Fire*, and *Hard Exit*), the American Ghost series of black-ops thrillers (*Rogue, Reckoning*, and *Requiem*), the Jack McNeal Thriller series (*No Way Back* and *Long Way Home*), and the Deborah Jones crime thrillers (*Miami Requiem* and *Dark Waters*). He has a keen interest in geopolitics. He lives in Scotland with his wife and two children.

Follow the Author on Amazon:

If you enjoyed this book, follow J. B. Turner on Amazon to be notified when the author releases a new book!
To do this, please follow these instructions:

Desktop:

1) Search for the author's name on Amazon or in the Amazon app.
2) Click on the author's name to arrive on their Amazon page.
3) Click the Follow button.

Mobile and Tablet:

1) Search for the author's name on Amazon or in the Amazon app.
2) Click on one of the author's books.
3) Click on the author's name to arrive on their Amazon page.
4) Click the Follow button.

Kindle eReader and Kindle App:

If you enjoyed this book on a Kindle eReader or in the Kindle app, you will find the author Follow button after the last page.